STARVING MEN

Siobhan Finkielman

388 7777

AISN: B0876FTB4M
ISBN-13: 979-8655763241

Cover design: Book Cover Zone
www.siobhanfinkielman.com

Dedicated to Jarek, who never lacks sense

In 1649, Oliver Cromwell and his New Model Army landed in Dublin to quash a rebellion in Ireland. Their four-year stay led to the death of almost half the population, six hundred thousand people.

In 1845, Sir Charles Edward Trevelyan was placed in charge of Irish famine relief. His actions contributed to the death of a million Irish people as well as to the migration of a million more, most of whom never returned.

Both men died of natural causes at relatively advanced ages. Both remain celebrated figures in Britain to this day.

The Short and Nasty Prologue

John Bingham didn't know he was going on the run when he entered his former wife's house to find his children's nanny bludgeoned to death in the basement, her face bones cracked into the inside of her head and her white teeth littering the parquet floor beneath her. He didn't know he'd have to leave the country when he heard his ex-wife on the basement stairs, the breath being gurgled out of her by a man twisting a curtain cord around her throat. Bingham got an idea that running might be wise when the attacker stopped short his twisting and said, in a strange accent, that he was next. As he made a run for Bingham, the stranger tripped on something, likely the coughing body of Bingham's ex-wife, and the terrified man was able to escape out the basement door and up to his car and drive all the way away.

Bingham didn't have time to get a false passport made or to set up a shady bank account in a sunny place for the rest of his life. What he did have was enough wealthy friends to fly him directly to Nice, then all the way down to Nairobi. And what really came to his aid was the fact that it was 1974, when the governments of the world were linked only by letters or a phone, and when a man accused of murdering his nanny and attacking his ex-wife could blend into the crowd with nothing more than a shave and a good tan.

The charming, intelligent, and ever-so-flawed John Bingham chose South Africa for his new, insignificant life, and the blanket of anonymity dropped down over the man formerly known as Lord Lucan.

It is today, and time has caught up with Lucky Lord Lucan. Eighty-two years old, white haired, and with the annoyingly crooked spine of age, Bingham's screams of pain are the only thing he has to protect himself against the knife being dug into his back. His fingers are locked from arthritis and he can merely flail them about like stubby sticks as each stab pierces through the skin and into the muscles – high near the shoulders, down at his liver, off to the sides where there's no lasting damage except for the stinging pain. At any other time, Bingham would be able to look out the living-room window of his small farm holding near Johannesburg. He would see his well-worked car on the dusty drive, the few chickens that deliver his daily egg, even his neighbor's house in the distance. Today, he can only see the window frame, as he tries in vain to grab hold of it to keep himself from being pushed to the floor, where his assailant stands on his face as soon as he's down there. There's no rush, there's no one around, Turlough O'Sullivan can take his time. Bingham's head can be crushed into the floor at leisure, and the old man can't even lift up his twisted bony fingers to protect it.

1. A Brief Visit to the Doctor

When I met that man who was going to do so much for me, I didn't want him in my office. He seemed like a ghost among the living, one of the *Sídhe* folk, the people of the mounds, who came up from the soil in the old Irish tales. Indeed he had clothes on, he could read and write, he could talk and make sense like the best of us. Few would have thought him in any good way remarkable, though he turned out to be one of the most remarkable men I've ever met. And I didn't want him in reception, making my waiting patients feel uneasy due to the glorious black bruise around his left eye.

I told him I wasn't taking new clients, but he said he'd been referred by a friend of mine. It wasn't a good time of year, I said, but he mentioned that L. Grady thought well of me and would I just have a few minutes to spare. It was an unusually busy day and I wouldn't be free for hours, but he was happy to wait in reception, with my collection of depressed clients. That was the last thing I needed, so a few minutes with him couldn't hurt.

Turlough O'Sullivan came into my office and sat down. Having got in, the first thing he said was that he didn't want to be there.

"You have to be here voluntarily for anything to help. Does Mr. Grady know you don't want to be here?"

"He told me I have to come. I want to move back to Ireland, and you're the gatekeeper."

"You don't live here now?" I asked him.

"London," he said. "I came over to see you."

"I can assess you, but we'll have to start at the beginning. And were you in a fight recently?"

"It wasn't a fight. I was running away and banged into a wall."

"Running away from what?"

"From the bodies of the eight men I shot in Libya two days ago."

"What?"

"That Libya thing, that doesn't matter. I want to get past that and end at what matters."

"You shot eight men and you don't think it matters?"

He looked at me like he didn't understand what I was saying. "I've shot a hundred men, and I don't think it matters. I wouldn't be any good to Mr. Grady if I did."

I tried not to pause. "Which side were you on?"

"Whichever side didn't lose eight men two days ago. It doesn't matter which side I was on."

"What do you think does matter? Is there a problem Mr. Grady has picked up on?"

His eyes moved to the side of the room, then out the window. Not evading, thinking.

"The part about my family. Mr. Grady may have had a problem with that."

"You had a difficult family background?"

An irritated sigh. "No, my own family. He thinks I wanted to kill them."

"And did you?"

"I don't know. I was far gone by then."

"When was this?"

"Years ago."

"You can't remember?"

"June 1996."

"And what has changed since?"

"What? Just check me if I'm okay now. That's all I want."

"It takes much more than that, I can't just..."

O'Sullivan stood up and walked out of the office. And I was glad he did, because he took his menace with him. But I knew he'd be back, because I was the only psychiatrist who'd take him.

2. A Long Two Years

That was two years ago, and I admit it was a strange time for me then. It might have been O'Sullivan's arrival that started me thinking, but whatever the reason, a photo of a dead man preoccupied my hours. It wasn't just his ugly actions that bothered me, it was the ugliness of his face: the Neanderthal brows, beady eyes, far too much hair on his jowls, no matter what the century. And a wide, disgusted mouth. I'd find myself in my office in leafy green Ballsbridge, with Charles Edward Trevelyan looking out at me from the photo in my hand. Dressed in his suit and a snarl, the expression that says to this day, "The famine has been sent by God to teach the Irish a lesson."

And on one particular day, when myself and Trevelyan were refusing to blink at each other, I squeezed his photo in my fist, squeezing the life out of the dead man himself. Then I unfurled it and stretched it between both hands, flattening it out on the desk. And when his eyes stared back at me, I squeezed again as tightly as I could, repeating his name as if I could wear it out.

"Is it love/hate?" a voice asked.

Someone was in my office, the door already closed behind them. I felt as embarrassed as if I were masturbating in my swivel chair.

"Sorry, I didn't hear you. Did you knock?"

"You didn't hear me."

The man, my next patient, came and sat in the cold leather chair across the desk from me. I put Trevelyan's picture in my drawer, where it joined the other balled photographs, the little army of crumpled faces that covered the false-bottom panel beneath, all hiding the two bonuses of knowing the people I knew: an extra passport and a heavy old Glock 17.

"So this is the second session, Mr. O'Sullivan," I said, "and we can begin anywhere you like."

True to species, Turlough took his time. His eyes moved over the room, seeing what his new shrink liked to collect or show to his clients. Obsolete medical books that would fall out of their jackets if touched. Certificates of education, sterile signs of passing a test. Nothing about making it through the student-drink-driving days and falling into the lecture room just in time for an exam. Three carved wooden monkey faces, the size of children's faces, hanging down in a straight line on the wall.

"Where are they from?" he asked.

"Africa."

"Are they lucky?"

"They are. How did you know that?"

"Did you get them yourself?"

"No," I said, smiling, "they were a present from a friend, after they'd traveled down there."

"Down there? Down where?"

"Oh dear, I can't remember."

"Africa's a big place. It's not really a 'down there' place."

"Have you lived in Africa?" I asked him.

"Where have you been?"

"Em, Spain, on holidays. London, of course."

"That's it?"

"Mostly. Where else would I go?"

"The world's a big place."

"So why are you so determined to get back into Ireland?"

Turlough let out a little smile, a slip that vanished as soon as it came. Then the usual clouds assaulted his face and he shook his head, angry at himself, and looked at me as if he would have handed me his soul to save him.

"Doctor Gleeson," he said. "I think I'm going mad."

*****

Turlough rarely missed an appointment, while the money came through each month from an account that wasn't his. And yet so many bits of this man fell to my floor during those sessions and sat there broken, looking up at me without expression, that I sometimes thought I could never help him at all. He told me about days he forgot to eat, days he ate too much, years he couldn't remember and incidents he could never forget. An out-sourced IRA sniper who burned in the Afghan sun, still on contract overseas despite the war at home being over. Barred by the IRA General Council from residing in Ireland for as long as they saw fit.

Turlough had no relationships, no hobbies, no movies or songs that he hated or quite liked. Random daily rituals had become his children to nurture. And queerest of all, he had no political leanings, though he was at the center of everything.

I had started him on fluoxetine, twenty milligrams per day and then up to forty after four weeks. That was the base, the place where we could set a foundation for the cognitive therapy to kick against the OCD. The Prozac took effect eventually, and although I couldn't say he was a changed man, his face was more relaxed when he came into the office.

"Are you sleeping well?"

"I'm sleeping well. The thoughts are the same."

"What do you do when you get them?"

"They're there all the time. I can't always do what you told me to do. There'd be no day left."

"You're going to fail," I said.

"Huh?"

"You're going to fail a lot, and that's okay. What do you do when you get the thoughts?"

He looked up and to the left. And back to me with an embarrassed smirk.

"Before I flew over here this morning, I had a shower. And I hung the towel on the back of a kitchen chair, near the radiator, so it'd be dry by tonight. But out on the street, I thought, couldn't that radiator heat up the towel and set it on fire? And that was stupid because it wasn't an open flame.

"I focused on where I was going, took the breaths in, like you said, calmed myself down. But I couldn't get the thought out of my head. The place was going to go up in flames. So I walked back to the flat and went in and the towel was nowhere near the radiator. I felt good, for about half a second, because the thought wasn't hounding me anymore. And then I got so mad at myself. A bloody towel, and sure, would it even matter if it burned down the flat? I'd get over it. And I took the towel and threw it out the window and down to the ground. And then I came over here. And now I can't stop thinking that one of my towels is getting wet in the garden."

There was nothing new in anything he said. I'd heard it all before, in different forms, from other clients. But before I could encourage him that he could get beyond it, he said,

"Sometimes I think I should burn down the flat. Then I wouldn't be afraid of a towel."

And when I got home later that night, I was still wondering whether that wouldn't be true.

3. Maggie's Goodbye

"Have you ever shot anyone in the stomach?"

Detective Margaret O'Malley didn't know how to answer. She wanted her nieces to think she was invincible, but they were only ten and eight, so she decided to say no.

"What about in the finger?"

"That'd be a difficult shot."

"In the hair?"

"Off you go," Denise said from the sink, and the kids wandered out to the hall, where they went through Maggie's bag.

"You're going to miss this," Denise said. "London isn't as green as Ballyhack." She was only a year older than Maggie, but she already looked like their mother used to, vaguely sad and definitely tired as she stood watching the long garden and the rising fields beyond.

"I don't get down here that often," Maggie said. "I'll miss you lot, but most of my friends are in Dublin."

Denise continued her stare across the fields. "Do you remember Dad saying it was the sun that switched people on every morning, that it reset their body clock? And when the Celts came to Ireland and there wasn't any sun, it was the sight of the green that did it."

Maggie remembered her father standing in the middle of the kitchen, delivering his heavy pronouncements to the two daughters he always seemed like he was surprised to have.

"He said a lot of things."

"Go easy on him. He would have loved to have seen you in uniform, upholding the law and all that shite."

"And Mam would have collapsed if she knew I was single. I should be spitting out the kids by now."

"Like me?"

"I didn't mean it in a bad way."

"I don't mind. If I never do anything else, I suppose I've done something useful."

"And you're doing it on your own, which is twice as hard. But what I meant is that Mam would have preferred me to be anything else but an officer."

"I guess it's better she's dead then. Where did you get that bruise?"

"Which one?" Maggie asked, touching the side of her face.

"That one."

"Badminton. I fell on the court."

"You'll have to give that up."

"I can't, I love it. You can be standing there, and the shuttlecock is lobbed at you so hard that you think it'll fly up to the roof, but then it suddenly stops and drops, floating down like a feathery angel, and you know you can get to it. No matter how violently it's flung at you, you always have a chance."

Maggie was relieved when Denise didn't ask any more. There was no use telling her that the bruise was a three-day-old souvenir from a man suspected of planting a bomb under a prison-officer's car. As Maggie followed her sister into the hall, she gave her aching shoulder a sly rub from where it had been slammed into a door frame during his arrest. She picked her bank cards and makeup off the floor without wincing, then she kissed her nieces and hugged her teary sister.

"Denise, it's only London. I'll ring you every day."

"You won't."

"Then I'll post funny pictures on Facebook of people I'm arresting. Would that make you feel better?"

Denise nodded and held back the tears, and Maggie thought there might be something more to her sadness, something like a wish to be flying off herself.

"Come over to me," Maggie said. "We'll see the sights together."

"You'll be chasing after drug addicts the whole time."

"I'll squeeze you in somewhere. I mean it, drop over anytime."

Denise promised she would, and Maggie had to leave her sister standing in the porch. The journey ahead was a two-hour drive from Wexford to Dublin, a choice between straight up the country on one motorway or along the east coast on another. She didn't even consider using the smaller national roads, through the towns that had hardly changed in a hundred years. She took one last look at Denise's house, the white bungalow that had been the family home many years before, still with its two huge windows to the front, like wide-open eyes looking down to the sea. Her mother used to complain to her father about why the kitchen and living room were at the back of the house, why the bedrooms got the good view when the occupants were asleep in them most of the time. *Ireland has the sea around it but the green inside,* he'd throw back at her, and nobody knew what he meant. Maggie still didn't know, and she didn't wonder, as she got into her car and left for the drive back to Dublin and her last week at Harcourt Street Station.

4. Turlough's on the Way

It could have been head trauma, drug-induced psychoses, or the tiniest tumors that turn the quietest individuals into society's most wanted, but more often than not, the people who sat before me in the cold leather chair were there because of a few small years in their painfully long lives. Too many memories that spat themselves out as addictions, depression, or neuroses like OCD. Turlough opened up easily about his adult self, but he did everything he could to protect the child he once was, to avoid recalling the memories that would make that child feel pain again. It took him months to go into detail, and many more months to do anything about it.

"Sometimes I don't know if what I can remember is the truth," he said.

"That's very common."

"How do you know if things are real?"

"The memories? You don't. And often it's better not to force yourself to remember, because the brain likes to make things up to form complete stories. It's best to work with more of an impression."

"An impression?" He scratched his ear and looked down at the floor. "I'd be asleep and I'd get a box in the head in the middle of the night. That left some impression."

"Who was it?"

"A priest. Isn't it always a priest. My father died from a bullet, and my mother couldn't cope with the lot of us, so I ended up in a fine Catholic institution."

"How long did it last?"

"Years. It stopped when I left Derry for Dublin."

I let him tell me as much or as little as he wanted. And I listened over the months as he described a list of things that I was well used to hearing and to sticking in a treasure chest at the back of my mind. Treasure, of course, is the wrong word, but if I'd visualized the chest as an old black box with broken leather straps it would have sat in my consciousness, highlighting itself, shouting it was there. So it was a shiny gold pirate chest I had in my head, Disney-benign, quiet and resting and nice enough not to trouble my working brain. Filled with the things I had to keep but didn't want in the first place. My treasure chest to keep me sane, the thing my clients paid me for. And the gun in my desk was the locking mechanism should it ever spill open.

"A few years ago," he told me, "I thought about visiting him, meeting him face to face in some old priests' home or whatever. Seeing what he had to say. But maybe I couldn't stand to be in the same room as him, and that scared the life out of me. I'd be letting him off admitting what he did."

Turlough lifted his face as if wakening up. "In any case, the thoughts were getting too bad. I couldn't organize a thing, let alone a trip down to some shithole to see a skeleton in his fucking stinky chair."

"Those meetings can help. But you never know until you're in the situation."

"Do *you* think it would help?"

"It might provide some kind of reconciliation."

"Reconciliation with him?"

"Reconciliation with your past. Don't worry about him."

"What'll I do, doctor? I don't want a loose thread hanging around my neck for the rest of my life."

"Do you know where he is?"

"He's in Roscommon, in the middle of nothing. The nearest thing he can touch is the cows."

"And what would you want out of a meeting with him?"

"I'd like to see him before he dies, tell him I made it and I forgive him. He's a bastard, but I forgive him." He thought for a second and said, "Would it help if I took someone with me?"

"It would. A family member or close friend perhaps."

"I don't know anyone."

"No one at all?"

"I had a friend a few years ago. And I had a few friends a few years before that. The family's all gone."

"I can go with you if you want," I offered.

"Would you to do that?"

"I would, of course."

"It'd be easier if you were there."

"But if you feel uncomfortable at any time, you have to tell me and we'll take control and leave the place. Do you understand?"

"I do, I will," he said eagerly, but then he looked out the window and the hope on his face turned to concern.

We settled on a time and a meeting place in Roscommon for the following day – the sooner the better, according to Turlough. And I was happy to help in such difficult circumstances. When he left me alone in the office, I thought about my own friends and, despite our frequent disagreements, how much I valued them. And then I remembered they were coming over for dinner that evening, and I broke into a bit of a sweat.

5. The Dinner Party

"I'm a bit early, Michael." Ken Skeffington grinning at the door. Fifteen minutes early, and I could have punched him in the grin.

"I'll have to leave you to amuse yourself," I told him, but he followed me into the kitchen and kept chatting away, blocking every shelf I had to get to. I loved cooking but was useless at it, and I knew well it was the wine and the arguments that my friends were returning for every few weeks. Ken's arrival brought me out in a migraine for the first time in my adult life. The singing pain at the front of my head bent down with me as I lifted the raspberry sponge out of the oven.

"Let me get the door for you," Ken said at the sound of a knock. But then he wandered into the living room, still talking about some filthy new staff member in his department. I was wondering which way he meant it when the doorbell rang, and I ran out to welcome Jean O'Halloran and her friend coming up the path behind her. By the time I was back in the kitchen with the smoking roast, I heard Alastair's loud, warm words filling the porch.

"You're a bit hassled," Ken let me know.

"I am. Would you pour the wine for anyone who wants it?"

He took the bottle and went into the dining room, and I swear everyone still had an empty glass by the time I got in there. Ken was the chief radiologist at St. James's Hospital in Dublin, and I marveled at how he'd got the job. Sitting with him were Jean, the assistant head of nursing at St. James, and her pal Suzanne Murray, who I'd never met before and who sat in scared silence for most of the evening. And Alastair MacFarlane, the retiring chief of surgery at the hospital, over for dinner and, more importantly, a whiskey. He let his wife know that our gatherings were vital for keeping up with medical advances, but she must have wondered how he remembered anything by the time he got home with a slur and a smile.

"I'm writing a novel," Ken was saying. "It's science fiction but it's very good."

"Interesting. What's it about?" Jean asked with the static face of disinterest.

"An apocalypse happens, and the only people who survive are the ones who've had Botox. It's an evolution thing, and Botox gives them immunity."

Guffaws all round for something that wasn't such a bad idea after all.

"So the Hollywood ladies are left to fend for themselves?" Alastair said in his furry Scots accent. "And don't men get Botox too?"

"They do," Jean said in excitement. "And acid peels. They could only help the plot."

Ken was annoyed that they had run away with his book. "It's a dystopia, not a comedy. They have to eat each other to survive."

"But if a flaw in the immune system killed everyone, wouldn't the food still be there?" I asked. "Couldn't they keep growing things?"

The budding author looked at me, and I wasn't sure whether he was trying to fit my revelation into his manuscript or work out how to slap me without being seen. But Alastair thought it was a wonderful idea and asked how long it would be.

"I'm aiming for a novel, and I'm at 20,000 words at the moment."

"That could well be a best-seller," I said to make amends. "Definitely a best-seller."

"I don't know about that, but I'd like to be published."

"Haven't you been published lots of times already?"

"In medical journals. They don't count."

And for some reason, everyone nodded.

Mini salmon puffs for the starter, hard to get wrong when you buy them. Roast chicken for the main, easy enough, with a good sauce to counter dullness or dryness. But the highlight was my mashed potatoes, a simple thing that can be hard to get right.

"These are like silk," Suzanne said out of the blue.

"Thanks for saying so." I might have blushed if my face wasn't already red from the wine. The compliment meant twice as much, coming from a mouse.

"How do you make them?"

"You have to start with a good potato. Russets are the best, but they're hard to find in Ireland."

For the other men at the table, it was the perfect opportunity to fondle their wine glasses and drink down deeply.

"I use Roosters," I explained. "And I pass them through a ricer. Then I add butter and lukewarm milk, about a third as much as there are potatoes."

"Well, that's excellent," Ken piped in. "Let's drink to the potato."

So I toasted my own efforts. And by the time the sponge was out and the fifth bottle of wine was open, I hadn't noticed that my migraine had gone.

I couldn't miss Roscommon the next morning, though my throat was tight and my stomach raw. As I went out my front door, I kicked into something I didn't see and heard a *thump thump* I wasn't expecting: a white plastic bag with caramel-colored potatoes tumbling down the steps.

And a note: "Thanks for a great night. Here's a few Russets I found this morning, Suzanne."

What a surprise, and from one so quiet. I set off in the car wondering where she had found them and, more importantly, whether I should add cream cheese to my mash that night or leave the potatoes as they were in their beautiful naked selves.

6. A Quick Hello

The priests' home was a huge Georgian building, an old Anglo-Irish estate that the Catholic Church had converted decades before into a pleasant-enough locked castle for abusive priests. A sizable wall ran around the perimeter, high enough for 80-year-olds to have a hard time throwing their leg over. A few men in wheelchairs littered the grounds, left on their own with their Parkinson's and bilious memories. Hopefully still believing in hell.

I had picked Turlough up at the side of a stony pub, and he wasn't too talkative as we drove to the home. He was as white as a ghost when he got out of the car, and he steadied himself with one hand on the roof.

"Just give me a minute."

"You might feel panicky, Turlough."

He put the other hand to his chest.

"Can you remember something good?" I said. "Can you remember telling me about when you were in Afghanistan, at the border with the trainees?"

"Is that meant to be pleasant?"

"But you didn't get one thought the whole time. You felt in control, you said."

"I knew what to do."

"You fired off a round to scatter the border guards, but they were used to being shot at..."

"And no one had mentioned that to me." He broke into a weak smile, still clutching his chest.

"And they ran after you and you dropped the gun…"

"Miles of sand, and I ran. And then I collapsed."

"But you were laughing…"

"I was laughing so much I collapsed. I hadn't one OCD thought the whole time. My mind was as free as a bell."

"Remember that feeling. Today will help you have that feeling for good."

"I'm having a heart attack."

"You're not. I'm a doctor."

"You do heads."

"I had to do everything when I started."

"Were you no good at the other stuff?"

"Crap. I'm only good at pretending to listen to people."

Turlough's smile widened, and he repeated to himself, "My mind is as free as a bell."

The color wasn't back in his cheeks but he stood straight and let out a long, slow breath. He nodded at me and we went through the main doors, where we were hit by a smell of chlorine. I was happy to show my credentials to anyone who'd want to see them, ready to explain that after two years of therapy, one of my patients was looking for closure. There was no one at reception, and we stood a short while before Turlough winked at me and went behind the desk and scrolled down a computer screen to the name he wanted. Then I followed him up two flights of wide stairs and down a white corridor of doors.

"Are you alright, Turlough?"

"I am, I think I am," he almost stopped to say.

"Remember, we can leave at any time."

A nurse came out of a door and walked towards us. Turlough gave her a nod and walked by, and I did the same. He was concentrating, thinking about his heartbeat, controlling his pulse, taking command of himself like I'd taught him to.

"This is it," he said, looking at the name on a door. He opened it and I followed him in.

Turlough halted inside, his eyes fixed on the skeleton coughing in the bed.

"What do you want now?" it croaked over at us.

The engagement was going to be difficult. The priest was cranky at even existing, he'd be doubly so at being accused of child abuse. I moved to the center of the room, knowing the single chair would be for Turlough. I was far enough away that he could talk discreetly if he had to, but close enough that I'd be by his side if he needed me.

Turlough walked to the top of the bed. When he looked at the face that was in it, he opened his mouth to speak, but he could only shake his head, as if trying to disturb the right words. Nothing came. Long seconds without sound. Only the priest looking up at him either waiting to hear speech or waiting for his memory to sharpen. And without any notice,

Turlough yanked the pillow out from under the priest's head and placed it over the face and pressed down.

"Turlough!" I said in fright. "Turlough, stop!" It took me a second to run and pull one of his arms off the pillow. The priest's head shot up from under it and the toothless mouth gasped for air and squealed any noise to be heard. Turlough didn't brush me off. With my hands still on his shoulders, he took the priest's bible from the bedside locker and smashed it into his head, almost knocking him out of the bed. He pulled the priest back to his pillow, and the squeals turned to groans.

"What are you doing!"

"As clear as a bell..."

"I can't be here," I said, "I can't."

Turlough turned to me, his body bent slightly and his hands locked on the pillow beneath him. His face was the picture of calm. "Go then."

I left him with the priest. Several steps to the door, hoping no one would come in before I could reach it. At the door and my chest telling me it'd burst if I didn't get out. My fingers on the handle and I opened it and smelled the pure disinfectant of the shiny floor outside. Out to an empty corridor and its promise of a small walk to safety. A small walk back to my life, a quick move away from Turlough and his murdering hands. At least that's what it would have been, if I'd moved down the corridor at all.

I should have walked away. I knew even then that I could have walked away. But the thought of leaving grew quiet as another thought ran up to meet it, battle it, drown it out. The thought that Turlough was taking revenge on someone who'd ruined his life. He was doing what he had to. An old man would die in his bed, a man who didn't deserve another breath, and no one would wonder about it. And as for me, it wasn't like I hadn't seen people killed in front of me before.

Some part inside shouted all of this at me, while another part screamed that I had to get away. And as silent as death, one of those parts reached up to choke the other, and my mind hung free in my head. The clean white corridor held me for a moment, then I turned back to the door and went in.

The priest's legs were shaking under the skinny covers when I reached Turlough's side. I put my hands up to cover the twitching feet and I dropped them down, feeling a shock when I touched the insteps and pressing hard to take that shock away. Turlough didn't look at me as we waited through the most important minutes of all our lives. Waiting to hear someone knock, to hear the end of muffled sounds. To hear from a conscience that wasn't there.

I barely remembered walking out, back down the corridor behind Turlough. The same nurse as before approached us and held up her head to speak, but as she did, Turlough turned to me and said, "You know, Uncle Jackie really likes muffins. I'll bring some into him the next time we're here."

I managed a nod as we walked by, and we took the marble stairs back down to the main doors and out to the car park. I thought my hands would be shaking at the wheel, but there was no trembling as I drove us through the iron gates and took the green country road away. Turlough spoke to me, a few words about loose threads, but I was too distracted to reply.

By the time I reached home in the darkness, any fear in me was gone, all the shock that I'd felt had left me. I had taken the first step off the soft grass and onto the road to hell – and I knew it, I knew what I was doing! – because I wasn't thinking about driving to the police and handing both of us in. I was only thinking about Turlough, and how he might be the man to help me with something that had stabbed me for forty years.

7. Michael's Question

When you've helped someone to kill someone else, a bond forms between you. Not a mystical bond that means you're brothers for life, just the simple *I know*. So when Turlough gave me an opportunity a few days later in my office, I brought up a subject that had lodged in my head since Roscommon.

"It's strange," he said, "but you know everything about me. The shit that happened to me and the shit I did. It's a lot of big secrets to be keeping."

"That'll always be confidential, you never have to worry about that. But if it makes you feel better, maybe ..." I was stuck for words.

"Maybe what?"

"Well, you know about me, too."

"That had nothing to do with you."

"I know."

We weren't friends, but we were close in a different way. I was a psychological crutch for him, holding his fantastically horrible stories inside me, as I was paid to do. But now that I needed a crutch myself, having lasted on four hours sleep for as long as I could remember, it made sense to ask him for help, and to pay him in return.

"Turlough, something's been annoying me for a while. I'll tell you about it, because you've always been honest with me. There's no one else I could ever mention this to."

"We both already have secrets," I went on, "and maybe another will be good for your therapy, knowing we trust each other entirely. But maybe it won't. What do you think?"

And with his next words, he shocked me into what should have been reality:

"Who do you want me to kill?"

I snorted a laugh and he smiled.

"Ah, no, it's nothing like that," I said.

"That's what it usually is."

"Does it sound like that?" Faux disbelief. "Well, I don't know. Maybe it does. There aren't many people who do what you do, so you might be used to hearing that. I just want to track someone down, see what he's up to."

"That's not what I do."

I didn't know what else to say, and I was prepared to drop the subject right then.

"Where is he?" he asked.

"It could be New Zealand. I'll pay all your expenses, of course."

"You'll pay me for more than that. It's a job. And if I find him, do you want me to go knocking?"

"I don't know. Maybe I'll forget about it."

"Suit yourself. I like the Kiwis."

"He's not..." I crossed my arms and sat back in the chair. I brushed my eyebrows with the palm of my hand. Then I looked at him and said, "Have you heard of Lord Lucan?"

"Are you serious?"

"I know it's a tough one."

"It's been decades since that name's come up."

"All our conversations are confidential, aren't they?"

He gave me a jeering smile. "You'd be in trouble if they weren't."

"I mean on your side as well."

"Have you not been listening to me these past couple of years? There aren't many people I talk to. And with the shit I wade in, no one would believe me anyway. What did Lucan do to you?"

"Nothing. But this isn't really about him. There's another Lucan, one before him."

"His father?"

"Even further back."

"You're after a ghost? I'll need extra money for that."

"John Bingham is enough."

"What did the ghost do?"

I stood and looked out the window into the silent car park. I couldn't imagine how my words would sound to him, and I didn't want to see.

"It was Bingham's great-great-grandfather. I can't get him, but I can get people to remember who he was. He was let away with a lot of things, a great many deaths."

"And you can't let it go?"

I gazed at the greenery outside, the thick shrubs, the dark soil. I already knew what my answer would be, I just needed the strength to say it, now. In this office, right now.

"It's my OCD, Turlough."

"I suppose the Irish aren't a people for forgetting about the past. It *will* be a tough job."

"Finding him? I don't even know if he's still alive. I've done some research and ..."

"I can't stand Johannesburg. The smell is rank."

"Johannesburg?"

"And the crime rate is far too high."

"You know where he is?"

"It's a small world on our side of the fence, doctor."

"But the British police never found him."

Turlough sighed. He looked like he'd been talking for a year and wanted to leave.

"You don't drop a lord into the middle of South Africa when the country's about to explode. He chose the right place because he got lost easily enough, but he chose the wrong time and place for being a rich-sounding white guy. He had to have bodyguards, and none who were clean. The organization found out about him soon enough."

"They were there in the seventies?"

"There and everywhere."

"And you were his bodyguard?"

"He wouldn't have me. Hated the Irish for some reason. Something else came up anyway."

"What?"

"Sasol."

"What's that?"

"Never mind. Let's say I played my part in South African independence."

"And you'll do the same for us now?"

"For us? For you. This sounds more personal than patriotic. But are you allowed to ask me for something like this?"

"Definitely not. But I'm too selfish not to ask. And I'm sick of just peering into the shit."

"You want to fall in and drown?"

"If that's what it takes."

Turlough gave me the number of his personal bank account. While I wrote it down, I searched myself to see if I regretted what I was doing.

"I'd just like to know where he is."

He took a moment to act the psychiatrist. "If he dies in the course of things, how would you feel?"

"I'm not sure." *My father was a good man.* "A part of me would not be sad. A significant part."

And that evening as I opened my historical notes to read, I realized I felt fine, having transferred 90,000 euro into my patient's account.

8. The Difficult First (Mayo, 1835)

The first began the fall during the day, when everyone could hear me and I didn't care. Dan's sister by marriage Peigín O'Gliasáin was with me in the house, and she was powerful. She had many herself and knew to keep talking, saying things over and over, soothing words I wanted to hear. I told Dan to wait outside, far away outside, cursing him, because he was making me worse, telling me not to worry and to lie back and it would all be over soon. Well, I was worried, I wanted to stand, and it was not over soon. He had gone to the neighbor's house and I was still cursing him. This was not going to happen again; if God gave us one child, it was more than enough.

My mother was a help, though she had a hard time on her own last one and the fright of the dead thing had not sat well with her. But she was good with the water and rubbing my hair like I was a child. I wasn't alone, she said, but when the pain shot through my belly and didn't leave, I didn't care who was with me and who was without. Hour after hour, and I thought I was going to be dead. The village kept awake for me the whole night, though my screams would have made it hard for them to sleep, and Honoria arrived in the dark. When Dan came back in, crying because she was the best thing he had ever seen, I told him that he was the finest man in Ireland and I could not have done it without him.

(Annie Ó Gliasáin, Mayo)

9. An Old Story

Maggie watched the rolling red line of breaking news keeping viewers up to date on the bloody death of John Bingham. It was her last day at Harcourt Street, and the images coming from Johannesburg couldn't have seemed further away from rainy Dublin: an isolated farmhouse being bleached in the sun, surrounded by miles of dry orange scrub. The British news channels declared that an Englishman had been found battered to death in a quiet town in South Africa. DNA tests would be carried out by the Johannesburg police, but the items in the home suggested that the victim was Lucky Lord Lucan. Maggie was only vaguely familiar with the name, and she was Googling his image when Detective Superintendent Foster opened the day's briefing as reservedly as ever:

"Now to this pile of kak," she said. "The Lucan case, after all these years. Scotland Yard sent the file over to us as part of the exchange of information program. They've no idea if anything was taken during the attack because they don't know what was there in the first place. He lived an understandably quiet life."

Foster's permanent frown line deepened. "They're going through the papers that were found in his farmhouse and there's a few fun details coming out. Lucan claimed he was innocent of the 1974 attack in his former London home."

"Of course he did," said Bartley Quinn, the youngest officer in the room. "They all do."

"Hang on to your gallows, Quinn. In his notebooks, Lucan said he was targeted because of his gambling debts. He owed thousands to a man named Harry Blackwell, and he believed Blackwell sent a collector after him for the money."

"That's fairly specific," Maggie said. "Is it substantiated?"

"The Yard is looking into it now. Anything important has been sent up to London to see if they can help. I'm not sure how helpful they'd like to be though..."

"They've always been open with us."

"Ah, it was a different world in the 70s. Forensics were basic, often confusing things more than they helped. And there might be a few people still alive who wouldn't want the case reexamined."

"They wouldn't do anything to hamper it?"

"They just might not be very enthusiastic."

Foster paused, and the officers knew to wait until she gathered her thoughts.

"That case was always iffy," she said. "We studied it when I was a trainee, especially the legal part, because it was the last case in England where an inquest declared a man guilty of murder in his absence. If it was today, it's unlikely Lucan would be convicted on the strength of the evidence that was presented. But that's not to say he wasn't guilty.

"Lucan and his wife, Veronica, had separated and she'd got custody of the three children. Lucan's gambling had bankrupted him by then, so it seems he figured if he could murder her and make it look like she'd run off, he'd get the kids back and have fewer expenses to pay.

"Police believed he entered the Belgravia home using his old key and, in the darkness, beat to death a person he thought was his wife. But it was the nanny, 29-year-old Sandra Rivett. When Lady Lucan came out to see where Sandra was, Lucan attacked her, but she fought him off and they both collapsed to the ground. She claimed he admitted to her what he had done, then he went to the bathroom to get a towel for her. She ran out of the house and raised the alarm in a local pub. Lucan fled, quite rightly believing he'd be the prime suspect. He was never seen again, and the theory was that he'd drowned himself in remorse. Evidently he didn't do that, because he's just turned up dead in South Africa."

Maggie took in everything she was hearing, with a level of interest she hadn't felt in a while. Most of the investigations she'd been involved in had been predictable gangland killings in which at least twenty people knew who the shooter was, and it was just a matter of time before someone spoke up. Her eight-year career had been short on real murder mysteries.

"Is the theory of what happened airtight?" an officer asked.

"Definitely not. For one thing, the nanny was beaten so hard with a lead pipe that the floor, walls, and even the ceiling had blood splatter on them. But when Lucan's ten-year-old daughter recounted seeing her father and mother come into the bedroom after the attack, she said she couldn't remember her father having any blood on him at all. He should have been covered in it."

"Testimony from a ten-year-old?"

"Don't ever discount it. The sight of a parent covered in blood would be hard for any child to suppress."

"But Lucan would have benefitted financially from his wife's death?" Maggie asked.

"Not really. He famously didn't believe in insurance, so there was no windfall coming from that."

"Who else could it have been? A random burglar?"

"There was a conspiracy theory floating about that Lucan hired a hitman to do his dirty work, but he regretted it and rushed in too late to stop it. Also, Lucan's sister told Scotland Yard that his children spoke about a boyfriend of Sandra Rivett's, someone who used to visit the house in a fancy silver car. He and Sandra had a row, and they broke up a few days before she was murdered. That testimony was never presented in court. The whole thing is a mess."

"What do you think, ma'am?"

"About whether Lucan was the murderer? I've no idea. And the thing that baffles me most will probably never be cleared up."

"What is it?" Maggie whispered.

"It's the lead pipe. I never understood why it was there."

"The murder weapon?"

"Not the one used on Sandra Rivett. There was another one, an almost identical lead pipe found in the boot of an old Ford Corsair that Lucan had borrowed and abandoned. That weapon had no blood or hair on it from either victim."

"Lucan brought two with him, just in case? And he left one in the boot if he had to finish the wife off in the car?"

"Maybe. But my problem with it is more basic than that. I've been in homicide since 1989, and I've never seen a premeditative murderer bring two identical weapons to a scene. If they brought two weapons at all, they tended to be different. A hammer and a knife, for example. A bit of lead piping is flimsy, to say the least, and our murderer brought two of them? And Lucan had knowledge of weapons – he'd served in the Coldstream Guards."

The blank look on the faces before her told Foster to continue.

"It's a fancy regiment in the British army, tracing itself back to Oliver Cromwell's New Model Army or whatever they were called."

"But the Lucan lady said it was her husband who attacked her," Quinn reminded the room.

"She did, and she went through enough in her life that she didn't need conspiracy theories swirling around her forever. But she had a disastrous relationship with her ex-husband and she was hit on the head during the attack. In the end, the case will probably never be laid to rest, especially now that Lucan's dead and can't add anything to the story. Unless you count the ramblings in his notebooks: he said he was walking in the fog when he passed his old house. He looked through a window and saw his ex-wife struggling with an assailant. He ran in and the man fled. Lucan insisted that he recognized the man, but he couldn't remember his name. And that's an unfortunate thing for his legacy if what he says about the night is true.

"So, that's a murder in high society for you. And the British public are still talking about it today. Now that Lucan's body has turned up, the conspiracy theorists will have one less thing to worry about, because we can be pretty sure he didn't drown himself in 1974."

*****

At the end of the briefing, everyone gathered around Maggie to wish her well in her new assignment and advise her on surviving the new city. She half-listened to their tips on blocking out the constant noise, but she wrote down their recommendations for the best Indian restaurants. When an argument broke out about how chatty she should be with the London cabbies for safety's sake, she had to call a halt.

"I'm a cop," she reminded them, "and I'm not flying to another planet. It's only London – a bigger type of Dublin."

"Proportionally speaking," Quinn said, "there are a lot more weirdos on the streets."

"And we're normal over here?"

"No, but we're friendly. The people in London can be fairly cold."

"I'm looking forward to it," Maggie said. "And if it doesn't work out, I'll be back in six months anyway."

"Not if you marry a foreigner. A nice Englishman, then you'll be stuck there forever."

"I'd have peace from you lot," she said, taking her colleagues' hands and hugs warmly and almost getting a tear in her eye when they brought out a cake in the shape of her face.

Superintendent Foster was the last to approach her.

"I'll miss you, Maggie," the boss said quietly, and with a sad look in her eyes. "These blokes don't know how to keep their fucking desks tidy."

"You should beat them, ma'am."

"I'm too old. But what I'll really miss is you being the idiot who's always first through the front door, whether there's ten scumbags in the house or it's a pensioner who's died in his sleep."

"I'll have to tone that down."

"You take it all seriously, which is why you're getting the transfer and why you might get the SDU when you're back home. Learn what you can in London, and don't let them give you any guff over there. I did a stint with the Yard back in the eighties, and we were fucking trampled on. Things might be better for the Irish these days, but you're still going to get the odd prick. You know how to handle odd pricks?"

"I do, ma'am. And you can rest assured I won't come back in six months' time speaking the Queen's English. I know I'd be eaten alive."

10. A Break for Michael

When Turlough finally phoned me from Johannesburg on the last day of July, I had forty bottles of wine in front of me and one in my stomach. It was a one-night stay at the Belfast Ibis Hotel that had been organized by St. James Hospital's social club, the Fun-Raising committee, and they asked me along even though I was reducing my hours of public practice. I had trained in St. James and spent twenty years working there, but cutbacks and the recession had doubled the number of people who were looking for help. Something in me would have split if I didn't change my life, so I closed my world around me in my offices in Ballsbridge.

Those offices occupied half the ground floor of a low red-bricked block that would have passed for luxury apartments if there weren't business nameplates on the main doors. My neighbor was a plastic surgeon to the stars, as he called himself, an expressionless but friendly man who joked that he could take twenty years off me with one needle. I joked back that I could take fifty-four years off myself with one needle too, but I couldn't tell from his face if he understood what I meant. We looked out over the same small car park and the immaculate garden, and our elegant shared receptionist was the opposite of a hassled public nurse at the end of her tether.

I thought about canceling the wine tasting because I was flying into Dublin that day after a short trip away and wasn't sure if I'd make it home to Sandymount to collect the car and drive the three hours up to Belfast. But I did make it in time, and I was glad of the distraction from waiting to hear Turlough ring at any moment. I took the M1 motorway out of the city, and the scenery changed from concrete to green.

Before the motorway was built, I'd used the smaller national routes, passing through every town and village, the road itself based on the 1,000-year-old dirt tracks that had linked those places. And now the motorway ignored them, passing out of Dublin and up through Meath and Louth, up into the North to become the N1 and then the A1, bypassing towns and extending to Belfast, as if that was the end of the world and where else would you go? I missed the long drive through Meath, with its prehistoric tombs and ancient Hill of Tara, the High Seat of Irish Kings. Meath was ferociously Irish in a way that had been stamped out of Dublin, whose English neoclassical buildings proclaimed, "you don't matter at all," and whose tall Georgian houses reminded people that their original owners mattered very much indeed. And so from Dublin to Belfast on a motorway that split the green, a roofless tarmac tunnel that took me from one country to another, from Ireland to the involuntarily United Kingdom.

A tight "It's done" from Turlough, and I turned back to the wine table and hearing about the blackberry nose and oak ambience of whatever bottle the sommelier was talking about in the Northern Irish accent I'd spoken as a child. I lifted whatever was in my glass to my mouth and toasted Turlough in my head.

It's done. I've finished it for you, Dad. There was a man lying dead 15,000 miles away, a man who hadn't known me and hadn't known the man who'd attacked him. I didn't feel happy, I just felt relief, and I toasted Turlough again.

"Is this a dating night?" Alastair whispered into my shoulder, already half gone.

"Why would you say that?"

"They're making us stand up. We're being forced to mingle."

"My date for tonight is this Valpolicella, so nobody better cock their eye at me."

"Don't be too hasty, the love of your life could be here getting plastered," and he looked at the guests over the rim of his glass. "Jean, is this a dating night? Have you mixed the wine in with the romance?"

"I didn't organize this one," she held up her hands in innocence. "I wanted the shooting range."

A burst of laughter erupted in the corner, as Ken amused the medical secretaries with his endless hole of personal anecdotes. The ladies were not quite believing what he said, but he was the chief radiologist and their eyes never left him. Whether spinning exaggerated misadventures with his X-Ray machine or describing his Botox apocalypse, he held the crowd well.

I left Alastair and Jean for the quiet end of the tasting table, to focus on Turlough's words, to think about having finally paid for a little justice. I wasn't there a minute when I heard a "Hello Michael" from a solitary figure behind me.

I looked at the person with a smile. A forest of white hair on his head and fifty wrinkles on his face, all pointing to two black pits for eyes. I tried to keep the smile going.

"Are you wine tasting?"

"No, no," he said with his usual Northern Irish softness. "I prefer the Guinness."

"Is everything well?"

"We'll have a chat down here," he said, and I followed Mr. Grady wherever he led, sobering up with each step. We took adjacent seats at an empty table.

"I just dropped by to see how you are."

"I'm fine. What do you need?" I tried to focus.

"I have a few things for you to look at."

"Send them over anytime."

"We need a new quartermaster. Southern only." He stared at the unruly wine tasters as if there was no one there. "See who'd make a good job of it. No one too young. No one who'd want to start things up again." And not really addressing me, he added, "But also no one who'd send two tons of plastics out of the country."

"That seems to be happening a lot," I sympathized with him. Since the IRA ceasefire of 1996, and especially since the Good Friday Agreement two years later, the people of Northern Ireland had to drop the arms and become a new model army of friendly citizens. In reality, they split into two new model armies, and our organization's weapons at least had seen more movement than ever before, being hidden, dug up, shipped out, sold off. Former combatants now had time on their hands and the need to make a living, and what could be easier than selling the things that shouldn't be there?

"Don't you worry about that!" Grady barked, with a fierce expression matching his words. He covered the lower half of his face with his hand and looked at a couple of revelers as they passed by. When he took the hand away, he had assembled some kind of a smile. "Don't worry about that. Just think about the profiles."

He suddenly said my name. "Michael Gleeson. Your dad was a great man. I'm glad you're with us. Oh, and while I'm here, have you seen Mr. O'Sullivan? We can't find him anywhere." The lightness was still on his face, but his stare was solid.

"I haven't seen him since his last session a few weeks ago."

"Not to worry, we'll find him. We always keep tight tabs on men like that. Otherwise they'd kill us all."

"He does know how to distinguish who he is from what he does."

"And what is he?"

"He's a patient with too many memories."

"He's a child who can kill you without either of you noticing. Don't ever forget that. If I'm still sending you unhappy men many years from now, it would help if you're still alive."

I needed a moment to answer, but Grady didn't give it to me. He stood up.

"I've a million other things to do tonight, not least looking at a few peace walls."

"Should you go out the back door?" I said, looking around the room. "I'm not sure where it is ..."

"The back door? Am I not just a civil servant meeting an old friend at a wine-tasting hooley? It's not like we're plotting to blow up the country." And leaving his glass untouched, Mr. Grady gave one knock on the table and was gone out the front door, marveling at the antics of the attendees as he went.

I didn't know how, but it sounded like a warning, and I should have been glad of it. But as I sat there with the wine to my lips, the bodies and high talk around me, I seethed. The blood drained from my stomach and out to my fists, up to my sweating face.

History doesn't belong to them.

Using Turlough to find Lucan may have been a bad idea, but I might never have got the chance again. Dad would have known how to handle Mr. Grady – he would have told him to eff off and mind his own business. He would have reminded Mr. Grady that he's working with the British and Irish governments now, that he should keep his bloody black pits on that.

I doubt Dad would have said anything at all.

"Who was that?" Jean sat down beside me.

"How are Ken's stories coming along?"

"Silly stories about making mistakes. Can you give me a lift home tomorrow?"

"If I can stand." And I knocked back my glass. And then a refill, because I was sober now and could have pushed the whole wine table over and watched all the bottles smash to the ground. If they had their eyes on me, that'd be the end of everything.

When I slipped up the stairs to bed, for the first time since college I felt like getting sick. Alastair was long asleep, and Ken was entertaining the ancillary staff. I noticed it was Jean who was helping me up. I think she said something to me. But I think I was alone when I fell onto the bed and didn't wake up until the next morning, my bladder stabbing me with the toxic bottles of liquid it held. I sat up to go to the bathroom and found beside me a large plastic folder containing ten other folders, all snapped together with an elastic band. One of Grady's men must have left it there while I slept. In noiselessly through the locked door.

When I went down to the breakfast buffet, Alastair was waiting for me. He didn't look lively, and out of everything he could have chosen, he had tea and dry toast in front of him.

"Not feeling good this morning?" I asked.

"Stomach's a bit dodgy."

"I might just have toast myself."

"You're getting like me. We're both getting too old to drink."

"Old and cranky."

"Actually, Michael, I hope you're not getting like me."

"What do you mean?"

"I better tell you before the masses arrive. I have a small growth. Nothing too bad so don't start sobbing. My PSA came back a bit high."

I missed a breath. "Why did you get tested?"

"I've had a few problems *down there*," he said with a grin that lasted a second. "It might be the prostate, and that's not a worry these days."

"Shit."

"You're not sitting with a dead man yet."

"Were you wise drinking so much last night?"

"I was. And we'll be doing it again. Now, change the subject, man. I've done my duty telling you. How are all your loons?"

"Shit. When will you know?"

"Wednesday. And that's enough of that. Your loons."

"My what? I don't think you can call them that these days. And they're all very well. Crackers, of course. Shit, Alastair."

"Please Michael," he placed his hand over mine. "I'm a head-in-the-sand man. The less I think about it the better. Dwelling on it would make me sick to my stomach, get the immune system aggravated, and that's the last thing I need."

"Okay. Shit. I can't think of anything else now."

I knew how he felt, what it was like to visit a clinic and wait a lifetime in only a few days, stop living until the results came back.

"Your patients are always a blast," he said.

"I don't want them dwelling in my head either." There was only one thing I could think of. "I can tell you about something …"

I scratched my head. With a few words, I'd already gone too far. Extra ears were what I needed, but I knew his wouldn't be sympathetic to what I was going to say.

"I may have done something that may not have been quite appropriate."

"That sounds kinky."

"It's to do with my other job."

He put down his cold toast and sat back from the table. "I don't want to hear anything about that."

"I know."

"I'm not listening, so say nothing to me. I don't even know why you're still working with them. You're not taking on any new ones?"

"No new ones."

"They're just criminals now. The fight ended with the Good Friday Agreement."

"The fight was put on hold with the Good Friday Agreement."

"Jesus, man, your heart is still bleeding the green."

"What are you talking about?"

"I'd say if you were stuck in a lineup with Patrick Pearse or some of those old Republicans, you wouldn't be out of place.

Although being in a lineup with them may not be a good idea, seeing as they were all shot dead."

He looked at me sadly and softened his tone. "I know you're trying to help those old shits with their bombings and crap, but don't go any further. Especially not now. What you're doing, your head shrinking, that's legal, even if they tell you they blew up a city, you don't have to let anyone know. But anything more than that is criminal, Michael. Especially these ones today, they're not freedom fighting. It's drugs and weapons today."

"I know, Alastair. That's why I'm bloody ..."

"Bloody what?"

"You know my background."

"You can't use that. You're too clever for that excuse."

"Excuse? Do you remember when Scotland lost the referendum for independence, and you cried, Alastair? You were in bits."

"I had one too many whiskies on me. And it was a little different."

"You felt it. You couldn't believe the result. You don't have to be ashamed of wanting your own country."

"We haven't killed for it. Not recently. I think being in Belfast is doing funny things to your head, man. You should get back down south and not worry about this anymore. Let the people worry about it themselves."

I moved in closer to the table. "I couldn't care less about them up here. I hated every second I lived here. If they haven't got the British out in the last hundred years, they never will."

"For some reason, I've a hard time believing you don't care."

"Are you guys kissing?" Jean's voice at our side, and the smiles came back to our faces as she placed her two plates of buffet food on the table and sat down. The chatter of Irish idealism stopped by a full Irish breakfast and an enthusiastic helping of continental pastries.

*****

Jean was my passenger on the drive back to Dublin, but before we left Belfast, I made a quick stop.

"You were born up here?" she asked, as we headed down Castle Street toward the quays.

"I was. In the Short Strand."

"That sounds beautiful. Beside the sea."

"It's on the River Lagan, and it's out of this world."

It was the only world I'd known up to the night in 1970 when we walked away and let it implode on itself. The day before my eighth birthday. You wouldn't get much back then, a toy and an orange, but you still got the few friends over and your dad might tell you you're getting big now and then go back to watching the telly. That was enough, or it would have been if the street outside hadn't suddenly been cordoned off with walls of tumbling barbed wire.

"My mates won't get in!" I cried to Mam, and she tried to calm me by saying they would get in, they just had to ask the soldiers there if it was okay to come down to Michael Gleeson's party. More wire went up and two armored cars appeared at the blockade at the top of the road, but I was sure they could still get in. The carpet of rocks on the street wasn't a problem, the near-sounding gunfire might be put on hold, the heavy chemical smoke would have drifted away in a day. But when Dad came in on the arms of two men and lay on the sofa, the circle of a black bruise covering his whole chest from what they said was a bullet made of rubber, I got the notion there might be a problem.

"Won't they think the party's still on? What if they show up?" I said to Mam that evening as the three of us were hurried through neighbors' houses to get to the port.

"I'll let the mammies know," she said, handing me an orange. I didn't ask her how. It would be three years before I was back on Bryson Road, three years of being happy in London, up until a foggy night that forced us home.

Now, driving with Jean, there were slightly fewer union jacks on the streets, a few less tricolors, no burnt-out cars, no roadblocks, no roadblocks of burnt-out cars. But something was the same as it always had been: the skittish unease that Belfast made me feel.

I drove us over the Lagan and continued a short way onto the Newtownards Road, then took a quick turn at a soft-looking church and proceeded down Bryson Road. A couple of large square buildings, then a line of terraced houses on the right. I wondered if Jean noticed that the left-hand side of the road consisted only of a wall, with a monolithic steel fence on top of it. But the fence was grilled, so the sun kept shining through as I drove to the end of the road and parked where it swung a corner into Madrid Street.

Out at the wall, I looked for myself and found me, tiny and on the side of a brick that was part of a series shaped into a diamond, adding a touch of glamour to the bleakness.

"I'm still here," I pointed, as Jean joined me to see what was so interesting.

She looked disappointed. "Micha? That's some kind of mineral?"

"No, there's no 'h' in that. This is the start of my name."

"You didn't finish it?"

"I was stopped."

She stared at it for a few moments before taking a look up and down the street and getting back into the car, saying it was *a funny little thing* and that she had to check her messages. I touched the brick with my fingers and as I did, something flew up into the sky from the other side of the wall and came down with the sharpest of cracks in the middle of the road. I took the few steps over and saw a pink and white sock with a weight in it, likely a few stones, and the outlined face of a cat looking up at me. 'Hello Kitty' it read. I got into the car before any other hopeful missiles landed on my head.

We were out of the area and hitting the A1 when Jean delivered her stinger of a question:

"Do you remember last night?"

"How do you mean?" I'm sure I came out in a rash over the course of one sentence.

"About us getting married?"

"What?"

"I said if we're both still single in a couple of years, we should get hitched."

"Did I agree?"

"You fell asleep. I thought I'd take my chance, seeing as the staff nurses are crazy about you."

"I think that's Ken's department."

"He doesn't run it very well."

Jean was one of the most reliable people I knew professionally, direct and efficient and always black and white, and the thought of a dalliance with that kind of personality scared the hell out of me. I'd had a few relationships in my life, and some had even lasted, but it always struck them eventually that no matter how loving I was, there was a part of me that was a million miles away.

"I'd never be good for anyone. That Micha back there, my name on the brick, that explains why."

"Something happened with it?"

"With it, and everything. One long messy set of years."

"You're a psychiatrist, you should be able to work all that out."

"I can work it out easily enough but dealing with it is another thing."

She didn't ask any more, and when I spoke again, I hadn't meant to. I noticed a sign for an upcoming turn for a large leafy suburb to the west of Dublin, a place I knew well, with a name I'd always associated with a shopping center there. The Liffey Valley Shopping Center, and Liffey Valley was what I called the place in my head. But the larger area had another name, something I knew but which only resonated with me then.

It was 'Lucan.'

"That's funny," I blurted out.

"What is?"

I stared at the sign as we passed it. His name went on, Lucan's name was continuing, in big black letters over the main motorway in Ireland. My hands were suddenly irritated by the steering wheel and I was sick of sitting down. *They're long dead yet they changed so much of us.* I drove even faster and made it to Jean's house with twenty minutes to spare.

By the time I was home myself, I had a pain in my head and a knot in my stomach. I was wound up to the point where nothing could calm me down, nothing at all. I thought I might feel better getting things out in words, washing my anger out, as the therapy goes, so I sat in my small home office typing rubbish. I deleted the words and started again. And when nothing better came out in the draft, I sat back in the chair, closed my eyes, and thought about Bryson Road.

*****

The night I'd carved my half name, we'd been back in Belfast two years and I was a man of thirteen. I must have figured that if I got my name down permanently, it'd be more likely that we'd never move again. Or maybe I was only thinking that if I got my name down first, the wall would be mine. And what a wall it would turn out to be, one of the early peace walls, though work had only started and you could still get through to Thistle Court and you could still get from Thistle onto Bryson Road. Where I stood, using the key around my skinny neck to carve my name into the sweet-smelling brick.

They didn't even bother with words, just a push of my head into the wall. That didn't knock me to the ground, it just surprised and riled me. Three fellas from the Thistle, forcing me to stay and get battered or take a run at one to get through them. I took the run and brought him off his feet and backward to the ground. I think it aired him because he was slow to get up, and that's when I should have run. Christ above, I knew even then that I could have run. I could have torn up Madrid Street and anyone there would have taken me in and the fellas would never have followed.

But I stood and lashed out, clipping the next one on the side of the head with flaps of my hand. He came towards me in some kind of funny run and started punching my shoulders, me well able to soak it up. The last one tried to get a few kicks in behind, but he kicked his pal as much as he did me and then he stopped and said it was time to go, that they had to leave Bryson before anyone came. I would have been happy with that, because I would have stood up to them and, with a few embellishments in the retelling, I would have come out on top.

One boom of a siren shook the street and our ears, and we stopped and stared at the army patrol vehicle that hadn't even bothered to turn on its lights. The doors cracked opened and two men got out, straight over to us, and one made a limp grab at the nearest fella, but he pulled himself out of his jacket and let it fall to the ground and he was over the half-finished wall and away to his home in the Thistle. I didn't know where he was gone, because a baton to the face stopped me looking. And this time I fell, my nose shattered into me, making me think I'd never have a face again. The older men sometimes said your body goes numb when you're being kicked and batoned on the ground, but I felt each strike. I could only wait for the next hit and wonder where it would be and then be surprised at where it was. Curling up to protect my face, and the blood was in my mouth.

And maybe I'm exaggerating now, maybe they only hit me a few times, otherwise I'd be dead. I don't know and I don't like to think about it too much; the brain likes to make up its own stories. The blows hammering down on me, and the seconds were hours, and I heard the sound of trainers running toward me on the terrible sandy surface of the road. A few shouts, the first voice I'd heard for ages, and the two men in green were down on the ground. I can't remember gunfire, though one of my eardrums had been banged to bits. What I can remember is a man's face at my own, saying in a normal voice that it'd be okay, I'd be okay, and we have to move you to a doctor's.

I thought it was my father, but I had to settle for the chest of my uncle, as he held me and half-carried me down Madrid Street and out of harm's way. My father's face changed when he saw me at the door, and the quiet man got a look of death in him that never went away. It's hard even at that age to get the hate into you; my young head still believed everyone was good. But it had started to knock, and it settled on me like a poncho a few years later, the night my father went for a pint along the Falls Road.

*****

I opened my eyes. The draft was still on the screen in front of me. A draft email to a friend, to Turlough, about his thoughts on a second job, seeing as the first went so well, and could he find another person for me? I took two Nurofen and read what I wrote.

I deleted the message. I'd asked about finding an individual in England, someone on the low end of celebrity. Not hard to track down. I must have gone mad. All those years of listening to dreadfully lonely stories from patients were catching up with me. My treasure chest creaking open. It must have been that, because this was an innocent person I was asking Turlough to find. This person, and Lucan already dead. Their ancestors were among the worst men ever to cast a glance at Ireland, but there was no blood on the descendants' hands. The sins of the father stayed back there, back with the black hearts. I didn't have a time machine. The ancestors. Who were probably still laughing at us, sniggering in their graves from deep in the ground, laughing at how they got away with killing so many. We were innocent, and they had taken everything, land and lives. And the descendants of those men, they were innocent, too. Innocent, but laughing at us by being alive. Still beating the sense out of us when we were thirteen years old, when we just wanted someone to read our name off a sweet-smelling brick in our own country.

Dad, you'd laugh if you knew what I was up to. You'd wonder why no one had thought of it before.

I pulled the email out of the recycle bin and sent it off to Turlough. Then I opened my folder of notes and moved out of the present and into the past.

11. The Fog (1845)

They said about the place that it was a fog that brought it, but we never saw that. However it came, it settled on the fields, and the heavy air that kept it there went in and out of the houses. Like the air of a morning before winter, when you know all around is starting for sleep, but you might still get the sun that day and you'd think for a moment you'd be back in the summer. But the morning didn't lift and it was damp and wetting everything it touched.

And when the other men came to Dan to see how his were doing, he left with them for the high field. Something small might be amiss, and our hearts would drop and we'd think on what to do for the months to come. We had a cow and her calf, and if it came to the worst, my parents could help. Or the neighbors, as we had done for them the year before.

When Dan got back in the evening, he looked nothing but confused. They had walked all day to the high field and then to the fields beyond, and every green leaf they found was black and curled. The potatoes they took up were just as they should be and that was a hope, and an effort was made to get many out in the day and the days after.

And in the days after that, the ones from the ground that we had in the house rotted away and the smell from them filled the room and rose to the roof.

We asked around if it was everywhere, and no visitor from the next county brought good news. The few who came from even farther told the same story. And so it went on, as the blackness that hung in the air came into our chests and settled on our minds. We killed the calf for winter.

(Annie Ó Gliasáin, Mayo)

12. Evan Scott's Story

Evan Scott wasn't too happy that less than half a million people tuned into his car show each week, when that car show was undoubtedly the best thing on Channel Four. He didn't get a first-class degree and spend fifteen years working his way up from the bottom of the production room for this. The show's producers were imbeciles who knew nothing about cars, and his only consolation was that they received less than a third of his salary and could be fired for looking at him funny.

Stepping out of the Channel Four van at a quad-bike track in Newgrove, Staffordshire, Evan Scott wondered what the increase in viewership would be if one of the show's drivers crashed. Maybe not a death crash, but a moderate amount of scarring. Maybe one of the other hosts, live on camera. He wasn't to know that by the time the evening news came on, there were 20 million people watching his show, and it wasn't the car reviews or quirky vehicular escapades that they were tuning in for.

It was an outside broadcast from a sandy field in the middle of nowhere. Instead of quad bikes, Evan Scott told the producers to find a pair of 1937 Rolls Royces to race around the course, an entertaining speed trial to see whether either would survive the hard track and high dunes before rattling into pieces. The cars had to be pushed onto the track and coaxed into starting, and Evan Scott had to stand beside the rolling cameras and enthusiastic locals before getting the all-clear that the engines had decided to do their bloody job.

The bullet arrived as a sound that none of the people had heard before. It was such that it seemed like an invisible thing pushing the air out of the way, affecting the line between where it came from and where it ended up and leaving that line hanging in midair. The shot *fumped* into the back of Evan Scott's head and smashed his face into the camera, knocking the cameraman to the ground with Evan Scott's body on top. The viewers saw eyes and a nose blast toward them, a shake and a cloudy sky, a screen smeared with blood. The only sound was the shrill of screams, and it was enough.

Turlough let out a little laugh, something he rarely did. He had seen Evan Scott on television before, and the broadcasts had always stayed in his mind. The content was usually remote and unimportant, but what resonated with him while looking at this complete stranger was his name, sticking out like a wooden stake in the heart of an otherwise normal body. And now he was glad that his current employer had gone ahead with this assignment, even if it had meant watching car shows to find out where the next live broadcast would be, chasing Evan Scott up and down England with an Arctic Warfare Magnum hidden in his trunk. Turlough was happy to have found him, and very happy to have finally sent a bullet through the brown-haired head of Evan Scott Trevelyan.

13. Second Dinner Party

Alastair couldn't make it for dinner. He'd started the first round of chemo, and the tiredness had set in. A four-inch growth in the prostrate, fixable. An eight-incher in the pancreas, not great. No other signs of metastasis at least.

I considered canceling the night, but I needed something to think about other than my friend. So I thought about pork loins and potato gratin, the tiramisu that I'd buy. Crates of beer brought back on the ferry from Holyhead. And I left work at four o'clock this time, in case Ken called around even earlier than before.

"Did you get my message?" I asked Suzanne when she and Jean came through the front door.

"I did, you're very welcome."

"A great bag of spuds."

We were only one guest short, but the dining room seemed empty. I felt we should be talking about Alastair, but I didn't know who knew about his condition. And then a phone call stopped me wondering, and I left my guests to step into the hall.

"No problems," Turlough said, and the world stopped around me. Two words that meant more than all the patients I'd helped in my life, any good thing that I'd done. The million dead could now be quiet in their graves, and Charles Edward Trevelyan would be rolling in his. Whenever he'd be mentioned in the future, his name would be linked to this killing. Someone like him would never happen to us again, not without knowing that, no matter how many years in the future, we'd get them back. It was a shield for Ireland, a defense for the years ahead. Turlough was still talking to me, and I didn't hear a word.

"Is there another one?" he'd asked.

"Another three. And the next is a bit trickier."

"That could mean more money."

"The item that you used, can you get it for me?"

"The item?"

"I can't say it. The thing that had the effect."

He thought for a moment. "That's gone."

"Can you get me the same one?"

"Why?"

"Does it matter?"

"No, but you don't want one of them lying around."

"It won't be lying around. And I'll pay what I have to."

"I suppose it's the least of my worries."

And as brief as ever, Turlough hung up. I took it as a yes.

I was floating. I couldn't catch my breath, and I didn't need the air. The psychiatrist in me was saying well done, the Short Strand lad in me wanted to scream out loud. And when I soared back into the dining room, the excitement of Ken's words only added to the feeling:

"Have you seen the news about Lord Lucan? They bloody well found him. Battered to death in Johannesburg."

"I heard about it," Jean said. "Suzanne, do you know who Lucan was?"

"I do, of course," the mouse politely answered.

"He went on a shooting rampage, killing his mother- and father-in-law, and then he disappeared."

"Oh, for god's sake, Jean," Ken laughed. "He killed his nanny and tried to kill his ex-wife."

Jean remembered something to reclaim the focus. "Oh, did you see the footage of that man being shot on camera? I had to look away. It was the Trevelyan guy, and his face was all over the screen."

"If that name's not poison over here," Ken said.

Not to me, not any longer.

"Who was Trevelyan?" Suzanne asked, and Ken was kind enough to answer without condescension.

"The man who was shot was a Trevelyan. But one of his ancestors dealt with famine relief in Ireland, and he cocked it up big time."

"My father told me I was named after the man in that song," I said, "The Fields of Athenry."

"Trevelyan?" Ken wondered. "But that's not your name."

"Not him, the one who steals his corn."

"A bit creepy to be named after someone who's shipped off to Botany Bay."

"I think my dad was more interested in the stealing part."

"He hoped you'd steal things?"

"If it meant saving people. In any case, it was a lie, because the song was written in the seventies."

"That's a strange thing for your father to tell you."

"Sometimes he got things wrong."

"And that's two very strange deaths," Jean said, raising her glass. "Lucan and Trevelyan. To brighten up our dinner party."

I already imagined there'd be another death by the time we'd meet again, only I hoped it wouldn't be Alastair.

14. Suzanne's Story

It was fine being back with her mother, though Suzanne kept an eye on the Internet to see if a cheap apartment came up in any half-decent area. She couldn't raise a teenager in a really bad area, especially a child like Kieran. Best to stick with Mam, best to stay on the outskirts of Dublin.

Mam's daily routine had changed little in widowhood from what it had been in marriage: out to buy flowers in the morning, over to the huge draughty church to prepare vases for the altars, and then into Tallaght village to buy spuds, chicken fillets, and two tins of spaghetti hoops. And in the evening, Suzanne and her mother would eat and watch telly, with their plates on their laps.

"He'll have to see someone," Mam said during an ad break in *Celebrity Big Brother*. "His insides must be affected."

"He won't go again. Mixing vitamins into the spaghetti will have to be enough."

Their talking stopped when Kieran came through the door.

"A kiss for the women," Suzanne said, and he begrudgingly hugged them goodnight and went out again. He had the figure of an eight-year-old, with no spots on his face and that face as pale as a sheet. His clothes still came from the younger children's section of Tesco, and if he had any friends, they would have been twice the size of him. He was fourteen years old.

"We won't always be around," her mother said quietly.

Hearing again the one thing that broke her heart, Suzanne couldn't avoid the tears, though she wouldn't let Mam see them. She knew her mother was as worried as she was, as upset by the fact that for the past four years, since his father had walked out, Kieran would only eat spaghetti hoops and a few boiled eggs. It was the stupidest thing in the world, but spaghetti hoops and boiled eggs were ruling their lives. Suzanne had to change the subject, to something as far away from spaghetti hoops as possible.

"Mam, did you ever hear of a guy called Trevelyan?"

"Was he an actor?"

"I don't think so. Maybe an English fella who was in Ireland during the famine? It was the same name as that man who got shot, the car man."

"Ah yeah, of course."

"Do you remember the famine one, though?"

"Ha, I wasn't there at the time."

"I know, but did you hear anything about him in school? They were talking about him at the dinner I was at, and I wish I'd known more."

Mam screwed her face in an effort to remember. "I'm not sure about school, but my father told me about him. And the Black and Tans."

"The Black and Tans were more recent, I think. Trevelyan was way back."

"Yeah, that's right. He killed all the Irish."

"A lot of us, anyway."

The theme tune of *Celebrity Big Brother* came back on, when Mam suddenly announced, "Charles Edward."

"What's that?"

"Charles Edward Trevelyan was his name. He wasn't the boss, but he worked for the government. He sent all the crops away."

"But there weren't any crops. Didn't the blight kill everything?"

Mam looked at her daughter in amazement.

"There were loads of crops, Suzanne. Oats and the thing you make beer with, wheat, sent off to England. Millions of cattle. Did you never hear that?"

"Never."

"That's why my father started in it."

"Started in what?"

"In the war against the British. Grandad O'Reilly. He was nearly killed too, only one of his cousins dragged him away."

"You never told me this."

Mam registered that she had, indeed, never mentioned it.

"He had a few hard things to do. It sat heavy on him, so he never talked about it."

"What did he do?"

"Three Black and Tans."

"What do you mean?"

"He killed three Black and Tans. They were brutal."

"When was this?"

"1920 or thereabouts. Everything happened around then. Was there anyone nice at that dinner?"

"They were all nice."

Mam laughed as a fist fight erupted on *Celebrity Big Brother* and the camera assistants had to run in and stop it. Suzanne gazed at the telly, her mind many miles away from the shouting on screen.

"You know your work with the church?" she asked. "How do you feel about your father having been in the war?"

"Suzanne, you're mixing up a lot of things there. It wasn't like that."

"But the church wouldn't have allowed killing. They would have spoken against it."

"I know the priests told people to fight the British. It was a war."

"It must have been a different time."

"Are you kidding me?" Mam spoke softly. "It was a different world."

15. Maggie's New Job

Detective Margaret O'Malley (now Temporary Assignee, Homicide and Serious Crime Command – Metropolitan Police Service, London) had to sit in reception on the fifth floor listening to a hummed version of "What Shall We Do with the Drunken Sailor?" She had chatted with the chief superintendent's assistant about the likelihood of rain, but the conversation dried up and the humming restarted, and Maggie sat with the nerves washing over her. She wondered whether it would be too much to tell the assistant that this place was huge and she was shitting herself.

Chief Superintendent William Booth was the man she had to meet. A very British name. He was probably more like a sergeant major than a police officer, the kind with thick white hair and a matching mustache. Maybe a hound or two at his heels, a rhino gun in his hand.

"Are you Detective O'Malley?" she heard, and indeed a tall, white-haired, white-mustached man was standing beside her. There were no hounds about him.

"I am, sir." She stood up, feeling the cold sweat on her back.

Booth extended his arm for what felt like a personal handshake. "Welcome to Scotland Yard. We're enormously busy right now so …"

Here it comes – he was going to tell her to fuck off to the basement. Find a table and look busy, read a list of names or whatever. If the floor's dirty, no harm in cleaning it.

"...we need as many people as we can. We'll get a coffee in my office and go through everything you need to know, and you can tell me how you see yourself contributing."

Maggie was overzealous in confirming what a great idea it was.

"How many cases have you had?" he asked.

"I've worked on eighteen homicides in the past three years, sir, five as lead."

"We can probably bump up those figures over here."

"I hope so. Well, not that I hope anyone is..."

A uniformed officer appeared in the doorway. "Ballistics are back on Trevelyan."

The officer looked at Maggie, and Booth nodded to speak away.

"Sixteen-hundred meters."

Booth's mouth dropped open. "Show the detective around, Gemma," he said, before hurrying out the door after his officer.

The assistant said she was delighted to, but when both of the phones on her desk rang, Maggie told her not to worry, that she'd stroll around herself.

She walked down corridors lined with open doors, people rushing through them, and the place was alive. The security badge around her neck let her wander in peace, working out which rooms were for what, where the canteen was, what the bathrooms were like. Excited by the buzz, not interested in the cause. Everything began to seem familiar – the movement, the figures, the sounds. And by the time Gemma found her to show her where her desk was, Maggie had already blended in. This was the atmosphere she'd felt at home in since she was eight years old and sitting in Ballyhack Garda station eating Milky Ways, watching people complain about their broken windows, seeing the odd youth being cautioned or arrested. Only now she was Margaret O'Malley, an experienced Irish officer in the very effective halls of Scotland Yard.

"I'd say everything is similar to back home," Gemma said as she showed Maggie around the floor. "Though the Yard is slightly more advanced. And we never get a break."

"I'm going to get lost."

"Probably. Stick to the sections where everyone looks the most worried. And remember the Red Lion."

"What's that?"

"It's a pub down the road, if you want to blow off steam. And I'm sure there are Irish clubs if you feel homesick."

"Are there English ones?"

Gemma just laughed at the question. "Today is your settling-in day, but you'll be straight into it tomorrow. Briefings are early, and Booth likes everyone to be at them."

"Should I know anything about him? Does he have quirks?"

"Quirks? You just have to do what he says."

Maggie felt less at ease after her conversation with Gemma, and the overcrowded Tube home didn't help her mood. It was raining heavily, and she smelled like a damp dog during the 20-minute journey to Camden. Her newly rented flat was one of several in a large Edwardian house that had seen better days, but the kitchen was modern and the walls were thick. She changed her clothes and switched on Sky News, catching the end of an update into the Trevelyan shooting.

With one eye on the TV, Maggie used her laptop to look up the name Trevelyan. The newly dead TV presenter appeared first in the search results, followed by a page of information on an individual from the 19th century. Curiosity got the better of her, and she clicked on a link to a creaky site dedicated to "The Fields of Athenry," a tune she could hum but didn't know the words to. She saw that the song was about some guy who was sent to Australia for stealing food, "Trevelyan's corn." Trevelyan worked under the Lord Lieutenant of Ireland, whatever the hell that was. As she read the words, the tune came into her head:

By a lonely prison wall,
I heard a young girl calling,
Michael they are taking you away,
For you stole Trevelyan's corn,
So the young might see the morn,
Now a prison ship lies waiting in the bay.

A corny song about corn, she thought. It was a little extreme to send the man across the sea for trying to keep his kid alive, but rules were rules. She wondered what she would have done in the same position, but she didn't have a child and she didn't have a husband. All she had at that moment were her new job and her small rented flat. And they were two things that suited her fine. A boat to another country wasn't the worst thing in the world. A plane to Heathrow might have been just what she needed.

16. Meeting Terry in the Rain

When the General Register Office was closing for the night, I stood in the draughty porch, watching the rain batter the ground as if it hated it. The office held most of the genealogical records of Ireland and was located in the heart of Dublin, Werburgh Street, named after the irritatingly square church of St. Werburgh next door. I closed my coat around me and headed into the rain, leaving Werburgh for Fishamble Street, moving from an Anglo-Norman road into Viking Dublin. People had walked Fishamble for more than a thousand years, and while most of them were looking to buy fish, I was now looking for my car.

In the wet and the wind, a hooded man jumped in front of me. I sprang to get around him but he blocked me again.

"Dr. Gleeson, I've a few things for you."

I jolted with my name, but the vagueness of his words meant only one thing. I yelled at him to run with me to the car, and as we reached the doors, I wondered if he would have followed me all the way down to the nearby River Liffey. Inside, he pulled back the hood, and I saw a youngish pale face with dark shadows under the eyes.

"The one on top is important," he said, handing me a wet plastic folder.

"When do you need it?"

"As soon as possible. And Mr. Grady wants to know if the others are finished."

"They're finished. Give me a few days with this one."

His business was done and he opened the door, letting the cold rain whip into the car. But he closed it again without getting out. He might have been looking for a break in the weather, but he reminded me of some my patients at the start of their first session, when they have too much to say and their mouths are bound with tape.

"Do you mind doing this?" he finally asked.

"Looking at the profiles? Of course not. Once it helps."

"It confirms things we already know."

"Do you mind coming out in the rain?"

"It's my job."

"I know you get paid, but ..."

He put his fingers up to his head, flattening his wet hair, then he placed his loosely locked hands on his lap.

"I don't do it for money. My father was a Republican."

"And it rubbed off on you?"

"I suppose it did, but maybe not from him. The men back then, you could trust them. And the big idea made sense."

"Does it still?"

He tried to gauge my expression.

"You would have made a good psychiatrist," I helped him along.

"It's all gone quiet, of course, but there are still a lot of misguided people who should be in different fields."

"Lying in them?"

"I don't know. Just away."

"If you're ever worried, remember the big picture."

"I will. That matters more than any of us," and he opened the door and got out.

He shouted at me through the rain, "The name's Terry, by the way," and then he was gone.

17. Straight In

When Gemma showed her into the main briefing hall the next morning, Maggie's eyes widened at the size of it. It was as big as a college lecture room, with bare white walls, a central podium, and emergency exits up front. Maggie took a seat near the middle, craning her neck to take in the empty space.

"You're humming," she heard from behind.

She turned around to see a man with rolled-up sleeves and glasses that were more for function than style. He moved in closer, as the noise increased with the officers filling the hall.

"You've met Gemma? She loves the "Drunken Sailor.""

"It's catchy."

"You're new and Scottish?"

"New and Irish."

"Almost there. Over for good?"

"Six months. Some of your lads went to Dublin to work with the Criminal Assets Bureau, and I got to come here."

"Lucky you. I hope London won't scare you away."

"Scumbags are the same everywhere."

The officer had time to introduce himself as Alex, "definitely the top forensics detective" with the Homicide and Serious Crime Command, Maggie's new department, before William Booth spoke from the central podium.

"Case RC-168. The victim is Evan Scott Trevelyan, a thirty-four-year-old television presenter who was shot while on location. A gunshot to the back of the head, taken from an exceptional distance. This opens up the field to more than crazed fans, though they can't be ruled out. Staffordshire police are overseeing the investigation, and we're helping out with ballistics and possible terrorist links."

Someone in the audience asked why it could be linked to terrorism.

"It's to do with the shot. It was taken from 1600 meters."

The room shocked into sound.

"Provos or the new guys?" Maggie asked over the noise.

"Excuse me?"

The hall went quiet.

"What kind of terrorists?" she said, less loudly.

"The IRA haven't been openly active for years. I can't see what they'd get from this. And terrorism can mean groups or loners nowadays. All we know is that there was a vantage point 1600 meters away, and the shot has been confirmed by ballistics. The bullet missed a cameraman who was standing in front of the victim. We don't know if that was on purpose, but even if it wasn't, we're still talking about a marksman. Military level."

Maggie thought about the poor man's face being splattered on screen and, caught up in the animation of the officers around her, she hoped she'd get the case.

*****

"You're on Lucan," Alex told her when she was back at her new desk. He handed her forensic documents on the murder in Johannesburg, along with personally assigned passwords to access the Scotland Yard databases.

"I didn't get Trevelyan?"

"Not when you're just in."

"Lucan is just as good."

"Well, if he had been killed in London, he would have been. But Liam Doran will be working with you. He's fairly Irish."

A man appeared beside Alex and took a gob-smacked look at Maggie. His brown hair had no grey, but his bloodshot eyes didn't do him any favors.

"I'm with you?" he grunted.

"You're with me," she said. "Stuck with the new one."

He took a seat, but as soon as Alex left, he dropped his head into his hands and said, "I'll be the anchor."

Maggie's cheeks flushed with annoyance. It was only her second day, but these people were rude. "Screw that. You've been here longer but ..."

"I mean I'm going to weigh you down. You see my face?" He pointed at the offending article, its drained complexion not helped by the fluorescent lights overhead. "I've looked like this for four weeks. We've a new baby and my life is shit, vomit, crying, and no sleep. First week back from paternity leave and all I want is a simple burglary. You're Maggie? I'm Liam, nice to meet you."

"You're Irish?"

"Half and half, so both. Or neither."

"One of your parents was English?"

"No, but I was born here."

"So you're English?"

He eyed her wearily. "Who knows? I support Arsenal but was also dragged to mass every Sunday as a child. Over to Galway for the summers."

"Congratulations on the baby." Maggie thought for a moment. "They must trust us a lot."

"Who?"

"Booth and the higher-ups. If Lucan is famous over here, why did they give him to us, the Irish-flavored ones?"

"He's famous if you're seventy. And it's not a gift; the case isn't ours. We're only helping out Johannesburg, and they'll get any credit. The focus is on Trevelyan, as well as the other 120 murders that have come in this year."

Maggie slumped into her chair. "I thought it would have meant more. And you think it was just a burglary?"

"Given the area, that's very likely. The crime rate in Johannesburg is up 40 percent in the past five years."

Liam took two folders from his desk and spread the contents out before them: photographs of every room in Lucan's farmstead, especially the crime scene itself, along with reproductions of fingerprints lifted from the house, and photocopies of Lucan's notebooks.

"So a guy goes on the run after attacking his ex-wife and nanny," Liam said, "he hides for decades, and then he gets battered to death. But in his notes, he claims that someone else attacked the women in 1974, someone sent by a man named Harry Blackwell." He sat back in his seat. "Do you know much about the case?"

"I got an outline of it back in Dublin. It seemed more exciting then."

"That's probably because of this hitman nonsense. It's fed conspiracy theories since the seventies. The theory was that Lucan hired a hitman to kill his wife, but now he says in his notes that a hitman was hired to get *him*. Either way, I don't think it has anything to do with his murder last month. If someone was still looking for him, how did they even find him? The Yard has been following up leads for decades and none has ever come up with the goods."

Maggie despaired as Liam spoke. She may as well have been sitting in the basement. She had left her life to come over here and was dumped with a case she wouldn't even get credit for. Her hard work in Harcourt Street had put her in a solid position, and now she was stuck with a partner who was barely awake.

But as she began to read Lucan's notes, a tiny excitement crept through her. She knew she was reading the exact words Superintendent Foster had talked about only a few days before. And what words they were – a combination of fine handwriting and gibberish:

I should be glad to be here, but what kind of life has this been? Dust in a dusthole.

My wife said I was following her and of course I was! We do everything for our children. Nobody believed it, but I saw a fellow with her. I'm not an imbecile. Why would I say this now? Of course I went in. Why did they think I was there?

I believed it was some level of trick. The room was black and my poor lady wife on the stairs. I was set to tackle the man when he saw me and spoke, he spoke in that muck accent and I knew who it was. I heard him, and when he moved into the light I saw the little sprite. I'll tell you! He was small, but I saw him. They don't care about their children. We do everything for our children.

Those damned neighbors are knocking. I'm not dead yet. I'll find Harry Blackwell in heaven or hell, if he doesn't find me first. Forty-thousand pounds, though I know I owed him more. We do everything for our children, and Harry did too. If only I could remember his name.

"A little sprite?" Maggie said with distaste.

"Aristocrats use funny terms."

"And what about 'he was small?' The attacker was short?"

"A small man could attack two women."

"How tall were they?" Maggie searched on the Internet for images and descriptions of the women. "Both five-foot-two. That's tiny."

"About the same as you."

"I'm five-seven."

"You look shorter."

"I'm sitting down. So you think he was lying?"

"Definitely."

"But when he wrote all this, he had nothing to lose."

"Relax, we don't have to figure that out. We just have to chase up Blackwell, find any links between him and Johannesburg. If any of his associates were there last month. If any of them are even still alive."

Maggie nodded and stretched her arms. She closed her eyes and started to hum. Was Lucan lying or telling the truth, in the way that a distracted eighty-year-old might? Foster had called it an iffy case, and it was only going to get murkier as time went on. Soon it'd be a legend, then a ghost story, and then completely forgotten.

When she opened her eyes, Liam had dozed off.

"You need a coffee," she said, "but you're not getting one. Look at this." She swiveled the screen around to show him a picture of Lady Lucan, her husband standing beside her.

"Lucan's a giant," she said, "at least a foot taller than the wife. And someone sent a small man to get him? That would be terrible planning."

"That's because he's lying. And this isn't our case."

She swiveled the screen back. "Have you found anything yet?"

"Bits and pieces. In the seventies, money did go from a South African account into an account under the name of Henry Blackwell. He's listed under company records as the owner of a pub in Woolwich from 1965, and prison records have him doing time for minor assaults and running a gambling outfit. There's no surviving family, and anyone I've checked who was linked to him in any obvious way is dead."

"Is that suspicious?"

"Ha, not at all. Those kind of blokes didn't live long in the first place. Young violent men."

"That's all we have?"

"It's a small door," Liam said with little hope in his voice, and they left for the drive to Woolwich.

18. Gone

It was Alastair. Quick, and as painless as it could be, and the man I saw in the hospice bed looked nothing like the extrovert I'd known for three decades and drunk eight bottles of wine with a few weeks before. A yellow rubber corpse sucking the room's attention to it, with nothing to say in his lilt of an accent. I stood in silence with his family, watching the dead man say nothing in his pajamas.

I had visited him that day, and part of me wished I hadn't.

"You're looking better," I told him when I sat on his bed. I gave him some kind of a hug while holding one hand to his face. Feeling the boniness of him.

"You're a terrible liar."

He sat up as best he could, looking thinner when I saw more of him.

A nurse came in and checked his drip, asked us if we needed anything. Then she glided out again.

"I don't know why you never married," he said. "You were surrounded by nurses your whole life. Did none of them take your fancy?"

"I was never lonely, Al. Always busy."

"You always had something on your mind."

"Usually work."

"Not that." I caught him staring at me, but his face brightened. "You never told me what you did."

"What I did when?"

"When we were in Belfast. You were going to tell me about something inappropriate you did. Was it to do with a patient you were working your magic on?"

I couldn't smile with him.

"Oh, it was something else," he said. "Something to do with the half people who come in to see you."

Alastair's eyes dozed while he let me consider my reply.

"I was always waiting for something and I didn't know what."

"Have you found it?" he said quietly.

"I've found someone to help me."

"Let it go, Michael."

"I'll let it go when they pay me for my father's neck. I've done nothing about it my whole life. The nearest I've done is listened to wrecked old men's stories about how they won the little fights and lost the struggle."

"What did you do?"

I took several moments to answer, not sure if I could answer at all. But the sound of Alastair's snores loosened my tongue.

"Lucan and Trevelyan," I whispered eventually. "I've taken one from each of them."

Alastair opened his lips, and in his dozing state, he started to repeat what I'd said. He only managed "Lucan," before the humming machine by his bed sent out one faint, flat tone.

"Alastair?" I touched his upper arm. I felt his pulse. He died with the name of Lucan on his lips, and I cursed myself.

*****

The family tried to make the funeral as uplifting as they could, with food and a free bar and encouragements to talk about Alastair. But everyone wore black and no one laughed too loud.

I couldn't sleep that night. I sat in the living room and then moved into the kitchen. I opened the back door and the sharp air hit my face, my thighs, my bare feet. I crouched down. How cold is this? Almost autumn, a house with insulation and no heat on. Six degrees outside, maybe. Ten degrees inside? What would it be like to have sold the winter clothes, then the summer clothes, to be left with only a thin cotton shirt or a slip of a dress.

I had been thinking about Alastair, or maybe something else. I walked into the garden, feeling the cement patio under my feet, then the short grass and hard soil. I sat under a tree and took off what I would have sold. My pajama top and bottoms, my underwear.

I laid down. Alastair's dead in the ground now, dead like this. And all those people who lay in the ditches with their children in their arms, they knew what was coming. This was how they died. This was the cold they felt.

Dear Alastair, the next is for you. The Scots and the Irish, brothers in suffering and brothers in hatred. A pair of twisted brothers.

I was freezing by the time I walked back to the house. I lay on the bed and pulled the duvet over me. A pillow instead of a rock.

A man at the table beside me, not my father. The fucking exams were tomorrow and I was in a panic. I couldn't find the books. Did you put them away? "This is all you need," he said, opening an old encyclopedia. "That's history," I said, "not biology." He pointed to a picture that filled a page. "That's ground, isn't it? That's soil. That's photosynthesis. That's the earthworms you're learning about. How they move and get fat when the soil is good and the food is the bodies, the bodies of whole families lying in the ditches. Read it! That's all you need to know." "It's not," I said, "there's other things, maths and chemistry, art and English..." "The land is all you need," he said. "When you have your own soil, you have own your food, and no one can govern you. Look at it!" The book was gone from the table. "You're killing them again!" he shouted.

I woke up to the dark, wet from sweating. My first thought was relief that I didn't have to do exams anymore. As my brain clicked into consciousness, I remembered how he'd never let me study. He wouldn't let up about the dead in the ditches. He was crazy about his fucking dead in the ditches.

My brain must have been hanging around the same neighborhood, because I woke up the next morning not thinking of exams or Alastair or the cold, but of a shriveled head sitting on a stick. And I felt relief.

19. The Novice

"Do you think Lucan had anything to do with that nonsense?" Maggie said out of the blue. She was still thinking about Booth's words during the Trevelyan briefing – *possible terrorist links* – a sentence that crawled over her skin.

"What nonsense?"

"The IRA."

"It's unlikely. And they're long gone now."

"The guns are gone, but the men who held them are still alive." Maggie looked out of the car window at the dull rainy day, the depressed shop-fronted streets, the litter snapping across the windscreen and into the wet gutters on the road. She and Liam were driving to Woolwich, the area in southeast London where Henry Blackwell used to live. He was the only named individual they had in the Lucan case, the only place to start.

"I suppose the Republicans did go after high-profile targets from the seventies onwards," Liam said, "especially when they brought the fight over here."

"The London campaign."

"That's it. It went on until the nineties. They attacked politicians, famous buildings, various pubs and shops. Did you hear about it in training?"

"Training was more about current threats. But I've read a few articles over the years."

Maggie went back to looking at the litter.

"Do you like London?" Liam asked.

"There's a lot of people."

"You're not from a city?"

"Nah, a small town in Wexford. A beautiful place. The older I get, the less I hate it."

"That sounds like you got out as soon as you could."

"I wanted to be an officer, and there wasn't much happening back home at that stage. Dublin was fine, but sometimes a change is nice. What's the job like here?"

"It can be rough at times, but I suppose that's the same everywhere."

Maggie watched the people getting wet on the street, the wind pushing them on their way. Everything was working normally for them, they were thinking about their shopping, wondering about their dinner. It would only take one wrong turn or meeting the one wrong person out of the thousands they'd know in their lives, or the few seconds when their spouse got a little too angry and their lives would fade away.

"We see some shit alright," she said. "I've been lucky with work up to now – mostly drug gangs shooting each other, and even they don't seem to enjoy it that much."

"And now the boring Lucan."

"That's not boring, no matter what you say." Her eyes lit up as she looked at him. "That's a bloody adventure. My boss in Dublin loved the case, and she made everything sound interesting. She was as tough as nails and with the mouth of a docker."

"You'll be happy to get back to her when you're finished here?"

"She's retiring, and it nearly killed me when I heard. I was glad to get the transfer because I didn't want to be around when she left."

"That's a weird reason to leave Ireland."

"I also have my eye on the SDU, the Special Detective Unit. Emergency response, hostage negotiation and all that. You have specialized units for it over here."

"A section where you're not busy most days."

"It also covers counter-terrorism, and that's not slow anymore. That's where I want to be. And there's the place."

The pub they were searching for was on Woolwich High Street, and it was called Harvey's. It had been The Pig and Bucket when Blackwell owned it, and whether or not it was a dive back then, it was now either a cocktail bar or a wine bar. A fancy place selling glasses of fancy. The handsome barman behind the glass and steel counter was happy to have his first visitors of the day.

"We're Detectives Doran and O'Malley from Homicide and Serious Crime at the Metropolitan Police," Liam said. "We're looking for information on someone who owned this building around 1974. Henry or Harry Blackwell. Would anyone here remember that name?"

The barman said he'd been the manager since the business opened three years ago, and there was no one there from before that time.

"Was there anything left when you moved in?" Liam asked. "Documents in the attic, any photos lying about?"

"Nothing. The place went through several owners by the time my boss bought it."

"Maybe you have regulars," Maggie suggested, "people who would have drank here before you opened?"

"The old folk around here don't care too much for banana daiquiris. We're aiming at the younger Greenwich crowd. Sorry about that."

The officers thanked him and headed for the door.

"We might be in again," Liam said, "if we can think of anything else."

"I'll be here ...," the barman began, but he suddenly ran at them from behind the bar. He grabbed the front door and held it open, not for them, but for a delivery man coming in with a crate of rattling bottles. Liam and Maggie stepped out of the way.

"You know something?" the barman said quietly. "We use a distillery warehouse that has supplied this area for years. Back in the nineties, definitely, but maybe even further back."

"What's the name?" Maggie asked.

"Griffiths. We stuck with them from the start because they're good on the standards. Tonics and juices. But they gave us a bit of hassle when we opened."

"What kind of hassle?"

"They said we should stick to beer and spirits, said they'd been delivering to Woolwich for years and knew what the locals wanted. But my boss went down the wine-and-cocktail route. Turns out the distillery was right."

"So it was more advice than hassle?"

"Yeah. I'll get you their card."

Griffiths was a wholesale pub supplier in Portsmouth, a two-hour drive away on the southern coast. The officers weren't out of London before Liam fell asleep in the passenger seat. The snoring started on the A3 motorway and didn't stop for miles. Maggie glanced at him as he slept, knowing he'd probably be mortified to be caught with his mouth open and his thick hair sticking up from where his head had slid down the seat. An unrelated stranger seeing him so vulnerable. He opened his eyes to see her staring at him, and her own eyes returned to the road.

When they arrived at Griffiths, they found a huge, fully functioning warehouse and delivery depot right at the water's edge, where the drinks and snacks would come in and be sent around the country immediately. The reception had revolving doors and was manned by two ladies in matching skirted suits.

Liam opened with a grin. "This is probably a wild goose chase, but we're looking for someone who may have worked here forty years ago."

The receptionists laughed that neither of them were alive back then. A whisper together came up with a name, the only person who could have been around at the time. He used to work in the warehouse, but now he helped out with maintenance.

The officers were shown to the accounts department, where they found a man halfway up a ladder. He was well into his sixties but didn't seem to notice. Tanned and healthy, his youthfulness was aided by two armfuls of tattoos, tribal and skulled and modern.

"They're fine arms," Maggie said in appreciation.

"Thanks very much. Some old, some new." Paul Priestley had a downlighter bulb in his hand and was about to exchange it for one in the ceiling. "What can I do for you?"

"We're looking for information on a man who was around forty years ago. You were delivering with Griffiths back then?"

"I did a lot of things. Who was it?"

"A Henry or Harry Blackwell."

Priestley took the old downlighter out of its socket and dropped it to the ground. "Didn't he own a pub? In Woolwich, I think."

"Did you know him?" Liam asked.

"Not personally."

"But you know the name?"

"Blackman, you said?"

"Blackwell."

Priestley didn't get the new bulb in before he came down the ladder. "I can hardly remember anything from back then."

"Blackwell died in the eighties," Maggie told him. "We're actually wondering about an associate of his."

Priestley gazed out the door.

"Did they hurt, getting them done?" she interrupted his thoughts.

"The tats? Nah, I'm hard as stone." He rubbed the exhibition.

"Blackwell may have known someone else..." Liam said.

"Who?"

"A man called Bingham."

The tattooed man looked at the floor, kicked at a hole in the carpet, and could have passed for a schoolboy again.

"Mr. Priestley?"

"I never knew him."

"Do you know who he was?"

He had no answer for them, and Maggie had to break his silence. "Would you be happier getting a coffee in the canteen?"

"I would." And the nice old man with the beautiful arms dropped his bulb to the floor and ran out the door.

"Stop!" Liam shouted, but Maggie was already sprinting after Priestley. He made it to reception before she jumped at his legs, bringing him to the ground. A hard kick to her shoulder had her reeling enough that Priestley was up to his feet, but Maggie grabbed an ankle to topple him over.

Liam was now above him, hoisting him off the floor while Maggie was up and cuffing his hands. The officers got him into the car, and Priestley protested all the way back to Scotland Yard. It wasn't until he was in a detention room and the camera was recording that his talking died down and the questions began.

20. Michael Finds Barney

The next one took a bit of work, because the records were so flaky about the descendants. This wasn't a monster of the famine, but two centuries before, a man who stood like a giant in the Irish Sea and cracked a steel pick down into the country, shattering its bones and its teeth and its head. He was so big, so great a suffocation, that I was more than happy to step out from the 19th century to go looking for him and his line. But it was difficult, because even though he had nine children, most of those lines died out. And I was going to wipe out one of the spots on one of the remaining lines.

The Great British Historical Society had carried out most excellent research on the family and were happy to share it with anyone, especially the indirect descendants, people whose eagerness to find a link between themselves and the great man would bring them celebrity down the local pub. And then perhaps unease when they realized what their own lives were in comparison. But there was always another night down the pub, another group of people who hadn't heard who they were related to.

And so to the Internet and the family trees, something I couldn't have done a few years before. The genealogical sites, lists of local housing authorities, LinkedIn, census rolls, all reducing the numbers to a small group of people who lived in the right vicinity, could be reached easily enough, would be taken without much trouble. And then to the choosing:

someone with a particular kind of humanity. And then to the phone call.

"I have a name for you, and all the details."

"Is it local?"

"Local to you, London. You'll need time for it, so free up your calendar."

"I'll need money for that."

"You always need money, Turlough. How about doing this one for free? Patriotism."

"No. What's the name?"

"Barney Hutchinson." I spelled out "Hutchinson" in case he got it wrong.

"That's it?"

"That's it. He's a builder in Ilford. Separated, kids grown up. It shouldn't be a problem."

"Okay." He sounded disappointed.

"If you hang on a sec, I'll get you the address and instructions for afterwards."

"Is it complicated?"

"It's not complicated, but it will take a while, and I'd like to see it. I want to touch it." I went off the phone to get my notes, a pile of handwritten labor I'd spent weeks on.

"I'm here. Are you ready?" I hoped he hadn't hung up.

"I am."

I gave him the instructions and the address of a house in Southampton where we were to meet. I told him I was a useless cook and I might need help in the kitchen, doubling his wonder.

"All this for Barney Hutchinson? I've never heard of him."

"Not him you haven't, but there's one detail about him that's important."

And I gave him that one detail, and everything became clear.

21. Opening Up

"Why did you run, Mr. Priestley?" Liam began.

"I didn't want to be arrested."

"Why would we arrest you?"

"I don't know."

"You thought you might get into trouble for having known Blackwell?"

"Aye, that's it."

"What was he like?" Maggie asked.

"Blackwell? One of the old lads."

"What age were you when you knew him?"

"Twenty or so. It was before I got married. My wife wouldn't have any of that afterward."

"Any of what?"

"Blackwell's stuff was under the table."

"Is your wife still alive?"

"Why?"

"We'll have to search your home."

"That won't happen."

"You're not helping us at all."

"Will you take these handcuffs off?"

Maggie reached over the table and unlocked the cuffs. Priestley apologized for kicking her and gave his wrists a rub. Then he said, "I want immunity."

"From what?" Liam asked.

"I might have taken a few things. They're in my house."

"What things?"

"A few bottles of drink. From the depot."

"That's theft. We can't do anything about that."

"I didn't steal them. They were damaged goods. The labels were on upside down."

"We might be able to do something," Maggie interrupted. "Let them know you helped out with the case."

"That's not certain." Liam flashed her a look.

"It depends on whether you help us, Paul."

"What do you want to know again?"

"Henry Blackwell, and his connection to Lord Lucan. Can you remember him, Lucan?"

"I seen he's dead."

"He is. We want to rule out any British link. Do you remember Lucan?"

Priestley dropped his head down. He looked older now, more like a man his own age, swimming into the deep end of a hostile room with two officers staring at him and another scowler standing at the door. But when he lifted his face up before them, it seemed like he was describing the best movie he'd ever seen in his life.

"That cunt was beautiful."

"Lucan?"

"Yeah. You couldn't take your eyes off him. Tie, suit, and the hair always Brylcreemed. The mustache Brylcreemed too, it was big enough for that. He had everything going for him, except he was a gambler. They've got fifty pence left, and they still think they can win it all back."

"Try to focus, Mr. Priestley," Liam said gently, writing his own notes despite the camera being on.

"Well, Harry loved him coming into the Pig and Bucket, it brought in a bit of class. You know, they got his name wrong in the papers: he wasn't Lucky Lord Lucan, just Lucky Lucan, not that it matters. Anyway, he started borrowing off Blackwell, then he started not paying it back. Harry went easy enough on him at first, but things were shifting in London, and Harry had to pay more himself, to other fellas, to stay open."

"Like the Krays?" Liam asked.

"What? No, of course not, they were locked up by then." Priestley couldn't believe the idiot sitting opposite him. "No, but some of them were just as bad. The drugs were settling in, and there was no room for maneuver."

"So you saw Lucan a few times?"

"I saw him a lot, up until he lost everything."

"He lost it all?"

"It was embarrassing really. Him trying to get to a card table, and no one would have him. I heard all this, now, secondhand. We'd just be having a laugh, and I'd get the stories off my mate Joey. But everything changed when Harry's place started going under, and he needed the money back. That's when Lucan did a stupid thing."

"What did he do?"

"He wasn't a hard man, but he was desperate. He knew if he couldn't get this money, it'd be more than his looks that'd be gone. But he still had who he was, he still had the charm. He started hanging around with Harry's daughter, Charlotte, or whatever fancy name they'd given her. She was only in the pub a few times, but it was enough. She fell for him big time."

"What happened?"

"Ah, he said stupid things, said he'd run away with her if Blackwell didn't let him off part of what he owed."

Maggie seized her chance: "And Blackwell went after him for that?"

"Ah no. That wasn't it. You'd want to be crazy to do that." Priestley looked over at the brick wall, as if there was a window there and he could see out. "It was a bit sad, really, but Lucan must have dropped her, because Blackwell found her dead in the bath. Poor girl topped herself. Blackwell lost it then, I think."

"He hired someone to kill Lucan?"

"I don't know nothing about that, lass."

"You never heard anything?"

"Nothing. I had to lay low for a while."

"Why? You had nothing to do with the girl's death?"

"No. Jesus, no. Harry went a bit funny, and I thought it best to stay out of his way."

"Did you give this information to the police after Lucan disappeared?"

"Nobody asked me. A lot of people knew him."

"The inquest found him guilty of murder," Liam said. "Did he have it in him to attack two women?"

"I suppose he must have."

"You said he wasn't a hard man."

"I'm not a shrink. Who knows why people do things? Can I go out for a smoke?"

Priestley was escorted out by an accompanying officer. Liam stretched his back, and Maggie walked around the room.

"Did you hear what he said?" she asked him.

"Which part?"

"When I asked if Blackwell went after Lucan when he threatened to run away with the girl, he said, 'That wasn't it.'"

"As in, Blackwell went after him, but not for that reason? I suppose it's something. And I can't believe Priestley ran away from us because he was worried about a few bottles of drink."

"If Blackwell sent someone in '74 and they messed up, could it be the same person who succeeded this year?"

"They'd be ancient by now."

Mr. Priestley came back into the room, and Maggie asked him if he'd like anything to eat. He said he had to take his medication, so water and a sandwich would do nicely. Chicken, with none of the green leafy stuff on it. The accompanying officer was dispatched.

"Is it heart medicine you take?" Maggie asked, trying the personal approach.

"Epilepsy. I used to get the fits, but 1 don't get them so much these days."

"That must have been tough when you were in school."

"I didn't have it in school. Don't forget the salt and pepper, lad," he said to the officer returning with the water.

"We're just throwing this out," Liam said, "but if Blackwell sent someone after Lucan when his daughter died, who would it have been?"

"Someone close to him, I suppose."

"Someone tall? Someone small, maybe?" Maggie asked.

"I'd say Blackwell knew all sizes of people, but I don't know who it was."

"It would have been a man anyway?"

"I doubt if a woman would have the strength in her, though my wife would have given it a go. She didn't much care for Lucan after the trouble with the girl."

"Did your wife go after him?"

"If I tell you she did, will you lock her up?"

"Can't do that," Maggie smiled. "Would she know who Blackwell might have sent?"

"She wouldn't know anything." Priestley folded his colorful arms in front of him. "Lucan attacked those women, that's what it said in the papers."

"But your wife would have known the players back then?"

"She knows nothing."

"She lived in Woolwich?"

"Stop talking about her."

"If she knows anything ..."

Priestley stood up. "I'm gone. If you say one more word about her, I'm gone. I don't care if she finds out about the whiskeys I've taken."

Liam tried to placate him, but Maggie was having none of it. "Why can't we talk to her?"

"For fuck... You just listen to me. We made a deal, her and me, that those days wouldn't be mentioned again. She saw me nearly dead because of them, and I won't bring that back up. She's an awful bitch sometimes, but she stuck with me when the whole world collapsed. I won't see her hurt."

The officers apologized and Priestley sat down. The room went calm, but Maggie was bubbling inside. She'd begun to watch for the one wrong word, the little way in. She started again.

"How did you get epilepsy?"

"I fell."

"On the ground?"

"On the ground."

"Was it a fight?"

"Didn't you hear me?"

"I know some things are private, but this case isn't about you."

"You could call it a fight. I didn't put up much of a defense."

"Did you prosecute them?" Liam cut in. "If it was within the last three years, we can go after them for you."

"It wasn't in the last three decades."

"Was it Blackwell?" Maggie asked.

"Why would you say that?"

"He was fairly violent. Didn't he do time for assault?"

Priestley looked up to heaven. "Not much of a surprise." It looked like he was going to speak, but nothing came. He scratched his face and stared at the table. Maggie saw that he was clamping shut and the momentum was going. She had to reach deep and fast.

"I'm new here, Maggie's my first name. I'm not sure how long I'll be staying because I'm not great with hearing orders. Is that what happened to you, that you and Blackwell had a fight over work? Because it just gives us a better look at who he was. You don't have to tell us anything personal, anything that makes you uncomfortable. We just need to hand something into our bosses and then to close the case."

Priestley sighed and looked up at them, and the officers were surprised to see bloodshot eyes. Watery eyes.

"Sometimes it helps to let it out, Paul, even the ancient stuff."

He nodded and closed his eyes, keeping them closed through the first words he delivered.

"It was the worst day of my life. It was a horrible sad funeral. So many people crying for the dead girl. And some of them wouldn't have had much love for Blackwell. They came for her. Beautiful and lovely and he did everything for her. She softened him up over the years, so much that he was thinking of leaving it all, moving the family to Spain.

"I don't remember everything, but I know his wife was in bits. She couldn't walk, and every time she stopped and collapsed to the ground, the procession stopped behind her. She was shaking and collapsing, and Blackwell just stared ahead. The world was finished for him.

"And I did a bloody stupid thing." Priestley paused. "My missus, before she was my missus, she asked me to look after this kid in the church, a nephew of hers or something. She said he wasn't faring too well. He looked fine to me, but I guess he was squashed into the aisle, with the sobbing all around. I took the lad outside to cheer him up." Priestley took a deep breath.

"I was only young myself, so the only thing I could think of was showing him how to box. He said he'd just started 'big' school, and I told him how to hold his fists up, if any of the older lads came near him. He was throwing the punches soon enough and trying not to laugh. That kid was a cracker, full of life, and he even nearly hit me once. And when I pretended he got me, right on the cheek, he let out a merciful laugh, funniest thing you ever heard, and he was still laughing when I felt someone beside me. I turned and..."

Priestley stopped, and the officers waited.

"...I knew right then I was gone. Blackwell had come out from the church. He started yelling that his daughter was dead, screaming about respect. The lad was frozen, stuck to the ground, and Blackwell raised his fist to the boy. I roared it was my fault, and it was one blow that he gave me that knocked me to the ground. He laid into me after that, and he kept it up, until I felt nothing at all. Someone tried to pull him off, but they were floored too. And then my mate came running out and there was no stopping him. He pulled Blackwell off me, started punching his boss in the side of the head. He got him back on the ground, down on the pebbles of the church, and Blackwell lay there, a huge man moaning for his girl. I swear to god, my mate saved my life that day. While they were burying the daughter, I was sent off in an ambulance. I nearly got the last rites, too."

"Were you okay?" Maggie asked softly.

"Ah, it took a while. My teeth had to be made for me, and I was stuck with the epilepsy ever since. Blackwell was a tough man when he wanted to be. At least he didn't go for the lad."

"You must have been grateful to Joey."

"Joey?"

"You said Joey was your mate. I took it that he got Blackwell off you."

"I never knew a Joey."

Liam flicked back through his notes. "I have it written down, Mr. Priestley."

"Ah, we called each other funny names back then, whatever you had handy. I'll go out for another smoke, and then I'll have to go home."

Paul Priestley stood up and shuffled outside.

Liam was about to speak, but Maggie had gone out the door. He found her at her desk, searching the Internet.

"Christ, what a story," he said.

"But is it true? I don't know about over here, but back then in Catholic Ireland, a suicide wouldn't have got a funeral."

Maggie found what she was looking for. "Protestants didn't allow church burials for suicides either. How did Blackwell get around that, whatever his religion was?"

Maggie located an obituary for Charlotte Lucy Blackwell, as well as a news report from the day describing the large number of Londoners who turned out to pay their respects. The report ended with the words, "Henry Blackwell had the means to arrange a beautiful funeral at St. John's Church and a burial on the grounds of Plumstead Cemetery." A photograph accompanied the piece, a color image of the mourners, Blackwell himself named and partly hidden behind a person in front.

"Maybe the rules were bent for him, maybe he paid for it," Liam said. "Does it say who the priest was?"

"No, just the church." She was about to close the screen when a name caught her eye. It was the attribution under the photograph, a Carl Waters from London. Maggie searched and found a few Carl Waters on LinkedIn and Facebook, a few businessmen in England. Nothing about a photographer in the seventies or eighties. She began to check all the police archives.

"Why is he important?" Liam asked her.

"If he took the photograph, he must have been at the funeral. And I bet all of Blackwell's men were there. The newspaper wouldn't have sent a rookie to cover a gangster funeral. He probably knew who everyone was."

"That's wafer thin."

But Maggie suddenly stood up. "Where's the evidence room?"

"Why?"

"There's something belonging to a Carl Waters still in evidence, from 1974."

The basement was a warehouse of well-organized shelves, and in the 1970s section they found a single box for Carl Waters, containing two plastic bags. The first held a heavy Pentax camera, but it was the second that brought a smile to Maggie's face. She took up the bag and stared through its plastic at a stack of color photos. She could only see the top one, but it was enough. Faces were staring back at her, and those faces weren't smiling. Their owners were wearing black and clearly at a funeral.

22. Consigned to This (1846)

My father was Danny O'Gliasáin and he was not a quiet man. He loved the sound of words, the hearing and the speaking. He said *An Gaeilge* was a cantering horse – singing with the wind and strong and alive and it could not be stopped once it was started. Like your mother, he'd say, but only when she was out of the house. The horse in canter was the Irish tongue, and the English words were the strike of the animal's shoe being made and fitted, hard and direct. A horse will run without shoes, he told us, but the shoes take it faster and with less pain. The English words were spells that would keep us safe in the future, and we listened whenever he brought a new one home.

"Consign" he would say, and that we could manage. "Consideration," he'd say, and that we could not.

"Eviction, Annie," he said to my mother and we noticed it not for the word but the dread on his face.

"Did you meet him?"

"I did. He said the rent is the same, no matter how the ground is."

My mother let out a curse that he scolded her for, but he held his tongue when she cried.

"It's three times what we could pay last year, and this year we have nothing." Her words were stopped with a slight call outside, and when she returned, she looked at my father as though she'd seen a white woman sitting in a tree.

"Now we have more," she said, as her mother and father came in behind her. They had found a hare half-dead on the road but their house had been knocked to the ground.

(Honoria O'Gliasáin, Mayo)

23. Dear Ruth

The practice was wearing me down. My mind was filling with so many people who couldn't live without a few easy pills or cope with the dismal layers of a stressful job and unhappy marriage. I wanted to help them all, I wanted to shout, "change your job, change your spouse," but I was being paid 400 euro an hour not to. To stuff my chest with misery, to add to the mess in my head.

One client was nearly the end of me. She was borderline anorexic and, at twenty-two years old, a late starter. It was either a recent trauma or something very deep, pushed back only to come tapping when she was beyond the speed of youth. Her parents had taken her to several psychotherapists, and I was the first heavy-hitter on the psychiatrist list.

"It won't stay down, nothing will," she said in a pre-emptive strike. "So we can't even talk about food."

"What would you like to discuss?" I said, taking my notepad out of a drawer, one stuffed with articles on the Irish famine. There were more recent pictures too: Ethiopian babies, a line of concentration camp survivors, a starved torture victim in Utah. Anything to understand it.

"I want my parents to back off," she said. "I don't need them jumping down my throat the whole time about eating."

"It's their job, Ruth. You can't blame them for that."

"Ouhh," she said, wiping a teary face. "I blame them for everything."

"Why?"

"They stuck me in a new school, when I didn't want to leave the last one."

"Why did they move you?" I noticed the corners of my eyesight blurring.

"I know! I did want to leave at some stage, but not to go to Saint fucking Rita's."

"And Saint Rita's had a problem with eating disorders?"

"It was posh, so nobody ever ate there. There was a competition to see how far you could throw your lunch across the basketball court."

"Ruth, it's often in cases like this, with people who share the same difficulty, that they experienced something frightening or inappropriate when they were younger. Did that ever happen to you?"

"What? No way. I've never met any creeps. I *do* know loads of people who have though. All of the girls at Saint Rita's were abused."

"All of them?"

"I'd say so."

"Okay. Well, it doesn't have to be abuse, just something inappropriate or unsettling."

Ruth thought about this for a moment, and her eyes moved up to the right, where the creative part of the brain is located.

"There was this one guy," she began. "He was a friend of my brother's. Dermot Jennings was his name. He was creepy to me once or twice."

She looked for my reaction and I nodded, saying, "And did this...," but I stopped the sentence. She'd given a tiny smile, a smile you'd hardly notice. The smile of *duping delight,* satisfaction that she was getting away with a lie.

"I'll tell you what starvation is," I said.

"What?"

My migraine hit full on. I was listening to an unhappy young woman blame all of her problems on going to a posh school. I only noticed then that I'd scribbled back and forth on my notepad, written the same three names so many times that I'd made a wet hole through the pages. I ripped out the page and stuck it in my pocket, trying to refocus.

"It's nice to be prepared. You start by getting that hungry feeling that you have when it's lunchtime and you could murder a McDonald's. You're not very energetic, though you could still throw your lunch across a basketball court. And after two or three days, you get this funny taste in your mouth, kind of like nail varnish remover. You know that smell? That's the ketones, ketone bodies. They're increasing because your store of sugars is low. It happens with monks on a fast. Like Gandhi."

Her leg, bent over the other at the knee, started moving up and down. She had made the decision to leave and was subconsciously getting her muscles ready.

"And then, like, say after several more days, and the ketones are running out, your body gets desperate but it's not giving up. It starts to eat its own muscles."

She put on her cardigan.

"And this is the interesting part," I talked faster. "You don't have any energy, and your stomach might fill out, which is weird, because you'd think it'd be the opposite, and then the pain kicks in, Ruth, the pain starts."

She stood up and put on her coat.

"Hang on, Ruth, you should know what you're getting into."

She headed for the door, but I was ready, with a handful of pictures grabbed from my desk, and I raced around and blocked her way.

"Look at this – this is what happens to *real* starving people. They get every fucking infection there is and their skin flakes off and they don't even know if they'd like a cheeseburger because their brain is so wasted. This is starvation, Ruth! This is starvation! And if you want to kill yourself, that's fine, but think about your bloody family! Think about what it'll do to them!"

I stuck a picture of a starving person in front of her face.

Swearing to high heaven at me, she ran out the door. And I looked at the picture, worn out by it all. And the picture I'd showed her was of my mother.

24. Pulling it Out

"We found a few pictures, Mr. Priestley," Maggie said as the old man was brought back into the interview room. "A photographer named Carl Waters was at Charlotte Blackwell's funeral. He left his flat the following day and wasn't seen for a while. Isn't that funny?"

"Hilarious. I don't want to be here."

"This won't take long. The police found Waters' camera and developed the pictures. And I bet Blackwell's best men are in them. Would seeing a few jog your memory?"

"Can I go out for a smoke?"

"Sit down," Liam said, fed up that he had to be there as well. He opened a folder and took out several large color photos of a procession of mourners. "The autopsy said it was an overdose of painkillers and that the bruises might have been caused by the body hitting the river banks."

"Charlotte's body?"

"Carl Waters. He turned up in the Thames."

"I don't know nothing about that."

"Look at the pictures."

"God above," Priestley said with a smile.

"That's you in the entourage. I'm guessing that's your future wife next to you?"

"That's us alright. She was beautiful, still is."

"But look at the other mourners. Is there anyone of interest?"

Priestley looked at the images in front of him, while Maggie's eyes never left him. A few of the photos he regarded with knitted brows, and some made him smile, especially those of his younger self. Some folks he couldn't recognize and he quickly moved on.

And then he looked at one photograph for a little too long, but with no emotion at all. When he finished with it, Maggie turned that photograph around to face herself. It was a picture of a man in a trilby hat and jacket, tall and aloof and not interested in smiling for the camera. But he didn't seem threatening, because he had a child by the hand.

"Who's that?" Maggie asked, turning the picture back towards Priestley.

"I don't remember his name."

Maggie raised her eyebrows. The photo had interested him enough to stare at.

"Could it be Joey?"

"No. That's Richard something."

"So there *was* a Joey?"

"Maybe, but that's Dickie, Dickie Mitchell. He fought in the army. I didn't know him that well."

"You're pictured with him a lot. And he's holding the boy's hand in most of them. That's a funny thing to see in the seventies, from such tough men. Where was the mother?"

Priestley sighed in annoyance.

"The thing is," Liam said, "Carl Waters was a press photographer, and a very good one. You have to be organized in that job, because you have to know who you're taking, either before or afterwards, or else the pictures are useless. Do you know what I'm saying?"

"No."

"Carl Waters could have written the names down, and maybe those names are somewhere. You know how it goes: if you're caught out in one lie, everything has to be examined. And we're not even looking for someone who may have attacked Lucan's family all those years ago; we're looking for someone who attacked him this year. And there's nothing to suggest you know who that is, so far."

Priestley's neck reddened. "I don't know who killed Lucan and I don't know who attacked his family. But the man in that photo is not Joey."

Maggie wondered why he'd volunteered the name again. "Is Joey in any of them?"

"I don't know."

"Was he there?"

"Not everyone turned up."

"Wouldn't it have been a bad sign if he hadn't? Blackwell might have been angry."

"Blackwell was always angry. And Joey might have been away."

"On holiday? People didn't travel far back then."

"Maybe he was overseas."

"Where?" Liam said sternly.

"Maybe he was on an island."

"What? Which island?

"I don't know! Ireland is an island, isn't it?"

"Is that where he was from?"

Then Paul Priestley said the magic words, the words that meant more than anything that had been said so far in the interview: "I want a lawyer."

Liam sat back in his chair, knowing the interview was effectively over. He turned off the camera.

"Can I speak to you outside?" Maggie asked him. "And we'll get you a lawyer, Mr. Priestley."

The officers stood outside the door, keeping their voices low.

"Why does he want a lawyer?" Maggie began.

"I don't know and I don't really care. He has information, but I'm not sure how important it is."

"What about that Joey stuff?"

"He let the name slip out when he was relaxed in the last interview, so it was probably a real person. But if Joey even exists, he could be a hundred years old."

"And I suppose if we get a lawyer in, Priestley won't ever have to talk to us again."

"We'll save ourselves the bother and cut him loose."

The officers went back into the room. Priestley asked if they'd phoned for a lawyer.

"We can do that but..." Maggie began.

"Forget it. I want to get out of here today."

The officers took their seats tenderly. Liam began to speak, but Maggie cut him off. She jumped on the one weak spot in the story, the only thing they had:

"Was that Joey in the photo?"

Priestley gave a weak nod.

"Is there a reason for keeping him quiet?"

"I promised I'd never talk about him. Him or his boy."

"You promised your wife?"

"No. Him, Joe. He didn't hang around long after the funeral. Packed up his family and went home."

"Why?"

"Because he'd beaten up his boss. And also because of the boy."

"The boy?"

"His son, the lad I taught to box. Blackwell was a man in a million, and not in a good way. Men like that do funny things to make themselves feel better. Joey knew he could suddenly get some psycho thing in his head where whenever he thought of his daughter, he remembered the funeral and somebody laughing at her. Joey could never take that chance, so he took himself and his sick wife and his boy back to the only place he felt safe."

"That's a fairly weak reason to move his whole life," Liam said. "Was he that scared of Blackwell?"

"He loved that boy, he'd never let anything happen to him. Took him everywhere, and not only because the wife wasn't well. But maybe there's things I don't know. Maybe they wanted him back."

"Who?"

"Whoever sent him over to London in the first place."

"Did he ever talk about who it was?"

"He never talked about much."

"How long after the funeral did he leave?"

"A few weeks. I only saw him once after I got out of hospital, and the place they went to wasn't one for the visits. The place with all that trouble, you know?"

Maggie's throat tightened. "Trouble? The Troubles? Was it Belfast?"

"Yeah. It was in the news over the years."

"And he had a history there?"

"Look, I don't know. And I wouldn't have understood him if he'd told me. I was only interested in the ladies at that stage."

Maggie sat forward in her chair. "This is shit, Paul."

"Excuse me?"

"It's all shit. You're talking about a tough man who worked for a crime boss, someone who came from Belfast and may have had dubious links to start with, and you're telling us that he had to move himself and his family back home because he stopped Blackwell from killing you? What's the real reason he left?"

"That was it."

"Was it Joey who went after Lucan?"

"What?"

"You're trying to hide him. And winding us in circles is worse than saying nothing at all. Who went after Lucan? Who broke into his house?"

"I don't know. I was only twenty..."

"Twenty is old enough to do anything."

"Stop, now. I don't know who it was."

"Lucan's nanny was an innocent in all this, and somebody bludgeoned her to death. Don't lose your humanity because you feel some stupid loyalty to someone who could beat the head off another human being."

"I don't have to be here..."

"Sandra Rivett's blood was everywhere," Maggie interrupted, suddenly remembering Superintendent Foster's briefing, suddenly recalling the details. "All over the floor, the walls, even the ceiling. If it wasn't Lucan, someone else got off with that crime. Who did Blackwell send to get him?"

"I don't know."

Maggie stood up. "Of course you do. You'd have heard all the rumors."

"I didn't!"

Liam put his hand on Maggie's arm, but she wouldn't be stopped: "It was such a big deal, everyone would have known."

"I don't know. He was crying, he was crying..."

"Who was crying?"

"Blackwell was. I was half dead, and Blackwell was beside me, sobbing his eyes out."

"So what?"

"It might not have happened at all."

"What might not have happened?"

Priestley looked up at her with tears in his eyes. Then he looked back down and sighed a weight out of himself. "I can't..."

Maggie banged on the table and he jumped. "Tell us, Paul! If you're withholding ..."

"It was the funeral! The last thing I remember from the funeral..."

"Is what?"

"...is Blackwell lying on the ground, crying for his girl, and..."

"And...?"

"And Joey Gleeson bending down to him, bending down to his friend, saying, 'I'll get him, Harry, I'll get Lucan and his family.'"

25. A Great British Landmark's Story

Something was stuck onto a railing spike outside Westminster Hall. It was to the left of the main doors, where lines of Londoners passed by on their morning walk to work. Many of them saw it and a few even touched it, but their "ews" turned to amusement when they decided it must be some kind of puppet, part of a protest or some annoying art project going on in the city. The thing was a head, with neither eyes nor hair, and it looked smaller than a normal head, one that hadn't seen the inside of an oven.

The shifting audience of gawkers came to the notice of the Westminster security police at the entrance to the building. The officers strolled over to unblock the sidewalk. They saw the head and the head gawped back. The eyebrows were gone, and the muscles behind were arched into a look of surprise. One of the more sensible policemen thought it might be an archaeological item, found nearby and posted on the railing for someone more knowledgeable to examine. An Anglo-Saxon head that had rolled out of one of the many historical digs around the inner city, stuck on a spike by a helpful, if busy, passer-by. It seemed like a sensible explanation, and the head's discovery was radioed in with more fun than haste.

The news cameras arrived before the police. It wouldn't be a major story, but it was spooky enough to fill a minute or two at the end of the headlines. *Shrunken Head Found in Parliament*. A few liberties taken with the details.

A police car appeared with three officers who verbally pushed the audience on their way. Photos were taken and a small cordon went up. The pedestrians still passed close enough to see the black ball and enquire from the officers as to *what the hell was that thing?* And amid all the bother and joviality, a single forensic anthropologist popped around from Scotland Yard. He took a look at the face and removed forceps from his bag. He tilted the head and looked into the neck. The circular spinal bone was there, but more surprisingly, there was dried tissue that should be long gone from an archaeological find. He looked into the neck again. He felt the blood leave his face before he fully knew what he was seeing. He filled his lungs with air and knew that to take another second to breathe was a second too long. He opened his mouth and let out a roar that shook all ears that heard it.

"Everyone back! Close the street! The place will be useless!"

The officers stopped mid-breath and looked at him, then they looked at the head.

"Get them away! For god's sake, get everyone away!"

The police ran to encircle him, yelling at the pedestrians to get off the street. The cordon was extended as far as it would go, the public was driven back without ceremony. More squad cars arrived within minutes, and an army of officers shut down a ring around Westminster Hall and evacuated most of the workers from adjacent buildings. The newscasters hung around until the edge of arrest, but the footage they got was worth it.

The head was photographed in detail and sampled in situ, while a search for the body was launched. Teams of police began combing the entire Westminster complex and its surroundings. The head would be in the forensic labs within two hours, and DNA results were there within two days. A new case suddenly shot into importance in the heart of Scotland Yard, piercing the force like the spike that held the newly dead crown of Barnaby Cromwell Hutchinson.

26. What We Know

"A severed head has been found on a railing outside Westminster Hall."

Every mouth in the room opened, as the image formed in their minds. Twenty police officers were crammed into the smaller briefing room, with Booth in the center of them, trying to keep everyone calm.

"You're getting handouts now, with the details we have so far. Security police spotted the head just before eight AM. It must have fallen or been taken off the perch at some point because the back of it smashed, and fragments of bone have been found at the base of the railing. The path itself is forensically compromised, because hundreds of people walked by."

"Is there a body?" Maggie asked.

"That hasn't been found yet. But the victim has been identified from the dental records of missing individuals, because he disappeared over a week ago. It's a builder from Ilford named Barney Hutchinson. From preliminary discovery, we believe we know why he was targeted."

Barney Hutchinson, so plain a name, Maggie thought. Who would dislike poor old Barney Hutchinson enough to take his head off and stick it on a spike?

"Some treatment was carried out post-mortem," Booth said. "The lab suggests the head had been dry-heated for several days."

Noses wrinkled in the room.

Maggie read the handout again. Full name: Barnaby Albert Cromwell Hutchinson. Sex: Male. Nationality: English. Ethnicity: Caucasian. Occupation: Construction.

She saw from preliminary discovery that Hutchinson was the defendant in an ongoing class-action lawsuit against his building firm. At least sixty people had purchased apartments or houses from him that collapsed to the ground. Three people were killed in the process, one an infant.

"Anyone working on Trevelyan will be pulled onto this," Booth said. "Staffordshire police will have to handle that on their own. Other cases will be put on hold as well. Because of his legal difficulties, the suspect list with Hutchinson is going to run into the hundreds."

"What about video footage?" Liam asked. "Westminster is in the middle of the city."

"There's none," Alex cut in. "We have stills from the perimeter cameras, but there are only six cameras up because they're paid for by the local authority, Westminster council, not central government. The council can't afford any more, and they've been telling the government that for years. We have a few black-and-white photographs, and they're at the back of the handout."

Maggie looked at the pictures. In one, she saw a tall figure with his hands raised, almost touching the head. The same figure was walking away in the next image. He appeared to be an older male, dressed in a three-quarter-length coat made from a heavy material such as wool.

Did you just put that there? Maggie asked in her head, before realizing that she'd have to shelve the Lucan investigation until this more gruesome matter was cleared up.

27. Grady in the Snug

L. Grady sat his regular pub less than 300 meters from the Irish parliament, the Dáil. The place was constantly moving, with people coming in to buy their pints and taking them outside to sit in the last of the warmth. If they saw him at all, most people could recognize L. Grady's face, and the ones who caught his eye by mistake gave a little nod and then looked away, back to the business of buying their Guinness. A slight flutter in the heart from locking eyes with a celebrity. A type of celebrity.

A waitress inched open the door of the snug, struggling to keep the plates in her hands while trying not to hit the head of a man who, according to the barmen, might have been quite a member of the IRA at one time. L. Grady's companion helped her in, taking the ham rolls off her and letting her fly out as fast as she could.

"That Dr. Gleeson is very pleasant," Terry said as he started into his roll.

"How's he getting on, tucked away in his office?"

"He's fine. I'd go to him if I ever needed help."

"You'd never have to, you're strong."

"I've never had to go to extremes."

"I'm sure if you did, you'd know it was for a good cause."

"That's what he said."

"Who?"

"Gleeson. He said we had to think about the big picture, about the country."

"I've never heard him mention it before, but I suppose the feeling must be in him, like it was in his father."

"Did you see the head on the spike?" Terry said, handing his boss a newspaper.

"I did. Have they discovered who it was attached to?"

"A man called Barney, but there aren't many details out."

"I wouldn't like to go that way, like some new kind of kebab."

Grady read the front-page news. It shouldn't have taken him long, but he couldn't take his eyes from it.

"It's a funny thing, Terry, but this head reminds me of something, and I can't remember what."

"Maybe it'll come to you."

"Maybe it will." Grady smiled. "And maybe it's nothing."

"What time do you have to get back for?" Terry stuffed the last of his sandwich into his mouth.

"Two o'clock. I've a few arms to twist about the peace walls."

"Twist away," Terry said, standing up. "I'll get the profiles off Gleeson."

"Wait. It might be an idea to check up on the old man."

"Gleeson?"

"What? No. Sure he's younger than me. Can you get up to Monaghan? Drop into old man McConnell, see what he has to say about those deaths in the papers. I'd go with you, only we grate on each other. He wasn't too happy about me getting the new job. Running between Belfast, Dublin, and London was a waste of time, he told me. He said I was abandoning the North. Even though that old eejit has been living down south for most of his life. I'll ring him, let him know you're coming up."

The young man left the snug and wandered into Grafton Street, with its elegant storefronts and expensive lanes and spots for quiet polite buskers and louder polite flower sellers. This side of the River Liffey held streets as narrow as they were high, as historic as they were beautiful, and he wondered how the sun managed to get down through the buildings and light up the faces around him. The street was packed with people who knew how to walk by each other without so much as a touch, without a push, though if either happened by accident, both parties would apologize with a smile and feel that their day had been brightened by the encounter. What a wonderful life it was down here, what a wonderful thing it would be if the North could come out of the shadows as well.

And in the snug, the Special Intergovernmental Advisor on Northern Ireland Affairs downed the last of his pint. "A head on a spike," Grady said to himself. The ham roll looked up at him and he reckoned he would have preferred soup instead. "And a Trevelyan shot in the head." He wasn't due back in the Dáil for a short while yet. He thought for a moment, scrolling his memory back through the years. Dates that stood out, men that loomed large. And then he closed his eyes and clenched his teeth. *And fecking Lucan, who no one even noticed.*

Hutchinson's head was sliced off and stuck in the heart of London. The Trevelyan kill was taken from several hundred meters. And Lucan was battered to death in a place that the British police never knew about. Grady knew a few men who knew where that place was, but only one of them could tip a fly from a mile away. Scotland Yard had sent their feelers out to the IRA over Trevelyan, asking the less tight-lipped members if they knew anything before giving Grady himself a call. But now Grady would have to call one of them back, a friend in the know, for a casual chat about the poor mounted head of Barney Hutchinson. With each passing moment, Grady became more certain that wherever the police were looking, they were looking the wrong way. He was sure they should be looking for a ghost.

*****

When he reached the Irish parliament, it was at the door of the Committee on Planning and Infrastructure that Mr. Grady showed his face, and when he saw that there were enough people inside to make it worthwhile, he went in and sat down.

"Is there some chemical in here that's been used to clean the room?" he asked during a break in discussion. The five others had been examining the budget for a bypass in Cork.

They didn't let it show, but they were glad of the change in topic.

"Something like bleach?" one of the members asked, curling his nose at the thought of it.

"It could be bleach, but I think it's sweeter."

"They might have sprayed the curtains with something," from another member, looking warily at the floor-length beige curtains.

"What do you need, Mr. Grady?" the chairman, Fergal Gibney, asked. "Would you like to help us with this budget?"

"I'd love to, Fergal, but I'm on about the walls again. I need help with the International Peace Fund."

The members were good enough to keep a check on their sighs, but the conversation about cleaning chemicals would have been more interesting.

"We have it under control."

"With all due respect, Mr. Chairman, the fund's just got a new donation of 500,000 dollars. That's not going to sit very long before some hippie thinks it's a great idea to use it."

"The walls have been delaying integration, they have to come down."

"They've kept the violence in check. You can't stab someone if you can't get to them."

"The goal is to get people not to want to stab each other. And you've never convinced us of what you think's going to happen. People don't want a return to the '70s. The walls have to come down."

"They do. There's a hundred of them now, little stabs into the North, each one. But I'll say it again – this isn't the time. The people on either side aren't ready for it. And I need help putting the brakes on the fund. It would just take one troublemaker who's watched the History Channel too often ..."

"Stop, Mr. Grady, you're too late. The Northern Ireland Executive approved their removal this morning. The dismantling begins in two weeks. The North will be able to look at itself again. But for some reason, you're still trying to block this."

"Mr. Chairman, when the walls come down and Northern Ireland looks at itself, it'll scratch out its eyes before hitting itself in the face with a brick. And then it'll set itself on fire, like one of those Tibetan monks. Because at this point in time, Mr. Chairman, Northern Ireland still hates itself, and no one seems to care."

28. Are They All Gone?

"Where's the potatoes?" I said, staring at my plate.

"What potatoes? It's chicken curry."

"I thought there were potatoes."

"You can't have potatoes in chicken curry." Ken looked at me in confusion as he ladled his goop onto the other people's plates.

"What?"

Suzanne tried to be helpful. "You can have potatoes in some curries. Doesn't aloo sag have potatoes?"

"Sag aloo. What?" Her words were lost on me as well. Eyes were watching me but I couldn't see their faces. Where were the potatoes?

"What happened, Ken?"

"What happened with what, Michael?" He was at my shoulder, breathing beside me. Somebody was beside me and he wouldn't go away. For a moment I thought it was Alastair, and my heart sank when I realized it wasn't him.

"Sorry, I was thinking about something."

"What thing? Will you be okay for the States? Shit. What about our trip to Belfast?"

"You're heading up?" Jean asked him.

"Next Saturday," Ken said worriedly. "I'm a keynote speaker at a conference in Queen's University. But there's no way I'm going on my own."

"Is there trouble there?"

"They're removing the peace walls that separated Protestant and Catholic areas. Neighbors will see each other for the first time in years, and it doesn't sound like they'll be embracing. But we'll stay in a fancy hotel. Michael can relax, get back to his roots. Isn't that right, Michael?"

"Bricks and fire and blood," I muttered.

I should have been happy, I should have been thrilled. The sight of a Cromwell head on a railing at Westminster had me buzzing for days. Lucan, Trevelyan, and Cromwell, the worst names in Irish history. I'd done it, and it had no effect. No one had made the link. The newspapers were shouting about the individual cases, silent about history. That's how much our history meant – nothing. I felt worse than ever.

I had to get to the bathroom. When I stood up, the blood rushed to my head and I barely made it out the door. I pulled myself up the stairs, halfway up before I sat down. Was this a panic attack? Was this what my patients described? This had to be a heart attack. I couldn't breathe.

There was a ringing in my head. Or in my ear. My phone was at my ear. Turlough's name was on the screen, he must have called me. I pressed the phone to my ear to hear him speak and I only heard the ringing. I'd called him. I hung up as quickly as I could.

A door opened and a pinch of noise fell out. They were laughing at me, Ken was getting them to laugh at me.

"Are you okay, Michael?" I heard.

Ken's face was at the bottom of the stairs.

"I am, thanks."

"You're wrecked, friend."

"I am."

He came up and sat by my legs.

"I can make potatoes for you if you like, but I don't think it'll help."

"Yeah, no. Thanks."

"Do you want to head home? I'll leave you home."

"Sometimes there's no air."

"Is it your chest?" he said in alarm.

"Not that type of air."

"What other type is there? Are you stressed at work? You'll have to see someone."

"You're here."

"That's not enough."

"I decided on five, but I don't think I'll make it. And three has done nothing at all."

"Three what?"

"My father warned me never to forget, but I couldn't even if I tried. I see so many of them, Ken, so many broken men."

He nodded slowly, with unhappy eyes I'd rarely seen on him. He put his hand on my arm. "You're a great help to your patients."

"Not to the ones in the organization. I can hardly do anything. It's the big fact they can't get over, that they devoted their lives and lost. I never want to see them losing again, the way my father did."

"Is it a company that sends people to you? If there are too many, you'll have to tell someone high up that it's too much."

"Who's higher than L. Grady? And he's wiped his hands of it."

"The only L. Grady I know is the government man. Is that who you mean? Does he have a company?"

"Not a company."

He pulled back from me, keeping his hand on my arm. "Are you talking about the IRA?"

"The name changes, but it tends to be the same."

"The IRA, Michael? Does the government send them to you?" He tried to reason it out. "Is it part of the peace process?"

"It's best not to mention this to anyone."

"No, no one." The color was gone from his face. "Shit, that stuff would depress anyone."

He stared into space, and we sat on the stairs with our fingers locked.

"Shit, man. If it's any consolation, I'm glad someone's helping them."

"What do you mean?"

"I'm not big into politics, but I always thought we abandoned them, you know, after 1921, after the country was split up. The six counties went to Britain, and the south kind of wandered off. Once we were making money, we didn't care. And they were miserable up there. No votes, no jobs, no lives for decades. The army was British, the police force, the power. And we closed our eyes. Nobody seems to talk about that."

I didn't see it coming, I hadn't expected his words.

"Thank you, Ken," I said. I may have said it twice.

I suddenly had to get out. I gave him an awkward side-body hug and made my way down the stairs while trying not to fall. There was a person at the bottom. Suzanne was there. I didn't know how long she was there. She turned away as if she had something on her mind, something other than the panic-attacked middle-aged man trying to get down the stairs without falling.

"What are you doing?" I asked.

She turned back to me. "Are you okay?"

"Were you listening?"

"To what?"

"What did we say?"

"I don't know. You seemed a bit shaky..."

"I'm okay," I said without warmth.

"I can go home with you if you like."

"What?"

"If you feel sick, I can stay with you."

"No."

I got my coat while she watched me. I put it on and she turned and went back into the dining room.

"Who is she?" I said to Ken as he showed me to the door.

"Suzanne? You know who she is. She's Jean's friend."

"Are they related?"

"No, I think they went to school together."

"Did she hear anything?"

"I don't know. But it doesn't matter. What goes on in your office is confidential, not illegal."

There were no other questions I could ask without sounding ridiculous, so I said goodbye and drove home too fast. I had two more surnames on my list, and I was going to do them, no matter who had their eyes on me, who the hell wanted to take me home. I'd known the names for years, I just had to do the sifting. I ran up to my front door and went in with an energy I'd forgotten I had, but when I tried to close the door behind me, I couldn't.

I gave it another, harder push, thinking that something was catching at the bottom. It sprang back at me. And there was a face.

"I'm here to collect, Dr. Gleeson."

"Are you Death?"

"No, sir. Just the profiles."

"Are you the same man as before?"

"I am, I'm Terry. Is that who you mean?"

"What do you want?"

My gruffness surprised us both.

"The profiles, sir. And I've a few more to give you."

"You're very familiar. Do I know your father?"

"My father's dead. A long time now."

No hesitation, no sign of emotion. A dealt-with death.

"I have the documents in here."

He followed me into my small office.

"There's one I have to ask you about," I said. "It's the Southern Quartermaster. Are there likely replacements?"

He pursed his lips as if it was a touchy subject. "There are, but he's been around for years. What would you do with him, sir?" It was the first time I'd been asked for operational advice from any of them.

"He's not in it for the cause."

"You think so, yeah?" The slightest emotion from him, the slightest anger. "I'll let Mr. Grady know. He's busy with the peace walls at the moment."

"Trying to have them removed?"

"Trying to keep them up. He says the blood will hit the streets again if they come down."

"That's funny."

"Funny?"

"I remember blood hitting a street when they were going up. But it doesn't matter whether they're up or down."

"Why not?"

"Because the North needs more than small measures at this stage."

"I don't know what it needs. But I know I need to get going, sir, as I've an hour's drive ahead of me."

I told him I'd let him out through the back garden, and we walked through the house to the kitchen door. I held it open for him as he went out.

"I don't like having to go to extremes, Dr. Gleeson."

"With your work? I'd avoid it if I were you."

"If a man had to go to extremes, would there be a way he could prepare himself for it, beforehand?"

"I'd try not to get into the situation in the first place. It's the men who don't wonder about it who handle it best."

"I don't know how they do it."

"They may have seen it in their fathers, and it becomes just another way to solve a problem. Has anyone asked you to do anything, Terry?"

"No, not at all. And I don't know what I'd say if they did."

He was entirely distracted, hardly noticing I was there. And I realized what a tough life he had chosen for the type of man he was. I couldn't even be sure that he wasn't about to cry.

"Have you anyone to talk to?"

He gave a weak smile. "There's not many people who'd want to listen."

"I'm here. Give me a ring whenever you want. Sometimes it's hard to get the right outlook on things."

"That would be good, sir. Even knowing that I could."

He said goodbye and went into the darkness and I heard the side gate open and close. And I wondered how I could so easily see an end to people when this young man found it so hard. But I didn't wonder too long, so I guess I had my answer.

*****

The house was cold but I kept the heat off. I went back to the office and sat at my desk. I read some of the new profiles before I couldn't read any further. There were details of men and women who had spent decades trying to take other people's lives, then years trying to find some lives for themselves. Grasping for purpose now that the fight for their country had moved into politics and got stuck there as if it was in jam. I went to bed hoping the details wouldn't linger in my head.

The details went out of my head alright. Not even a psychiatrist can control the wandering brain when it's left on its own in the dark. And it's a funny thing to dream about darkness in the dark, but I had no choice. Just like I had no choice when I was sixteen years old and moved out of one darkness and into another.

I had the balaclava over me most of the time, turned around so the holes were looking out from the back of my head. They were probably making a statement with that, a symbol of the paramilitaries turned arseways. When I first had it on, the smell of it was noxious, my face against the woolly sweaty head of whoever had it on before. But by the end of the night, my tears and snots had made it my own.

Dad went out the last night I ever saw him. Off to a pub on the Falls Road to meet his brother-in-law for a few pints to help him get over Mam's death. As soon as the door banged after him, I was gone from the house the other way, taking a break from thinking about Mam, seeing what the lads were up to, the few I'd hung around with to learn what to drink and how to get the smell of cigarettes off you at the end of the night. Toothpaste, someone said.

Someone was talking about whether soap would work when we were approached by two army officers, older men, and them looking at me. My height meant I was the only one of us to get served in off-licenses but also the first to get singled out if there was any trouble. And most of the time, trouble to the British army in Belfast meant a group of lads hanging around anywhere, with nothing to do. They asked us our names and told us to fuck off home. We might have thrown a few choice words back at them, but you'd never give too much lip to a man carrying a black rifle that was almost half his length. We started walking. And I was told to stop.

I didn't say a word. One soldier stood away and radioed something in. My friends took turns to look back at me as they walked down the road, and a man I knew stuck his head out from his front door. While the soldier nearest me went through my pockets, another man appeared and stood at a corner down the block, about eight houses away. He wasn't a soldier. And coming in the opposite direction from my friends were two men, their hands held at the center of their chests, in the pockets of bulky jackets. The other soldier returned and asked me my name again and I nodded. And as the man at the corner was joined by another man, I wondered where the best place was for me to be. The corner men were closest. I looked at them, and their eyes were fixed on the soldiers beside me.

Then the corner men looked at me and I got ready to run. And then their eyes came off me and they looked behind themselves and something changed and they crossed over the road, away from me, and the sound of solid wheels grew louder as the street lit up. A Saracen came round the corner, a six-wheel giant taller than a man, the gun turret swiveling like a Dalek, ready to blast into dust any person, group, or house that got in its way. And I can't say I wasn't relieved, thinking I wouldn't be shot by a stray bullet aimed at the green jackets in front of me. But the feeling didn't last.

The Dalek didn't come alone, it had the company of a creeping Humber Pig, a lightly armored truck for getting in and out of streets, getting away, getting its passengers away. I was put into that, as if it were no more than a bus, and it was only when the twisted balaclava was yanked over my head that, damn me anyway, I started to fucking cry. When your sight is taken away, when you can't see if there's someone beside you and the reflex that closes your eyes if a blow is coming doesn't work because your brain can't see it, what do you do? Kick with your legs? Give the air a box with your handcuffed fists? Hope no one hits you.

The front of the balaclava was wet when we reached somewhere, and I was carted out and then in and sat down again. My hands were frozen. The talk started immediately.

"Nothing's going to happen to you."

I kept my mouth closed, shivering.

"We're not going to lay a finger on you, Michael. We just want to know where your uncle lives, we want to contact him."

I shrugged.

"Can you tell us that?"

Someone else was there but not speaking. Moving around. But the first one was the talker, and he had a fine English accent.

"Where does he live? Is it in Belfast? Michael!"

I jumped in the blackness. I was almost seventeen. Didn't they know I was only sixteen? I couldn't tell them anything, I didn't know where he lived. We never visited him, he always stayed with us.

There was a crack of knuckles and then a crack like a stretch, someone stretching their spine.

"We're not going to touch you. You won't be beaten or choked and your thumbnails won't be ripped out. None of those stupid things your pals may have talked about is going to happen. What we're going to do is take you over to a helicopter and go up in the sky and throw you out of it."

I think a "Wha?" came out of my mouth.

I stood up but there were hands on my arms, from people I didn't see, and I was frog-marched, half lifted, out to the air and I heard blades start their slow steady swipe and the wind was whipped up from the ground.

I was helped up a step and put sitting, and the swipes overhead got faster and louder. We were in the air when the hood came off and there were two men on either side of me and one man opposite. He had a map in his hand and he shouted my uncle's name.

I shook my head and looked out. It was dark, I couldn't even see the lights of a road. I felt like wetting myself, but it had been a while since I'd gone so it might not have been nerves. Higher and higher and the draught blowing in the open door. It would have been great were it not for the circumstance, it would have been a story to tell, my first ride in a helicopter, though it was night and I could only see the dark.

The man opposite came closer. "At 4,000 feet you're gone. Don't worry, you won't feel a thing." And then he sat back but time must have been running out because he soon spoke again.

"We're going to push you out, Michael."

"You're not."

"What?"

"You're not going to push me out."

"You think I'm lying? We're going to fuck you out that door," he said in confusion, with too many blinks, too much discomfort. I could tell even then when a person was lying. I had come from a family of distinguished liars – Mam lying to Dad about feeling just fine, Dad lying to Mam about not being involved in anything.

"You're not going to push me out because I don't know where he lives."

"Of course you do. He's your uncle."

"He's my mother's brother, and she's dead."

He slapped me with his hand, bumping me into the soldier beside me. They started fixing the handcuffs, checking my shoes, asking each other if the hood should go on. All of them lying in their actions.

And then they couldn't wait any longer. The man opposite grabbed my shoulder and, pinching into me, hoisted me over to the open door. A gale of freezing wind. He shook me, as if to push me out, and I held back the cries, my face an angry grimace caused by the wind. He said something and held me out further so that my toes were the only part left in the helicopter. I could see things now, lights down below. The white top of a building. What would it be like if my feet weren't on the ground. What would it be like to be out in the sky... He jerked me back in to the floor.

"Where does he fucking live?!"

"I don't know," I sobbed at him. Everything in my life had broken, one thing at a time. And all those broken bits came together on the sticky slanted floor of that helicopter and stuck onto each other, holding fast, into one tight ball of hate against the Englishmen in Ireland, past and present. It was a cry in my throat that stayed there all the way back down to the ground, all the way out of the helicopter and delivered to the front door of my empty house with a kick out the back of a jeep. The ache in my throat went away, and I was glad of that, though it only moved the short distance up to my head.

29. The Quiet Farm

A farmhouse in Monaghan in the green chest of Ireland might be one of the world's forgotten places, but Cathal McConnell knew there was nowhere finer on earth. The sky was in twilight and the collie had to empty herself before she sat in her kitchen basket and dozed and jerked and peered out for the rest of the night. Just as old and slow, Cathal stood at the back door, watching the thick line of light against the flat fields stretching out to god knows where. This was peace – green in the day and black at night, silent from voices at any time. He whistled Dolores back to him and the two of them went in together.

"Where were you born, son?" Cathal asked as he took a seat at the kitchen table, where Terry had before him reports on the current arms stocks, profiles from the psychiatrist, and printouts of recent news on the politics of the North. The young man was politely trying to distance himself from the iffy-smelling dog that was jumping up to his face to lick him in the mouth.

"Dublin, sir."

"From a big family?"

"Two brothers and a sister, big enough."

"I'd say your mam brought you up well. And your dad."

"It was my mother, and she did."

"And now you're in the IRA."

Terry wasn't sure whether that was a sting from the old man, but he didn't have time to decide before another question hit him.

"Do you have hobbies?"

"Hurling. I play a lot with the lads."

"Hurling and the IRA. One of those two taking up most of your time. Do you like playing up north?"

"I hope you mean hurling, Mr. McConnell."

"What did you bring to show me?"

"I have news reports, and profiles of some of the questionable members. A psychiatrist looks them over for us."

"Who would that be?"

"Michael Gleeson. He's from Dublin."

"He's from Belfast, he's living in Dublin."

"You know him?"

"I know the name. He's the man to see if you want your head fixed."

Cathal stood up and walked over to the kitchen window, where he filled the kettle with water and stared out at the dark. Then he whispered, "Can you hear that?"

The kettle began to boil, but what Cathal was listening to was the sound of Dolores snoring, like a fat middle-aged man. The two men smiled.

"That's peace," Cathal said. "And someone in the organization wants to end the peace."

"What do you mean?"

"Ah, you don't know. Grady didn't tell you. It looks like those deaths in the news are linked – the head, the TV man, and the old lord."

"But they don't have anything to do with us."

"Are you sure? Do you know the full name of the Hutchinson head? There's a sound in the middle of it that'll send a shiver down the Irish spine. *Cromwell*."

"I know *that* name."

"Barney Cromwell Hutchinson. And whoever took his head off his shoulders waited a long time for this moment."

"Is it some kind of statement?"

"It's too controlled to be just that. Whoever it is knows they can't take on the Brits and the unionists on their own. But they can remind people about the past. The southerners especially. Little killings, not a war, a reminder that Britain shouldn't have been here in the first place, centuries ago. Laying the ground for the thoughts that'll buzz the young ones and put the placards in their hands. And the guns, if it comes to that. Whoever it is has an itch for Ireland that never went away. They've waited until now to scratch it, so something must have changed."

"How do you know all this, Mr. McConnell?" Terry instantly regretted questioning the former head of the IRA Army Council.

"You don't kill the descendants of three of the devils of Irish history by accident. Only a handful of people in the world knew where Lucan was, myself and Grady included. And in my long life, I've only ever seen one man shoot a living target from a mile away. I actually saw him take out a mark from two miles away, but we didn't have the Guinness Book of Records with us at the time, so you'll have to take my word for it."

"And this man is deciding who to kill and going after them?"

"The man I'm thinking of wouldn't care either way who the target is, so I've a feeling someone else is pulling his strings. What has Grady been up to recently?"

"It's not him, sir. He asked me to come here to see what you thought about the deaths."

"Well, whoever it is, an example will have to be made of them. We can't have people going off on their own current. Things are already jumpy up north, and anything could make it worse. Petrol bombs are being flung over the so-called peace walls every so often, and now those walls are going. They look the other way, the Brits and the Irish down south, and everything just keeps collapsing."

"Maybe we should burn it all down and start again," Terry said quietly.

"I've been saying that for years. Will I stick us on a few Margheritas?"

"Cocktails?"

"Pizzas. I'm going to keep you for a while. You're young, you'll be able to work out a glorious future for us all."

Cathal was halfway to the oven when three hard knocks on the door made both of them jump. Terry stood up and Cathal stood still.

"Who is it?" Terry asked, and Cathal shuffled over to the door but didn't open it, saying as he went, "I wish they wouldn't do that. We have a bell."

He asked loudly who it was and hearing something that wasn't unexpected, he opened the door with the chain latch still on.

"You're doing it now?" He took off the chain and went outside.

Terry lifted up a kitchen knife and walked over to the door, placing the knife on the shelf of a coat stand and covering it with the end of a hanging coat. He was in a farmhouse in the middle of nowhere with a man whose fighting days were long gone. Thankfully, he was in a farmhouse in the middle of nowhere with a man who had seen many fights.

Outside, there were two SUVs, engines running and lights on. Men were lifting black boxes out of the trunks and carrying them over to a shed. No talk, just the sound of shoes on stony ground. Cathal nodded to the air as the last of the boxes was transferred. One of the men caught his eye and nodded himself, then he joined the others as they got in their vehicles and pulled away down the drive. The trees in the distance lit up when they reached them, then the lights of each car disappeared.

"Are you okay with this?" Terry asked the old man.

"I hope so. I organized it."

"Where did they come up from?"

"Cork. And I'm surprised Southern Command has anything left to give. But they might be needed if the killings continue. I don't like men with red hair."

"Excuse me?"

"They make me nervous, men with red hair."

"You mean Redser?"

"Was that his name? I suppose it fits."

"You can't trust them?"

"I've never heard that. It's because they're vampires."

"What?" Terry laughed.

"Lilith was a vampire, and she had red hair. Lilith – Adam's first wife."

"Who?"

"Adam and Eve. But first it was Adam and Lilith. She was a wild one, wouldn't lay down under him or some such tale. Was kicked out of paradise."

"And she was a vampire?"

"She was, or so they say. Then again, Adam was also a redhead. 'Adam' is from the Hebrew word for red. So God created two redheads as the first people. Two vampires. And we've been eating each other ever since."

30. Shopping

"That guy was an asshole," Liam said to the table as he brought over the pints. It was himself, Alex, and Maggie in the Red Lion after work. "That Hutchinson guy, building houses with cheap cement, and when they fell down, he just closed his company and opened a new one. I'd say a few people had it in for him."

"He didn't deserve to end up on a stick," Alex said. "But there's a list of 300 persons of interest now, buyers stretching back for years. When will you be finished with Lucan?"

"We're finished. We got one name out of three interviews, and there's no point in checking up on that unless we like looking in graveyards. Isn't that right, Maggie?"

Maggie was staring at the bubbles in her pint. She roused with her name and didn't mean to change the subject.

"How famous was Lucan over here?" she asked.

"Oh." Alex thought for a second. "My parents used to talk about him, and there were crazy theories about whether he was still alive. Like the Loch Ness monster."

"Everything about that case was crazy," Maggie said, still distracted. "The testimony about the silver car that wasn't presented in court, the second lead pipe that was found in the boot. Lucan insisting that a small man was sent to get him."

"Christ, you know more about this than we do," Liam said. "Don't show us up."

Alex looked at Maggie sympathetically. "He wasn't well known in Ireland?"

"Older people would have heard about him, but I only associate the word 'Lucan' with a shopping center in Dublin. It's built in a place with that name."

"Was the place named after him?"

"I've no idea."

Liam put an arm around her. "Don't worry about it. We're finished with it now, and my wife has said I can stay out till ten, so I'm not sitting here talking about work."

"That's the problem – now that we're finished with it, it'll probably never be looked at again."

Maggie was glad when the topic switched to office gossip, though she couldn't contribute a lot. When she left for home, she bought a kebab and wandered around in the night air. The traffic was still busy enough to keep the place alive, and there was no shortage of tourists and well-heeled Londoners to stop her from feeling alone. It was the first time she saw the city center at night, and the scale of the floodlit buildings took her breath away. Standing in front of Westminster Abbey, she thought its yellow floodlights made the building look like gold. A turn to the left, and she was staring at Big Ben, just as golden as the Abbey. And leading away from the base of Big Ben was the extensive Palace of Westminster. It had the same golden sides, but it also had thin lines of yellow tape extending around its railings. Maggie recognized it as police tape, and she closed her coat tightly and scuttled back to Parliament Street, where she caught the next bus home.

Back in her flat, she turned on her laptop for however long she could concentrate. She wanted to check the latest news coverage on the Hutchinson find, but when Google opened in front of her, reading about the blackened head seemed more challenging than finding out whether the area in Dublin known as Lucan was named after the man himself. She looked it up.

What she found was that Lucan was originally an Irish word, *Leamhcán*, the place of the elms. The first earl of Lucan was created in 1691 by the English king James II, who gave the title to a supporter named Sarsfield who was born in Lucan. It then passed to a great-nephew, Charles Bingham, and it stayed in that family. The search was less interesting than Maggie had hoped.

There were other articles on Lord Lucan, conspiracy theories on his disappearance and murder that she'd read a hundred times, obituaries for the mysteriously departed. The only thing that impressed her foggy brain was a newspaper article on the fact that several home-owners in the west of Ireland, in a town called Castlebar, were still paying rents to the Lucan estate, and there was a petition to have those financial obligations quashed now that he was dead.

A single word caught her attention. It was in a section describing a second reason why the residents of Castlebar weren't too happy with their landowning Lucans: one of the ancestors, the third Earl, had evicted thousands of tenants from the area during the famine. His actions earned him a nickname, and Maggie had to stare at the word and read it aloud for it to sink in. It sounded like something from science fiction, not from the 19th century, and she wondered if it had changed in translation from Irish to English.

The nickname was the Exterminator.

What a name, she thought. He must have been a piece of work. And I've never even heard of him. Not like Oliver Cromwell or the other guys. I can't even think of the other ones now. The English lads who came over for a visit.

She closed her eyes where she sat, taking a small sweet break before she'd have to brush her teeth. Then she shut down her laptop and fell on the bed. *Did they all have weird nicknames back then? I can't remember if Cromwell had one. Maybe they called him the fecker. Probably something worse. Here he comes, that arsehole, Cromwell. That arsehole Barney Cromwell. Dad, you'd be a help if you were here. You knew all about that historical ...* Her brain stood still. She reassembled what she had thought. "Arsehole Barney Cromwell. Oliver Cromwell."

Holy shit.

Maggie jumped off the bed and opened her laptop, waiting for it to reboot through the slowest minute of her life. Then she spent the next three hours working, in full concentration, and the pints washed out of her as if running into the Irish Sea.

*****

First thing the next morning, Maggie gave Booth's door a solid knock and went in. The superintendent was finishing an early call to the Met's Assistant Commissioner, justifying the need for more officers for all the cases before him. She went straight over to his desk as he was hanging up.

"The murders are linked," she said.

"Which ones?"

"Lucan, Trevelyan, and Hutchinson."

"What? Lucan wasn't even killed in this country. And the suspect list for Hutchinson is over 300."

"I checked into Lucan's family history, and I found an ancestor called the Exterminator. He evicted thousands of people from their homes during the famine."

"So?"

"Hutchinson's middle name is Cromwell. Cromwell and Trevelyan, sir."

"What about them?"

"Oliver Cromwell massacred thousands in Ireland in the seventeenth century, and Trevelyan was in charge of famine relief a couple of centuries later, but he couldn't care less."

Booth scratched his head. Three high-profile deaths, and an Irish officer alleging they're because of British rule in Ireland. The tabloids would go wild.

"There are no similarities between the killings," he said. "It's a coincidence."

"The descendants of three of the worst men in Irish history?"

"Wouldn't an historian have picked up on this?"

"Not necessarily. Lucan's life was more about his disappearance than a predecessor who hardly anyone in Ireland knows about, let alone over here. And Barney Hutchinson's middle name hasn't appeared in the media. It's a common enough name in England."

"Lucan and Hutchinson had a lot of enemies, and anyone in the public eye like Evan Scott Trevelyan is always a target for stalkers."

"Do we have to wait for another death to confirm it either way?"

"Be careful with your attitude, Detective."

"Sorry, sir. I'm looking at it from the Irish side, and the link seems so obvious."

Booth took a moment to think. "Does Officer Doran agree with you?"

"He does. He suggested I bring it to you."

"I'll contact an historian to see what they have to say. But come back to the present until then."

Maggie thanked him and headed for the door.

"Sir, Lucan is closed on our end, but we came out with a name. A witness allegedly heard a man called Gleeson say he was going to get Lucan."

"Has that name come up in the case before?"

"No, but I can't figure out why the witness would have lied."

"A bad memory, maybe. Keep the name at the back of your mind. It would be great publicity if the Yard finally solved that old case, but we have to focus on the recent killings."

"So you don't think it was solved the first time round, that Lucan was the murderer?"

Booth looked at her, and he couldn't help smiling.

"That case was a mess," he said, reminding Maggie of the exact same words she'd heard back in Dublin.

31. The Bull

I was late getting over to Ken's. For too many minutes, I'd stood in my home office, staring at something I'd found in my pocket. It was the crumpled piece of paper I'd scribbled on in work during Ruth's visit a few days before. I now flattened it out on my desk, remembering how I used to do the same with Trevelyan's face. And as I read the names on the sheet – Lucan, Trevelyan, Cromwell – they didn't frighten me anymore. I squeezed the paper into a ball for the last time and put it in a desk drawer, knowing the names had lost their power in my mind, knowing I could burn all my handwritten labor, all the starving faces that had sat in my drawers for years.

When I reversed out my driveway, it wasn't a bag of potatoes I saw but Suzanne herself, waiting at my gate with her bike in her hand.

"What are you up to?" I asked.

"I wanted to see if everything's okay. You were tired at Ken's, I think."

"I was. All well now."

"I've a few more Russets for you. I thought they might help." She pulled a white plastic bag out of her basket.

"Oh, I have to go. And I've a flight tomorrow, so I won't be home."

Her face dropped as if I'd stabbed her.

"Sorry, Suzanne. Listen, you use the spuds, enjoy them for me."

That was all I could offer, because I had to say goodbye and pull away. I was late for Ken and the drive up to Belfast. My eyes focused on the road but I looked into the mirror once or twice, to see Suzanne cycle away and out of sight. I wondered why I had been so suspicious of her. And then my eyes returned to the road and to the sight of two men in a car, parked at the curb and looking at me. A strange thing at eight in the morning, strange enough for me to pull back into the side.

A bang on the passenger window made me jump. A figure stood against the door, blocking it, not showing their face. I was out of the car in a second. I didn't recognize him at first, and he got such a look of fright that I thought it was anger I was seeing.

"I have to get out, Dr. Gleeson. Can you move your car?" Mr. White, my neighbor, seventy years old and too startled for his age.

I looked at the car with the men inside and walked towards it, leaving Mr. White without a reply. Both of the doors opened and both men got out. I was ten meters away from the driver, walking like a bull in the middle of the road, fists tight and arms locked. The driver looked at me and then at his chest. There was a tattoo on his neck. I got ready for any blows that came, ready to throw them back. He reached into his car. I could only duck if a gun appeared, but I kept walking.

He took something out, something long and yellow and looking like a neon vest. A workman's vest. He pulled it over his head and lifted out a heavy bag. He closed the door and blinked on the alarm. Then he walked near me, by me, with a silent stare, and he joined his passenger on the curb and the two of them went down the road to whatever bloody pothole or wonky wiring they were working on that day.

I didn't anticipate the "Yes, of course!" I yelled at Mr. White in answer to his question. When I pulled away from the curb, I thought what a funny thing my life had become, what extreme lengths had opened up inside me.

32. Choices (1848)

By the end of the third year, most in Muraisc had sold their clothes. The warm winter things had gone to anyone who could pay for them, for whatever they could. Our father said the blackness couldn't last another season, that we could get back the rags or spend on new ones, dresses with colors and shawls to swallow us up. But to have the milk and oats now, the clothes had to go, and we sat shivering in our thin slips, our shirts and short trousers. There wasn't thread left to sew the holes, and the needle was long gone.

Some in the village had died that winter. The families had been too large. My parents had to choose between feeding my mother's kin or feeding us, never mind themselves. We moaned from the hunger so we got the watered oats and mushrooms, if any were found about, and my grandmother and grandfather sat together on the straw and got nothing. They didn't mind after some days, they were out of the rain and if my mother didn't cry, they wouldn't either. And we couldn't look at them, we pretended they were lying together talking about the weather or giving out about a neighbor. But my mother and father had to look at us, as the meat dropped from our bodies and we turned into somebody else's children. Bones and eyes, my mother said.

And when my mother laid Nancy beside the old ones, knowing she was to go, it was the first time in days that she looked at her parents, and they were long gone. She let out a small noise and hugged Nancy beside her, and my father said to us to turn back to the pot, to eat the warm grass from the pot. My mother lay with Nancy for a day or two, it was always dark and my youngest sister went off to meet her grandparents. I remember my father moving away from us across the room with Frankie in his arms, saying to my mother that he was behind her and not to turn onto him.

"Are you with them, Dan?" I heard her say when he was back with us, and I think he heard and I think he replied that he was.

And when it came the next morning and we could see more, my mother had her arm behind her, across her beautiful cold little Frankie. She was staring at Nancy in front, but the light in all of their eyes was gone.

(Honoria O'Gliasáin, Mayo)

33. Back to Belfast for Michael

The smell was the first thing. Invisible and everywhere. Part smoke, part rubber, part sweet plastic or whatever it is that's thrown on blazes. Each year, the unionists build their Twelfth of July bonfires, celebrating the Protestant Dutchman William of Orange for defeating the Catholic James II in summer 1690, thanking him for keeping his title as their overlord, the king of England, Scotland, and Ireland. Billy and James brought their battle to the beautiful River Boyne in County Meath, where James' defeat meant the start of the domination of Ireland in earnest, the Protestant Ascendancy. Unionists celebrate it and nationalists lament it, though nobody mentions that neither of us, Catholic or Protestant, needed either of them.

But the bonfires that burned their smoke into my hotel window weren't unionist. It was the last day of October, known as Samhain in Celtic times, the night when the door between this world and the otherworld opens and the ghosts of the dead appear. The *Daoine Sídhe* make an entrance and the millennia-old instructions for placating them are to give them food and dress up as one of their own to confuse them, though it's unlikely they would have looked like the Hulk or Cinderella as children become on what Samhain is today, Halloween.

Myself and Ken checked into the Stormont hotel, a little luxury outside the city center. While he went to Queens, I walked around the smoky streets. It was four o'clock in the evening and the bonfires were on every corner, though their effect was minimal with the light that was still in the sky. Pairs of police officers looked on anxiously as gangs of teenagers walked around in high spirits, some with half-painted faces or part of an old costume dangling from their waists. The children that ran down the terraces door to door took it more seriously; the bags of sweets in their hands told everyone that this was their day. But as the darkness dropped and the children ran home, the bonfires grew taller, and they and the otherworld screamed that this was their night.

The smell of smoke increased on the walk back to the hotel, but it was the visible smoke in the air that made me cover my nose on the Newtownards Road. I saw my hotel in the distance, and across the road from it, I saw the flames of a fire reach up to the sky. It was hard to watch without bumping into other people, middle-aged couples going back to the city or youths rolling rubber tires toward the burning mound ahead.

And what a mound it was. Twenty meters in diameter at least, and the wood and tires were still coming. The mood was excited, the beer was out, and, this being Ireland, it wasn't long before I got chatting to strangers. Among them a couple whose opening words to me were the expected "Isn't it big?" Several men asked me if I wouldn't mind moving back. To get higher, higher, the base had to grow. I even helped out at one stage, by throwing a headboard onto the fire in delight.

When his job was done, a man who had asked me to move stood beside me with cans in his hand. Would I like one, he inquired, and sure I couldn't say no.

"That's something, eh?"

"It is," I replied. "Almost as big as the Hill of Tara."

"The hill itself or Tlachtga?"

I looked at him in surprise. I hadn't mentioned Tlachtga – the Hill of Ward – because I thought he wouldn't have heard of it. Twelve miles from the more famous Tara, it was the place where the Celts lit the giant fire every Samhain, letting everyone know that the powers of darkness would be overthrown, light and life would come again. And what a blaze it must have been, 150 meters wide.

"You know it?" I said. "The bonfire to bring in the Celtic new year."

"Wash away the old. I'm Martin Nolan."

"Michael Gleeson."

"You're from down south?"

"I'm from the Short Strand, but living in luxury has ripped the accent out of me."

He didn't ask any more, and it took him a few minutes of thinking about something before he spoke again.

"This fire will burn the whole night. They can't stop us because they let the other fellas have their marches and bonfires and it wouldn't be seen as equitable, as they call it. But this is Tlachgta, the beginning. I've been hearing whispers that someone's finally settling the old scores, putting an end to our history. And we'll start a new one. So here, you and me, we'll drink to Cromwell, Trevelyan, and Lucan."

The heat and the laughter and the crackling wood, and I drank to his words. I said nothing, but I drank to his words. The pressure that rose in my chest wasn't from the fire, but from hearing, finally, that the link had been made. *They know, they all know.* I closed my eyes to feel the complete...

Someone shouted at us. Four men were beside us, and I was kidnapped for the night. Myself and Martin were corralled into helping with wooden pallets and bed frames and packing boxes, and the excitement was so great that I felt like a teenager again. The mound grew higher and wider. A ladder was found to reach the top, then replaced by another when it became too short. And by the time the day was up and I left for the hotel, my face was black and I smelled like ash.

"I'll see you again, when it's all over," Martin said.

I shook his hand and turned to leave as soberly as I could, hearing the quiet words behind me, "When I need help with the memories." I didn't look back.

As Ken drove us out of the hotel, taking me to Belfast International Airport, the fire was still burning but the customary fire-engine sirens that sing the end of Halloween were close by. The Belfast Tlachgta would leave a giant black pit at the start of the one-mile drive to Stormont Castle, the Parliament buildings, the place of power. I would have stayed longer, as long as I could, if I didn't have to catch a flight. It was a consolation that I was about to meet the other side of the family, the family of the Gleeson girl who'd survived the Great Hunger and got away. But as the plane took off, I hadn't expected to feel so low, with a hole in the center of my soul, from leaving the city I'd never admitted to myself, up to now, that I loved dearly.

34. The Different Kinds of History

What if Joseph Gleeson carried through on his promise?
was the question Maggie should have kept at the back of her
mind but couldn't get out of the front of it. She had spent
hours searching for Joseph Gleesons, looking for any who
lived in Woolwich in 1974, any who had been reported in
Staffordshire around the time Evan Scott Trevelyan was shot,
or any hint of one in Ilford when Barney Hutchinson was lifted
off the street. All she found were young men or dead men, so
she wasn't too reluctant to close her browser when William
Booth and two senior detectives walked into the middle of the
floor-length office and ordered everyone to shut up.

Booth made sure everyone was silent and facing him. He
cleared his throat and, in as neutral tone as he could manage,
he said,

"We have a serial killer."

The room stayed silent for one second before gasps of
"What?" were shouted from every corner. Officers looked at
each other to confirm they had heard correctly, and Booth
struggled to speak over the commotion.

"Trevelyan, Lucan, and Hutchinson. The victims have
specific connections to Ireland. An historian who confirmed
the association is going to speak to you now. Detective
O'Malley spotted the link yesterday."

Maggie was listening too intently to blush.

"The three cases are merged, and we'll be working with Counter Terrorism Command, with everyone reporting to me. Available officers who have worked with us before are being pulled from other regions. We're letting this hit the papers today because we need as much assistance as possible, but we have to control the reaction. We need to limit public hysterics, and to prevent a backlash against Irish residents over here. Everything after this will be in strictest confidence. No leaking mouths or you'll be fired. Anyone already assigned to any of the three cases, make your way to the briefing hall."

If she was pleased to have been proved right by an historian, Maggie was more worried about what the killings now meant. Someone was targeting British people because of the past, and that someone was almost certainly Irish. Her knowledge of the history between the two countries was a mixture of her mother's swearwords when it came to anything about the North, and five years of high-school history classes in which the Italian Renaissance always looked and sounded more interesting.

Liam was already in the hall when Maggie arrived. She sat next to him intending to gripe about their new killer when she was put off by the vibrations of his leg silently shaking under the desk. He was sitting forward and sucking his lower lip.

"Are you okay?" she asked in annoyance.

"It seems you were right."

"About what?"

"That the Republicans are starting things up again."

"I wouldn't put it past them, though I wouldn't have said they're this clever."

"Are you crazy? They had all types of people working with them. Engineers, accountants, police, politicians. They couldn't have lasted the decades without them."

"You sound like you're impressed."

"I'm impressed about one thing – it was never a matter of strapping on a belt full of explosives and running into a crowded place."

"No, just smiling Irishmen who'd stab you in the chest."

"Some people would say they had a cause."

"They thought they did, just like the ones today."

Booth's voice from the podium silenced the room. He introduced Professor Julian Beasley, the departmental head of Irish history at Oxford. The professor was a slight man who looked out of place among the larger uniformed officers and suited detectives watching him. He surprised everyone with a booming voice.

"With history, you always have to remember that interpretations change as new evidence emerges or old evidence is reassessed. People who lived centuries ago had different biases than we have today, and in a hundred years, officers like you may be sitting listening to some old fart in an oversized sweater describe us as savages.

"I'm here to talk about Oliver Cromwell, Sir Charles Trevelyan, and George Charles Bingham, the ancestors of your murder victims. Cromwell came first chronologically, and here's a picture of him, literally warts and all.

"Cromwell became the First Lord Protector of the Commonwealth of England, Scotland, and Ireland in 1653, after deposing Charles I during the English Civil War. Historians describe him as a man of liberty, a Puritanical hero who overthrew the monarchy. The British public love him, and he regularly appears on lists of the top Britons of all time. To the Irish, he's a mass murderer.

"Ireland had sided with King Charles and his heir, and after Cromwell quashed the rebellion in England, he landed in Dublin in 1649 to do the same thing. He used the New Model Army, soldiers who were religious fanatics, full-time professionals, and highly disciplined. He sent the message that any further rebellion would not be tolerated. The consequences were inevitable, though the exact number of deaths as a result of the suppression is debated to this day."

A mutter was heard in the room, and Maggie looked at Liam. She wondered if he was only clearing his throat.

"What's that?" Beasley asked.

"Six hundred thousand," Liam said, enunciating each word. He was sitting up straight, with his elbows bent and his two hands on his thighs, prepared for something, for movement or a fight. "I've read that 600,000 Irish died as a result of Cromwell, out of a population of one-and-a-half million."

Beasley nodded his head. "It was a lot, but war was a fact of life, and the English parliament had to smash any uprising in Ireland before it spread."

"He massacred everyone in Drogheda, and that was only the start."

"Okay," Beasley began, sitting back on the desk behind him. "Drogheda was a Royalist stronghold, and it was chosen for a full attack to deter other resistance."

"Four thousand people died there in one day."

"The number is closer to 3,500. But they were given a chance to ..."

"Irish children were used as human shields."

"Even historians debate what happened."

"But the rules back then said you couldn't kill civilians. In any case, it doesn't matter, because after that, it's like he went nuts."

"How do you mean?"

"He destroyed the country." Liam's volume increased. "Crops were burned everywhere, and that started a famine. And then he brought in a law that handed Irish land to the English. And if the Irish didn't like it, they could go to hell or to Connaught. That's what he said, be killed or move to the edge of the country."

"I've been to Connaught, and it's a delightful place." Beasley got none of the laughs he was expecting, only a stony-faced Liam telling him, "That's not a good thing to say."

Maggie looked at her partner as he spoke. He was staring at Beasley, confident in the passion he felt. Why couldn't she feel the same about the subject?

"This is unnecessarily heated," Beasley continued. "What's your name?"

"Liam."

"Ah. Would I be right in saying that one of your parents is Irish?"

"Does it matter? I've an interest in Irish history."

"It matters because what you heard may have been biased, just as what we heard came from the victor's point of view."

"You're right, sir," he said, locking his hands in front of him and speaking slowly and deliberately. "The point of view matters very much, because we have to know whether the killer got your version of the truth or mine. If it's yours, then the three murders may not even be related. They may have nothing to do with Irish history at all. But it looks like the killer got my version. And if it's one person with some blood-revenge thing going on, then he's going to continue, because he has an awful lot more people to choose from."

*****

While Beasley quickly changed his on-screen notes, Maggie took the chance to gripe.

"You're great at this stuff," she whispered to Liam. "I wish I knew more, but I can't stand it."

"You can't stand Irish history?"

"I feel like a fool. It's terrible that I don't know as much as you do."

Liam swung around to her. "Because I'm not totally Irish?"

"Well..."

"That's all I heard in school, Maggie, and now you're doing it."

"Doing what? I'm just saying I should know more about where I come from."

"For fuck's sake. You were only too happy to leave the place."

Beasley began speaking from the podium, saving her a reply.

"The next two individuals are connected, in that their actions occurred during the same event, the Irish famine. Or the Great Hunger, as it's now called. This is a picture of Sir Charles Edward Trevelyan, the British civil servant in charge of distributing famine relief when the potato blight hit Ireland in 1845. Trevelyan was a supporter of laissez-faire, which meant as little interference as possible by the government in economic issues. He closed food depots and stopped the import of maize, known as Indian corn, from America. He said he wanted to 'make Irish property support Irish poverty.' It had a bad effect, and a year later, a Public Works scheme was introduced under which people were paid a small amount for doing jobs such as breaking rocks for roads. It didn't work.

"Trevelyan made rather bad decisions, and that's why he's hated in Ireland. There's even a song about him that they sing at football matches, 'The Fields of Athenry.'"

"How many people died?" Maggie asked, trying to work up an interest in the subject.

"About one million."

"Shit, that's a lot," she said before she could stop herself.

"It is. And up to two million emigrated. The problem was that Trevelyan focused on economics. He was a government worker; he revolutionized the British civil service, reformed standards and admissions for civil servants. It was too easy for him to make decisions about people on another island, people who were part of the British Commonwealth but who..." He was lost for words.

"Was it genocide?" Liam asked.

"Technically, I don't know. Historians don't agree on how to classify it. It's genocide when you want to get rid of an entire ethnicity, when that's your goal. There's no suggestion that the British government actively pursued that policy. Trevelyan did, however, call the famine 'a mechanism for reducing surplus population.'"

Beasley changed his notes again and went onto the last topic, the Earl of Lucan. Maggie leaned in to hear him.

"I'll mention the recent Lucan in passing, because of his colorful life. Richard John Bingham, the seventh Earl of Lucan, was born into an aristocratic family in London. He married Veronica Duncan in 1963, but the marriage collapsed in 1972 and he left the family home in Belgravia. He lost custody of their two children and it seems he began stalking his wife and recording their phone conversations in an effort to get them back.

"In November 1974, Sandra Rivett, the children's nanny, was murdered in the house, and Veronica was attacked. She said it was Lucan who did it, but her and Lucan's accounts of the night differ. We know that Lucan drove to the home of his friend Susan Maxwell-Scott, telling her that he'd seen someone struggling with Veronica in the basement and that he panicked and fled, thinking he'd be implicated."

"Then he left for South Africa," Superintendent Booth said from the side.

"So we've found out. His ancestor, the third earl, was a man called George Charles Bingham. He was an officer in the British army who also had a family estate in Mayo, in the west of Ireland. That area was particularly devastated during the famine, because the soil is rocky and poor. When his tenants couldn't pay their rents, Lucan cleared them off his land to sell or develop it."

Beasley paused, looking at the figures to come.

"In one parish, Ballinrobe, he evicted 2,000 people and tore down 300 cabins so no one could get back in. The tenants were starving by then and had dysentery, smallpox, and TB. Some of the cleared land he turned into a racecourse for himself, and some he sold to other landlords. He also closed the workhouse when it would have been the only chance for many people. All of this earned him a nickname, 'The Exterminator'."

Beasley went silent, and Superintendent Booth spoke up. "Professor, we're working on the assumption that the actions of this ancestor are related to the recent Lucan death."

"It's possible that the two are not related, but Lucan's death comes at a funny time, what with the Cromwell and Trevelyan killings."

"What about the deaths themselves? Do they mean anything?"

"You mean how the victims died? Lucan was beaten to death, whereas his ancestor died of old age. And the Trevelyan individual was shot in the head, while his predecessor died of natural causes. So the only link is between the Cromwells."

"The spike?"

"That's it. Oliver Cromwell died a celebrated man, with a huge funeral at Westminster Abbey. But two years later the monarchy was restored under Charles II, and Cromwell's body was exhumed, hanged for a day, and beheaded. His head was stuck onto a spike at Westminster Hall."

"So the killer copied it?"

"It's unlikely to be a coincidence."

"Any thoughts on who could be next?"

Beasley brought up a list of names, along with their years of birth, important dates, and, if necessary, service in the British government. He was about to go through the list when he looked at the crowd.

"Do any names jump out, especially for anyone with Irish roots?

"Peel," Liam said. "Prime Minister Robert Peel."

"Yeah, he may not be in the class of men we're looking for, though. He tried to help by importing Indian corn into Ireland, and it cost him his job. He also set up a committee to look for a cure for the blight, which he would have given away for free."

"Was a cure found?" Maggie asked.

"No."

"Hograve and Lecky," Booth shouted up.

"What's that?"

"Hograve and Lecky. They're not on the list."

Beasley looked at his list. "No, they're not. Are they part of this?"

Everyone looked at Booth.

"They might be, though they're not well known. My grandmother used to scare my mother with the names."

"Your grandmother was Irish?"

"She was."

And Beasley searched for the names on his laptop and found a relevant website, and he and everyone else read about some kind of walk across mountains on what should have been a beautiful spring day.

35. American Cousins

A woman answered the door to a middle-aged man in a grey tweed coat and red scarf, a wool hat that he was removing.

"Nora? I'm Michael Gleeson. I think you got my letter?"

"You're family," she said in her South Boston accent, the Thanksgiving decorations adding to the welcoming effect.

"I guess I am."

I mustn't have sounded like a murderer or looked like a thief, because she showed me to her sofa and asked if I wanted tea. Then she called into the kitchen and instructed whoever was there to make it. A teenage grunt came back.

"I arrived from Ireland this morning," I said, "and I almost feel like I'm home, what with all the Irish pubs in the area. It's funny, but we don't have as many Irish flags in Ireland."

"We're very proud of our heritage here."

"Sometimes I think we're less proud back home."

"You don't need to show it off like we do. Though the neighborhood is changing. A lot of the old Irish families have moved out. The swanky folk want to live here now, doctors and lawyers. Oh, you said in your letter that you're a doctor?"

"A psychiatrist."

"And you wanted to know about Honoria Gleeson?"

"I did. It seems she emigrated to America around 1853. You believe she was your great-great-grandmother?"

"I think so."

"She was born in 1835 to Annie and Daniel Gleeson."

"I don't know much about that far back, but my father's grandfather was Daniel."

"He would have been Honoria's son. It was common to call the first boy after the mother's father."

I took my notes out of my briefcase. "Honoria landed in America, had Daniel and Florence, and Florence had Patrick Farrell, who was your grandfather."

"He was. But I could never work it out properly. I always thought I was missing a generation. Either that or they were very old to have children."

"Famine affects fertility, even the fertility of the next generation."

"Famine?"

"The Irish famine. That's why Honoria left Ireland."

"I thought it was for better opportunities. Famine sounds like a terrible thing."

"It is. It affects every..."

"Every...?"

"Sorry. By the dates in the family tree, Honoria's children had problems with fertility too. Being starved has consequences down the line."

"I was fine. I was in my twenties when I had Matthew."

"It sounds like it's readjusted now. You and your children are back to normal."

"Do you hear that, Matt? You're normal," she laughed.

The teenager came into the room with the tea and a shrug.

"Are you okay?" The woman stared at me.

Thinking about something. I've something on my mind.

"Sorry, I'm just trying to work this out." I thought I was staring at my notes, but it was actually the carpet.

"And Honoria came on her own?" she asked.

"It's likely she did. Her immediate family was dead by then. She couldn't save her last sibling, Katie."

"How did Katie die?"

"On a walk. There was a long walk through mountains."

"A climbing accident?"

I spit out a laugh and had to apologize. "No. They had to walk seventeen miles to see two men who were supposed to give them food, and she didn't make it."

"Oh, my. Who were the men?"

"They were English," I said, as if it would make sense to her. "Do you know much about the famine?"

"Not really, my parents rarely talked about it. They were working class, so money worries took up most of their time." She shook her head, not sure what she was embarrassed about. This woman in this American house almost hadn't existed, and she'd never found out why her ancestors arrived in America in the first place. Did they go through all that just to be forgotten? Not even forgotten: never known?

"Honoria was the only one of the family to survive," I said. "Her mother had to stop feeding her own parents."

"You'll have to keep your voice down."

The headache was back, but more than that, I could barely keep my eyes open. Gritty and dry and the plane hadn't helped.

"Your name's Nora?"

"Yes, I'm Nora."

"So many people had to change their names when they came over. But they couldn't change what they'd seen or done to survive."

"Matthew, I think the man needs his coat."

"It's Nora, isn't it?"

"Yes, my name's Nora. Should we call somebody for you?"

"I'm sorry, I'm exhausted. You'll have to forgive me. There's so much that's not known. Nora watched her grandparents die in a corner of the house, then her mother and sister and Frankie the boy, and her father must have gone too. She was left with a ten-year-old she couldn't save. But she made it, Nora made it over here."

"No, I'm Nora. You're talking about Honoria."

"Yes. Nora, Honoria. It's the same name. Nora's the shortened version. You were called after your great-great-grandmother, so someone must have remembered her. Someone must have known her story."

The woman softened. "It was a long time ago."

"My family line comes down through her aunt, Peigín, who took her last child and moved back to her people in Northern Ireland. And that's a story in itself." I returned all my papers to my bag and closed it over.

"Thanks for coming," she said before I'd even stood up. She got my coat and showed me to the door while I was still buttoning it. I was so tired, like the start of jet lag, and my eyesight was playing tricks. The periphery of one eye was entirely blurred and the other was starting to fog.

"Thanks for having me." The throbs in my head were pushing through my eyes, two rounds of pain at the front of my face.

I reached out my arm to touch Honoria's great-great-granddaughter for the one and only time. The woman didn't shy away. My fingers felt the ball of her shoulder and I was able to say slowly and sincerely, "She was the greatest person I ever heard about, and I've two more to do for her," before everything went white and I fell to the floor.

36. Moving In

"Forget about the curtains, Mr. Grady." Hugh Berry had heard enough from the Special Advisor on whether there was a funny smell in the room.

Berry, the Secretary of State for Northern Ireland, was in the Home Office in London with the Irish foreign minister, Caitriona Fitzpatrick, as well as the British deputy prime minister, representatives from the Northern Ireland Assembly, and Lieutenant General Otterson of the British armed forces. The topic was the worsening security situation in Northern Ireland, and whether anyone had any creative ideas on containing it. Mr. Grady was the first to have been asked to the meeting, given his unusual knowledge about the region and the unspoken belief that, if Republicans could be compelled to do anything, it would only be through him.

"We have to agree on security for the North," Berry told the room. "Along with the regular troops, there are now 200 soldiers from the Special Reconnaissance Regiment stationed there, and members of the Second Queen's Regiment arrived last Saturday."

"How many?" Caitriona Fitzpatrick asked.

"Eight hundred and twenty."

"That's too many," Grady said. "If they're on the streets, it won't be taken well."

"They're under instruction to remain in barracks until called out," Otterson said.

"There are minor incidents everywhere," Berry added, "and if there are any marches, we'll need more than police on the streets."

"Can I speak freely?" Fitzpatrick interjected. She went ahead anyway. "We'll send up as many soldiers as we can, but it's for peacekeeping, Otterson. If any of your lads get agitated, we'll have to pull out. We can't be associated with that."

"It's not the seventies anymore. Everyone wants peace in Northern Ireland." Otterson looked at Grady. "Everyone except one."

"Who do you mean?" Grady asked.

"I mean the nutcase who keeps going after famous names."

"It is destabilizing the North," Berry interrupted. "Nationalist parties are sticking their heels in when it comes to any kind of talks. They're thinking more about populism than what's good for the country."

Grady breathed in before answering, putting a check on his temper. "They're thinking about their electorate, and their electorate is getting nervous. Those walls should not have come down, not when the names of Cromwell and Trevelyan are on everyone's lips, north and south."

"Well, they won't have to think too long. Scotland Yard is certain that whoever's behind the killings will be caught, and the country can get back to normal," Berry said. "The police service will deal with matters in collaboration with Irish peacekeeping troops. And look, if a referendum on unification is ever called, it could be the end of the whole Northern Ireland question once and for all."

"It'll be the end of the North alright," Grady said. "The unionists won't be happy living under the Irish government. There's been no integration since Good Friday. Everything's exactly the same."

"Your organization won't have a mandate anymore, Mr. Grady, if that's what you're worried about."

"I don't have an organization, Mr. Berry..."

"None you can admit to," Otterson muttered.

"...and what I'm worried about is that Ireland tore itself apart with a civil war after it got its independence. I don't want the same thing happening in the North."

*****

The meeting ended when the number of Irish peacekeepers to be sent to the North was agreed upon. The Irish foreign minister and a weary Grady were the last to leave.

"So one of your number is running amok?" Fitzpatrick asked.

"It's not one of our number, and they'll be stopped soon enough."

"There's a lot of sympathy down south for them."

"For the victims, I hope you mean."

"You know, we'd be crippled if we got the North back. We're just out of recession, and our health service is struggling as it is. We don't have the money to take you back."

"The Brits won't let it go anyway."

"But if they did, it'd be hard. It'd probably kill us." The foreign minister folded her arms and gazed out the window. "But I suppose we've been through worse. The eighties were tough, and we survived the church and all its shite. Those banking arseholes. Ah, we could probably manage it. I'd say it'd be fine. We've come through the famine, for god's sake."

Grady began to walk away, but not before hearing, "as your lad keeps reminding us."

37. All Just Words

Nora Farrell couldn't have been more sympathetic for a woman who found herself with a crazy relative passed out on her carpet. I made my excuses and left, but by the time I reached the airport, any embarrassment had been replaced by concern. The British news sites were filled with reports of the killings, though no suspects were being described. I hadn't heard from Turlough in weeks and he wasn't answering my calls, and I suddenly thought he might have been caught.

The day I got home, I was searching through the newspapers for any hint that an Irishman matching Turlough's description was in trouble when the phone rang beside me. I was very happy to hear his voice, though it might not have seemed so from my tone:

"I couldn't reach you."

"I'm taking a little break."

"I have two more on my list."

"And I have more than one list."

"Is everything okay?"

Turlough paused, not expecting the question. "I'm fine. I might not have been entirely alone."

"I don't understand."

"I had to lay low, just in case."

"Oh. Should I do the same?"

"Don't take this as an insult, but you're very far from fitting the profile."

"Do whatever you have to."

I'd known for so long what he did for a living, and I knew how ridiculous my next words would sound, but the psychiatrist in me couldn't help it: "And try to keep as much stress out of your life as possible, to stop the thoughts from coming back."

I swear I heard him smile down the phone.

When he hung up, I went back to reading the newspapers, all the while hoping that he was very far, and very safely, away.

*****

The Irish papers couldn't help it. The twenty or thirty years that most of their journalists had struggled to stay hard-nosed, unbiased writers came up against the 800 years of history that sat on their backs. The early articles were the briefest, questioning whether the murder of Lord Lucan, Evan Scott Trevelyan, and Barney Hutchinson were connected, questioning the mental state of someone who'd try to avenge a country by taking innocent lives.

The words changed so gradually that only the finest spin-doctors would have noticed. Perhaps for the sake of space, the innocent victims became the victims. Perhaps for speed of understanding, the victims became the descendants. The editorials grew longer, and the discussions on public forums about British rule in Ireland became less restrained with each passing day.

After reading an article in the *Guardian* about police efforts to track the killer, I scrolled through the comments being made. The most recent ones had lost any moderate stance. I was being damned to hell by the largely English readers of an English newspaper. Someone claiming to be a psychologist even delivered their professional diagnosis of me, and I doubt I would have done a better job myself.

A lone Irish voice called the English "thieves," but their comment was removed a few moments later. And then a different voice arrived, one that was taking a tally, one that couldn't be banned for stating statistics. Eleven million in the Chalisa famine from 1783, a similar figure in the Skull famine from 1791, then Agra, Orissa, Rajputana, Bihar, Madras, and Bombay. Didn't famines go on all the time in India, someone asked. They did, the Indian reader said, but the frequency and severity under British rule was a marvel. It was a long time ago, someone else said. Three million dead in Bengal, the Indian contributor noted, when Britain took most of our harvest to feed its army, and your leader said the famine was our fault for breeding like rabbits. Look, it was a long time ago, it must have been some royal, the angry reiteration came back. It was Winston Churchill, the Indian reader said, and it was 1946. I'm embarrassed, that reader said, I'm embarrassed that there were almost 300 million of us at the start of the British Raj, only 23 million of you. We should have stopped you. No matter how small your country gets now, we should have stopped you.

In the case of Ireland, the numbers were different, but I knew exactly how that reader felt.

The British and Irish governments had a hard time proclaiming that the North wasn't affected by the killings, no matter how hard they tried. They noted that the peace walls were down, that everything was moving forward. And everything was moving forward, only not in the direction they described. Local fights outside pubs were put down to rowdiness, euphemisms were harder to find for isolated clashes on street corners in the middle of the day. And then a march was arranged for a Sunday. Organized by a centrist party, it was to be a small demonstration to request a referendum, in order to see what proportion of the Northern Ireland population wanted to rejoin the south. But to show it was to be held in good faith, it would culminate in a picnic with a bouncy castle on the lawns of Stormont. It was open to everyone, nationalist and unionist. And everyone came.

The march didn't get anywhere near Stormont. It left the small green outside the Odyssey entertainment complex with a couple of hundred people, and it reached the Newtownards Road with a thousand. Those in favor of the referendum filled the march, those against stood on the sidewalks. All it took was one foot being tread on, one shifty look, one old racist name that would mean nothing outside the country. One blow, one handy stick, one rock. And the beasts of oppression, both sides of it, came out.

Sixteen people were injured, one seriously, and a man named Martin was arrested for sectarian incitement.

38. Friends

"How's the baby?" Maggie asked. The only sound in the office was from the desk beside her, where Liam was reading with his headphones glued to his ears. She had spent the day interviewing employees of Barney Hutchinson and trying to crosslink them with acquaintances of the other two victims. It was after work hours, and she was only now getting around to packing the Lucan case away. She also felt it was a good time to apologize, and the baby was the best way in.

Liam took off his headphones and gave an exasperated sigh. "Sleeping is the hard part. The doctor says it's not colic, that she's too old for that. But he did say what the problem is."

"He did?"

"He said it's because she's a baby. They don't sleep when you want them to."

"I'm sorry to hear that." She smiled, as she filled an evidence box with the pictures and fingerprints sent from Johannesburg.

"I was a bit touchy in the briefing hall the other day," Liam said, "what with the baby, no sleep, and the historian putting his little spin on massacres."

"I'm the one who messed up. I didn't know how hard it was to have your feet everywhere."

"Feet where?"

"Don't worry about it."

Maggie flicked through the notes she made on Lucan's ancestry before feeling the need to break the silence again.

"I'm sure we learned all about Cromwell and the famine and those things in school, but they seem so long ago. Whoever's behind these killings, that history must only be getting stronger for them. It's backwards."

"I'd certainly say the killer is someone who never calls that history 'those things.'"

"They are 'those things.' They're in the past."

"For some people they're not. Is there anything you can't get over? Anything you feel passionate about?"

Maggie thought for a second. "I'm passionate about knowing there's a straight line ahead of me, that I'm able to see where I'm going. I wouldn't want crap from the past jumping in front of me, because that would make anyone go blind. So whoever's killing all these people, I'm the opposite. And I love badminton."

Liam raised his eyebrows and nodded to suggest it was a surprisingly good answer. Maggie looked at Lucan's notebooks for the last time.

...he spoke in that muck accent and I knew who it was. I heard him, and when he moved into the light I saw the little sprite. I'll tell you! He was small, but I saw him. They don't care about their children.

"So, Lucan saw the man, and the man was small. Liam?"

"That's what it says. A small man who looked like a goblin. Have you got a man?"

"What?"

"I've an excuse for being here this late – I need a break and the overtime – but you should be out enjoying London. Going dancing, getting mugged."

"I don't have a man at the moment."

"I've a few friends I could set you up with."

"I'm going home in two months."

"It's nice to have company in a new city."

"My sister will be here tomorrow and I'm always in the Red Lion with you lot. If anything, I need some time alone. The one thing I miss is the public chat, though – the conversations on the bus or when you're queuing to get your sandwich. But I suppose we never shut up back home, people never stop talking."

"The English might be to blame for that as well."

Maggie laughed. "Why's that?"

"You were colonized for 800 years, so you needed information, to hear it and to give it. Insecurity brought you closer."

"You're saying 'you,' Liam."

"You?"

"You mean 'we.'"

Liam gave her an appreciative look before putting his headphones back on. Maggie bundled up Lucan's notebooks and put them in the evidence box.

And finally, Carl Waters' photographs. Maggie knew that when they went into the box, no one would see them again for a while, if ever. So many faces, most of them dead by now. Maybe not the little boy. She looked at him, as he sat on his father's shoulders, smiling into the camera as if he didn't know he was at a funeral, didn't care that the brooding man he was sitting on was a henchman for Henry Blackwell. Whatever his father did or didn't do, the lad probably turned out okay, she thought, seeing as he looked happy. Holding the chin of the man who'd protect him. A man who might go after a lord for hurting a friend's child.

"Some of my mates are nice," Liam was deciding, as Maggie put the last of the photos into the box and sellotaped it shut.

39. The Finest Way to Live

A buzz came to the door. It was seven o'clock in the evening, already dark, but I didn't have the hall light on. It would have helped if I had, because I thought it was Ken calling around too early as usual and I got a shock when I opened the door to see Terry. He looked agitated standing in the porch, so I brought him through the hall and into the warmth of the small office, where he sat on the edge of an armchair.

"I'm sorry, Dr. Gleeson. It's taken me days to work up the courage to come here, and I still feel like getting sick at having to do it."

I took a chair opposite him. "What is it, Terry?"

He brought the heels of his hands up to cover his eyes and rotated them, as if trying to wake himself up. Then he said, "You don't really know me, and I know I'm taking liberties by being here."

"Everything is confidential. And there's nothing I haven't heard before."

"It's not about my head."

He rested his arms on his thighs and clasped his hands in front of him, seemingly waiting for me to read his mind. That was more than I could manage.

"Has somebody asked you to do something?"

"How do you do it?" he suddenly said. "How do you hear all those stories from your patients, see all those shitting profiles, and it doesn't drive you mad?"

"I'm not sure it hasn't."

"You seem sane to me."

"You don't really know me." I smiled, but he didn't smile with me.

"I need an outside mind. Someone like you, who's not involved in any of it."

He stood up and paced around the room, looking at what was on the walls but taking nothing in. It was only then that I wondered if I was in trouble. Had they found anything out, and was he here to tackle me, or worse?

"Would a whiskey help?" I asked, thinking that being in the kitchen surrounded by knives might be a better place to be.

"I'm not much of a drinker."

He sat back down and said, "They used to tell us the war never stopped, and that the rules of war were different to normal. But I know there are lines we can't cross. Not because it doesn't look good in the papers or the support falls off, but because it's not fucking right. And this is far from fucking right."

"I'll have to know what's wrong before..."

"Dr. Gleeson, someone in the organization is killing innocent people."

My heart jolted with the sentence. I felt my face flush and hoped the weak light in the room didn't show my discomfort. I breathed deeply and quietly and decided to get to the kitchen, but before I could stand up, he said:

"A lot of the lads come to me because they've known me for years or they just trust me. I suppose they know I'd never go to Grady and rat them out, no matter what they told me. And some of them told me that the police, the British police, got in touch with them asking if they knew who killed that guy on the telly."

"Which guy?"

"The Trevelyan guy. The police are sure it's one of us. And they think we did Lucan and Hutchinson too. And I was speaking to someone recently, someone high up, and he thinks the same."

"Who was that?"

"Cathal McConnell."

"I know the name."

"I can't be involved in this, but what the hell do I do? I can't go to the police. And I can't go to Grady because I don't know that it's not him."

"Why would you think it's him?"

"All I know is it's someone who can get a veteran to do jobs for them. And only a few people knew where Lucan was living. Grady was one of them."

"You've nothing more than that?"

"No. I was hoping you might have a clear head."

"I'm not going to be much help. I do know that whoever's killing those people wants to get the North back into Irish hands, and Mr. Grady's job is to keep the peace now. He's not thinking about unification."

Terry slowly put his hand across his mouth. Despite the dim light, I was sure the rims of his eyes lined with tears.

"I know that," he said. "I kept thinking he had some kind of plan."

"Mr. Grady may be a bigger challenge than someone trying to correct history." I sighed and moved closer to him in the chair. "Terry, always remember that *we're* the organization, we're the people, the population. It's our future too. If the big goal is still there, make sure you're on the right path to achieve it."

"I couldn't go against them. Nobody's ever done that and survived."

"I'm alive."

He looked at me in confusion. "Have you done something?"

"I'm sure I've done things Mr. Grady wasn't happy about."

"Like what?"

"I don't know. Deciding if someone from the profiles be kept in, or kept out."

"That would hardly get you into trouble."

"Deciding worse than that."

His brain was clicking away, processing the rights and wrongs of murder, trying to work out if there was any justification to any of it. And it was time to call a halt.

"I think you need that whiskey," I said.

I stood up and went down to the kitchen. I didn't take up any knives, I just poured him a drink, relieved to be putting a full stop to my words. When I went back into the office, he was already standing up.

"I have to go. I'm sorry for bothering you. I think the stress of everything built up in my head."

"I have people coming over this evening, but a longer chat would be better. I'm here anytime."

"You've helped me already," he said, walking out to the front door. "You're a good man, Doctor Gleeson."

"That depends on the perspective."

"What perspective do you have?"

"I was born into it, Terry. Born into Belfast when it was about to explode. With a father who knew only one life. An uncle who wasn't quite human. A background like that would focus anyone's mind."

I opened the front door for him. Someone was outside, on their way up the path towards us. Ken Skeffington was an hour early for dinner, and he couldn't have been more cheerful. He said "hello" to Terry and was ready to be introduced, but Terry just nodded and went out to the dark.

40. Little Black Heads

It's not an official national symbol but it may as well be. Say "potato," and most people think of Ireland. Even the Irish themselves will see an image of the spud and link it to home. And it's funny really, because we're so proud of something that killed nearly a quarter of us way back when. It's as if Africa had the mosquito as its national symbol, or like that joke about Christians wearing the cross around their neck: it's a symbol of their religion, yet Jesus might not be too happy to see the instrument of his death dangling around their necks if he were to drop by.

And so I was thinking when I showed Ken in. But my mind went back to Terry as I stood in the kitchen finishing my cranberry duck with rhubarb wine jelly and the king of the vegetables:

Roast Potatoes
1 kilogram Maris Pipers;
100 grams goose fat;
2 tablespoons flour;
Good quality sea salt.

Heat oven to 200C/fan 180C/gas 6 and place roasting tin inside. Peel potatoes and cut into even-sized chunks. Place chunks in large pot, cover with slightly salted water. On boiling, reduce heat and simmer uncovered for two minutes.

Meanwhile, place goose fat in roasting tin and melt in oven until piping hot.

Use colander to drain and shake spuds. Sprinkle with flour and shake again so damned vegetables are thinly and evenly coated. Place spuds into hot fat in roasting tin, turning the fucking chunks around to coat all over. Keep space between each.

Roast the devil's cocks for fifteen minutes, then turn over to brown all sides. Roast for another fifteen mins and turn again. Return to oven for a further ten to twenty minutes, until the shitting cancer-ridden cunts are crisp and golden. Sprinkle with salt and serve immediately.

My mind was not at ease. I'd only arranged this dinner because I'd ruined the last one, running off early and frightening Ken. One of my hands shook as I cleaned the sink. The slightest muscle tremor, and I gripped it with the other. I dropped both hands when Ken came into the kitchen.

"This might be my last dinner, Michael, unless you can kidnap more guests. Maybe not that young chap who was here, he looked a bit shifty."

"Are you always so honest?"

"I am. Lying doesn't work. It always comes back to stab you in the head."

"My problem is that I can't lie very well, and sometimes it would help if I could."

"It never would. You know, I went out with a super girl in my twenties, someone I should have married in an instant, but I slept with two of her friends. At the same time, mind you, so it was only cheating once. And it broke her heart. I saw it. It burst right in front of me." He looked enormously sad at the memory.

"So now I never lie. If a lady asks me if I'll be faithful, I always say no. It works out most of the time."

"I think you're actually a very fine man," I said, meaning every word. But the sound of the doorbell meant I hadn't time to ask him whether he might not consider being faithful in the future.

"Jean told me to drop over tonight, if that's okay." It was Suzanne, and I was surprised to see her.

"Is she coming?"

"I think she has a date. Is Ken inside?"

I told her he was and I got a corkscrew from the kitchen and went into the dining room, where they were chatting about something, something small. And it annoyed me beyond belief.

"Do you want to sit down? Let's sit down."

They moved to the table, still talking, and I opened the wine. Some of the plates were out, but I'd forgotten the cutlery. I felt the tremor in my hand again, and I wondered if I was going to shake the dishes when serving them, like a terminally-ill butler who'd come to the end of his time at the big fancy house.

"My bike was stolen from outside work," Suzanne was saying.

"From outside the supermarket?" Ken said. "Nothing's safe these days."

"Which place do you work in?" I asked.

"Tesco."

"Ah, that's a big one. What do you do?"

"I clean it."

"Very good, I'm sure that's good."

"What?"

"You know, I was in a supermarket recently ..." Ken began.

"I clean the floors," she continued, "and the checkouts, when there's milk on them. And the toilets, after the customers have been in." She stared at me, waiting for something.

"That sounds good."

"How does it sound good?" She took her time to speak, but she wasn't uncomfortable. "I work in a supermarket because I have to. I hurt my back."

"It's okay to work in a supermarket," Ken said cordially.

We hadn't started eating. Suzanne put down her glass.

"Something went wrong with a disc a few years ago. A nerve was being pinched every time I moved. I had to take painkillers, and then I thought I was taking too many, so I stopped and the pain came back. And then I got depressed. And when that started to lift, I got the job cleaning the supermarket. And every day I've been there, I'm so thankful that I'm not low anymore. I don't care what I work at, because I'll never be back in that darkness again. So, I clean the shit off the floors, the milk off the rubber thing, and I'm the happiest person alive. My life is white and open and not full of crap anymore."

I took in her expression of honesty, until I was suddenly pulled away by a smell coming from the kitchen. The oven was burning. When I opened its door, a ball of smoke punched me in the face. About twenty black potatoes sitting like little dead heads. I burned my hand pulling out the rack, and I threw all of the potatoes in the sink.

"The spuds are black," I shouted, and I was glad to hear them laugh. We had carrots and no potatoes, and a smell of smoke hung in the house while we ate.

"But we wouldn't be here if it wasn't for the spud," Suzanne was saying when I went back in.

"Don't you mean there'd be more of us if it wasn't for the spud?" Ken asked.

"That's true too, but if the famine hadn't happened, Ireland wouldn't have become a republic. Didn't it get people riled?" She looked at me, and I shrugged. I didn't know why she'd think I'd know. I was thinking about two other things at the time: twenty dead little heads and Terry's visit earlier. Something was needling me about it, something wasn't quite right.

"...because the Irish Republican Brotherhood started up here, and the Fenian Brotherhood started in America," Suzanne was saying.

"I don't know much about it," came Ken's honest reply.

"My mother told me recently that my grandfather was in the war," she continued. "He had to kill three Black and Tans. She thinks he killed one with his bare hands. Can you imagine doing that?"

"You have a hero in you," Ken laughed.

"Heh, I suppose. I've been reading about it a lot, but I still can't imagine what it must have been like. Can you imagine having to kill someone? Would we be able to do that if we were invaded again?"

"We still are," I said quietly.

"Still are what?"

"Invaded. The six counties are still gone."

"No, but it's different today," Suzanne said. "They can talk it out."

"They can talk all they want, but nothing's changed. The North's still part of the United Kingdom."

"Well, they can have the North, if it stops any more deaths."

"Would your grandfather agree with you?"

"He'd say the Republicans today are all murderers." She was smiling, but her face was getting red.

"Then he'd have to call himself one."

"He wasn't a murderer. They weren't murderers back then. They were soldiers."

"Soldiers in a paramilitary army. The Irish Volunteers weren't legal under British law, and we were under British rule."

"It was a different time."

"How so?"

"They were fighting for the country."

"We still are."

"But there are more Protestants up north than Catholics."

"That's because they were put there. In any case, there was only three percent more five years ago. It may have already swung the other way. You don't know what you're talking about."

"I don't know what I'm talking about?"

"It doesn't even matter what the percentages are, it doesn't matter about the religion. We're a bloody island. Our border is the sea. We know exactly what's ours, the limits of our land. Where our shared history ends, how far our culture reaches. The British shouldn't have been here in the first place, and they shouldn't stay any longer. But we let them get away with it, afraid to rock the boat. And what would your grandfather have said to that?"

"He wouldn't say ..."

"Would he be proud that we let the North be taken? Would he have been one of those who said 'let them keep this part, once we're okay?'"

"I don't know. He might have been Pro-Treaty ..."

"And look at what a mess the Treaty made, handing them the North. Your grandfather would be rolling in his grave, Suzanne, at the thought of things today. The thought that we've betrayed him. That you're betraying him now, with your words. Once the south is happy, we don't give a shit about the problems up north. Men and women died for the country, the whole of it, but they didn't die so Britain could take a little nip out of us at the end of 800 years. Rubbing our noses in it by taking a huge fucking region off the top! It's not a tiny little part that wouldn't be noticed, Suzanne, – it's a fifth of the country! What would your fucking grandfather say about that?"

"Don't you talk about him! He'd say the war has ended. He'd say they're all murderers now! He'd tell us to let it go. We're not fucking animals."

I stopped talking and covered my face with my hands, blocking her out. "None of us know what he'd say."

"He'd say you're a fucking asshole."

I dropped my hands down. "Who are you, Suzanne? Who are you? What are you doing here?"

"What do you mean?"

"You suddenly turn up with Jean, out of the blue. Just when I was getting things started. Who do you work for?"

"Tesco."

"Who else?"

She stood up and I did as well and I grabbed her. Ken put his arm on me to try and back me off, but I was going to find out who the hell she was even if I had to punch him in the grin that wasn't on his face.

"Was it Grady? Did he send you?"

"Michael, stop!" Ken roared at me.

"Are you with them?"

And then Suzanne stood tall. I let go of her arm, but she stared me straight in the eye without pulling back. Our faces were less than a foot away from each other.

"You're right. I did suddenly turn up. Right out of the fucking blue. I was underhand, Michael, I made Jean bring me here the first time. I told her I was depressed and needed a night out. But that was a lie, Michael. A big bloody lie."

"So who sent you? Why are you here? I'm going to finish it..."

"Finish what? I'm here because of a fourteen-year-old boy who I'd die for. Who I'd fucking put up with your stupid boring dinners for. Jean said you were a psychiatrist and I thought I'd get some free advice. Because at this stage, I need anything!"

"What?"

"It's my son, and he's breaking my heart. I need help for him. But now I know that help won't come from you, because the last thing he needs in his life is another shithead."

She stormed out to the hall and picked up her coat. She was gone out the front door before I understood what she'd said. I slumped into a chair as Ken raised his glass. He had earned his right to speak, and he did:

"Let's drink to the fucking Irish. At least we're never boring."

"Maybe if we were more boring we wouldn't be so screwed up."

Ken downed whatever was in his glass and poured himself another. "Tonight is the last straw, Michael. It's only going to get worse."

"I know."

"You have to get help with your head."

"I want to tell you something, Ken."

"Don't change the subject."

"Lucan was beautiful."

"Who?"

"Lord Lucan. Did I ever tell you I met him? Though 'met' might be the wrong word for it. He could have been a movie star. Not on the night I saw him, of course – he was a quivering wreck."

"Why?"

"My father was about to kill him."

Ken looked down to the floor. And then he looked at me, and he spoke with a complete and beautiful confidence that was shocking: "All this is beyond me, Michael. I don't need to hear any more. I don't like violence, I don't even like watching cop shows on TV. I just like X-Rays and women, and that's my life. But you have something inside you, and it's going to kill you if you don't get help. And I'd hate to see that, because I love you. You have a heart the size of a sea in you."

He finished his glass and went out to the hall to get his coat. His head appeared back in the dining room before he left.

"You know I mean that in a brotherly way?"

I assured him that I did, and then I heard the front door close and took in the silence. My mind started wandering, and I allowed the memories to come back, to the night that started it all. And by the time I was finished and needed something to take the taste out of my brain, I picked up the phone and called Suzanne.

*****

My first was always going to be Lucan, and it was no great surprise. I never forgot him, that handsome man with the imperious air, made dashing by a huge British mustache that made it seem like he was about to fly off in his Spitfire. But however attractive he was, you can't easily forget the face of a man you see staring at the battered head of his nanny in what was once his own home.

As in all good psychiatric tales, of course, the real reason I remembered him was not the man himself, but my father.

"It's best not to tell anyone we've been to this house," Dad said to me on the way there. "This man's long-ago granddad was a vicious fella, and he's not the finest himself." As he opened the black gate to the basement steps, Dad said, "If someone does something bad, they have to pay for it, Michael, somewhere down the line. The word for that is justice."

The basement was dark when we got inside, so I held Dad's overcoat as he moved in front of me. I tried to concentrate to hear any sounds, but I was pulled to the floor when Dad broke away. Snores, I heard some kind of snoring, and a slapping sound like you hear when it's raining hard. I sat on the ground and kept my eyes shut and my ears covered. *Sing about things, sing songs in your head.* But a bang on the stairs stopped me singing; something big being thrown into a wall. And I flashed opened my eyes without wanting to and someone was near me, at the place we had just come in. His face was chalk in the light coming in the open basement door, and a huge black line cut that face in half.

"Bingham!" Dad shouted to my left, and his overcoat rushed by me and there was a kick to my legs and the overcoat fell to the ground. *Dad, that's you. I'm sorry, that was me. I did that.*

"Christ! You fucking..."

Then a box to the head, and Dad wrenched me off the floor and almost had me flying in the air and out the basement door. Out after the man who had run away, but he was gone, his car clattering down the street in the fog.

There was nothing Dad could do to calm my crying as we walked home in the dark. By the time we reached our street, he was saying how he'd never take me anywhere again if I didn't shut up, and by the time we were at our front door, he was pleading with me to be quiet, telling me he'd take me everywhere with him and we'd go to the pictures or something the next day. And then he bent down and hugged the little head off me, saying again and again that it was his fault he tripped, it was his own stupid leg that did it, that he was sorry I had to be there, sorry I had to see. *I didn't see nothing,* I told him, and it was true: I'd kept my eyes closed like he'd told me to. And now standing in the fog, he brought his whole hand up to cover his face, and I covered my ears so I wouldn't hear the sobs. *I didn't see nothing.*

Dad was the quietest soul you could find for the times, so he must have had something on his mind when we called on the house that night. When I was older, I read that Bingham was a gambler, but Dad never had a liking for that, so it wasn't a debt he was after. I'm guessing he met Bingham in a pub somewhere or, more likely, when Bingham came in to get some busted thing fixed on his sports car at the garage Dad worked in.

And when I was older still, when I'd learned more about what my father was and the history we'd both been born into, I knew he wasn't talking about Bingham, but the earlier Lord Lucan, the one who had been around in the famine times. They never said much, my father's generation, about the things they were thinking of. The ideals of a united Ireland came in tiny, grand sentences – "Éirinn go Brách," "Tiocfaidh ár Lá," the less poetic "Brits Out." Words that hung in the air.

Maybe they were the air. But the words that carved themselves into my soul were the ones Dad said before we entered the house, before he put two pieces of metal into the lock on the basement door. He turned to me, and with a look that could have stopped a heart, he said,

"Never forget the people we lost." And then he told me to be quiet.

41. Breaking Through

Anyone else would have been mortified coming through Arrivals at Heathrow, but Denise knew what to expect. Maggie was waiting for her, waving an Irish flag and a British flag, shaking them so violently that the people around her had to give her more space. And Denise had her own flag in the air, a crap cardboard tricolor made by one of her kids.

"I thought the Brits would've kicked you out," Denise said with a hug.

"I hoped they wouldn't let you through customs."

And arm in arm, the O'Malley sisters walked out of the airport and into the nearest pub.

What's the job like, are there any nice men, have you been thrown off the Tube yet – Maggie was delighted to get the questions. And to hear that her nieces were doing well and Ballyhack was almost the same as ever.

"They want to twin the place with somewhere in America, but they can't decide where," Denise said in between pints. "The local council has its eye on Carmel in California, where Clint Eastwood lives."

"Don't they have to choose a town that's similar to their own?"

"Yeah, but they're building up the courage to ask the Yanks. And they're hanging Clint's photo everywhere to get us all excited."

"The place might be known for something now."

"You still hate it," Denise said with a smirk.

"No, but it was too quiet, I had to get out. Just like every other young person in every other old town in Ireland."

"I didn't leave."

"You found love, and it doesn't matter where you are once that happens."

"And look how it left me. A widow at twenty-five."

"With two kids, a family. That's more than me. I'll be sixty by the time I realize I need those things. And whatever career you think you're missing, you're still young enough to have it."

"I might do something."

"The Gardaí are hiring hundreds of civilians. Would you like that?"

"To join you?"

"You wouldn't be working with me, we'd kill each other. They're civilian posts, to let the police get back on the streets."

Denise looked nervously at her sister. "What about the force itself? I'm still under the age limit."

"An officer? Who'd look after the kids?"

"Templemore training college is only a two-hour drive from Ballyhack. I could get a minder. Or we could move closer."

"You've really thought about this?"

"I have, Maggie. I want to do what you do. I want to be as excited about living. The girls only see a tired, frustrated woman who could be much more."

Maggie pictured Denise in a uniform, in a station, even learning to shoot. And she lit up the pub with her smile. "Fuck it, Denise, I think you'd be brilliant."

Denise let out a breath of air that she'd been holding in.

"I didn't know how you'd take it."

"I'd be so proud of you." And then with a grin, "Of course, you'd have to get fit first."

"What are you talking about? I'm running around all day. I'm like a Roman slave to the girls, and they won't even appreciate me until they've had their own kids, and then I'll have to look after them too."

"They're worth it."

"They cleaned the toilet with my toothbrush and never told me."

Maggie struggled to keep the drink in her mouth. "How did you find out?"

"The toothbrush smelled like chlorine. That's not right, something like that's not right."

"I love them to bits. If they have a little spark in them, they'll be able to handle anything."

"Just like you," Denise said. "I wouldn't be without them for the world, but at the moment, they're little shits."

"Little devils, maybe, but not little shits."

"Little imps, then. My toilet-cleaning sprites. They'd shape up soon enough if I was a police officer."

"It wouldn't make a difference. We never listened to ..."

Maggie stopped. Her head didn't move and her eyes didn't blink.

"What's wrong?"

"He had to take him."

"What?"

"He had to be there." Maggie's face drained of color.

"For god's sake, Mags, what are you talking about? I'm over for one day, and you've already gone nuts."

"Jesus, Denise. The little sprite is a child."

*****

Maggie rang Booth's mobile immediately, the alcohol in her system overcome by adrenaline. He wasn't happy to be disturbed at home.

"I think the person who attacked the Lucans in 1974 wasn't alone."

"Are you in a pub?"

"Cinema, sir."

"He had an accomplice?"

"I think he had a child with him. Lucan recounts seeing a little sprite in his house. It never sat well with me that this was the attacker. Lucan was very tall, and it would have been foolish to send a much smaller man after him. I think Lucan was talking about a child, someone he didn't see until the assailant moved towards him."

"Maggie..."

"Lucan made a remark about 'them' not caring about their children. He might have thought that because the child was there, saw the murder. And now we have the name Joseph Gleeson, and we know he had a son who he had to take everywhere because the mother was sick."

"Veronica Lucan never mentioned seeing a child."

"She was hit on the head, she may have blacked out. Or the child could have stayed hidden."

"Detective, you spotted the link between the three victims, so I'm hesitant to dismiss your hunches. But this child thing is irrelevant."

"Why? It reinforces the suspicion that Joseph Gleeson was the attacker, because we know he had to take his son everywhere. And Paul Priestley said that someone sent Gleeson over to London, so he may have had paramilitary links, which brings us up to the present cases. If we could find Gleeson, we could rule him out of Lucan's killing, or rule him in."

"Priestley's memories are questionable, you know that. And if Gleeson is the same man who killed Lucan, he'd be very old by now."

"It's still possible, sir." Maggie paused. "Would I be able to interview Lucan's children? They're adults now, but maybe the Gleesons lived near them, maybe they knew the son."

"Are you serious?" Booth sounded flabbergasted. "Whatever happened on the night of that attack, those children have lived with this shit their whole lives. Conspiracy theories running from one extreme to the other. No one is going near them. You can't continue with this. No more resources on Lucan from this moment on."

Maggie knew from Booth's tone that she shouldn't protest. *Fuck.* She wondered whether he was blocking her because she was young. Maybe it was because she was Irish. Maybe it was because he didn't want the case reexamined. Or maybe it was because she was wrong. Her only consolation was that she'd asked Alex to do a small DNA analysis for her before *this moment on.* If nothing came of it, Booth would never need to know.

It was a leap to connect a man who'd gone after Lucan forty years ago with someone who'd killed him this year, but the more Maggie thought about the phantom assailant in the Lucan household, the more he came alive in her head. Somebody could have held onto a hatred for decades, and she wouldn't miss a lead. But she had to go back to Denise before her sister missed her, to plan for Denise's new career with this latest brick of a thought in her mind.

42. The Musician

L. Grady sat in his regular pub less than 300 meters from the Irish parliament, glad to be back from London. One person had already been over to shake his hand, but it was the two men coming towards him who held his attention.

"How are you doing, Terry?"

"Well, sir..."

Cathal arrived behind and pulled over a seat.

"You survived London, L.? Me and the lad kept everything warm for you while you were away."

Grady's eyes were still fixed on the young man. "Have you something on your mind?"

Terry said nothing for the longest moment. The words eventually came to him.

"I don't want my life to be in the wrong place."

"Excuse me?"

"I can't move in this direction."

"What are you talking about?"

"I was under some stress, so I saw Dr. Gleeson to talk it all through."

"Did he help you out?"

"I don't know. I know there's a lot that's private, that he can't tell me everything. But I have to ask, sir, are we behind those killings?"

"What killings?"

"The killings in the papers."

"Why would you say that?"

"Did he get a request from you? I saw something in his office, and I wasn't thinking straight."

"What did you see?"

Terry pulled from his pocket a sheet of paper that had once been white but was now covered in streaks of blue pen. In the center was a hole, where too many lines had been drawn and punched through. The words written around the sheet were many, and they were all the same: *Lucan, Trevelyan, Cromwell.*

"What's that?" Cathal asked.

"It was on his desk, and I took it."

"Did he see you?"

"He was in the kitchen."

"That could be anything," Cathal said, but Grady examined it as if it were a letter from the pope.

"I'm no psychiatrist," Grady began, "but it looks like something's affecting our Michael. Something's eating at him, when he's sitting in his office, listening to all those desperate stories from all those troubled ..."

"Did he do this for you?" Terry asked.

"Do what?"

"I looked in his desk. There were loads of things. Notes, pictures, sheets of names and dates, stretching back years. Was all that for you? I can't be involved in any of that."

"Was what for me? What are you talking about?"

"Choose people, did he choose people for you, the ones with historical names? There were Cromwells, sheets of them. All family trees, or whatever they're called. Ending in one person, the Hutchinson man who was killed. There were sheets of Trevelyans as well, and other names I didn't recognize."

Grady sat back and closed his eyes. All he could manage was a whisper, and all he could say was, "It's not us."

Terry started to speak again, but Grady raised his hand in the air to block any words.

"Would you get me a pint, Terry?"

The young man was surprised at the interruption, but it was an order, and he left to get a Guinness. Walking up to the bar, he couldn't imagine what they didn't want him to hear.

"Damn me to hell, Cathal." Grady spoke without haste, letting the idea sink in. "I couldn't figure out who Turlough would trust enough to do a job for, a job that had nothing to do with us. Who couldn't he say no to? Who would he trust with his life? And they say shrinks are nuttier than us all. I bloody handed Turlough to him. I got them together in the first place."

Cathal shut his mouth and sat back.

"Everyone on the Council was being watched," Grady continued, "and we spread it out further. Michael had more dealings with Turlough than anyone else, so we watched him in his house and kept an eye on his friends, just in case Turlough showed up and Michael passed him on. I never thought to look at dear Michael himself. But then Terry turns up at his door? A lucky surprise for us. I should have fucking known, Cathal."

Terry was back with the pint.

"Did you ever hear about Joey Gleeson?" Grady asked him when he sat down, while Cathal was left with his thoughts.

"I don't think so."

"Cathal's probably the best man to tell you about him, but I'll shorten the tale more than he ever could. Gleeson blew up Nelson's Pillar in Dublin in 1966. It was a big English stick, right in the middle of the city. A huge monument with Horatio Nelson on top, lording it over everyone for two hundred years. Gleeson would walk by it whenever he visited Dublin, and it annoyed the shite out of him. He was an awful quiet man, but what he didn't know about bomb making couldn't be learned. So he got the idea that we should burst it out of the sky. And he organized the whole thing, set the charges himself. And 'pop,' down it came, perfect. No other damage except this one big pillar collapsed into a tiny heap on the ground.

"But the stump was still there, and the Irish army arrived and decided to blow that up, for health and safety reasons. They set up such an explosion that it blasted every window out of O'Connell Street. Huge damage. They blew up the main shopping street in Dublin. It was the funniest thing."

"And that was Michael's father?" Terry asked.

"It was."

"And he's carrying on his dad's work? It's not us at all?"

"It is him," Cathal said without pause. "This is what he's been waiting for."

"You think so now, Cathal?" Grady said.

"A bloody psychiatrist with the heart of a Fenian."

"Do you know him?" Terry asked.

Cathal gave an angry laugh. "I know Michael well. Who do you think told him all about the Cromwells and the Trevelyans and the Lucans and stuck it in his head that he can't ever forget what happened to Ireland, no matter what goes on in his life? And it looks like little else *has* gone on in his life. He has his job, of course, but that's it. That and the memory of his father covered in blood and his dead mother who couldn't be saved and a man who told him his life was worthless if he didn't keep fighting. A fella who was in the bleeding heart of shit at the time, speeding up to Belfast to stop one more British soldier from breathing Irish air, ten more. And racing back down to the green and the quiet and dear little Michael Gleeson sitting at the table, trying to study his fecking biology."

Terry's mouth gaped open.

"The night his father died, he came down to us, me and the late wife. They'd moved back from London, and Belfast was a war zone. And Michael was heading for trouble. It's in him that he could slit someone's throat without noticing, once there's a reason behind it. Because that's the way his fecker of a dad was. I suppose we all had to be like that back then."

"Christ."

"Don't look so shocked, Terry. Coming down to Monaghan was the best thing for him. He felt secure for the first time in his life. And I loved the dumb little head of him, even though that head also irritated the crap out of me. I thought it was enough that he was getting the hugs and the praise, and that whatever I said to explain what had happened in Ireland, what was happening in the North, would soften him a bit, make him a proud Irish man more than a thug. He's become a proud Irish man alright. A ghoul of the centuries."

"Do you regret it?" Terry asked.

"Of course I do. He's going to die from all this."

"And what about the people he's killing?"

"British officers beat me to a pulp too many times to let any reason in now when it comes to that. My old father being clubbed to death in front of me knocked any sympathy out of me years ago. But we should have seen it, Grady, we should have seen this coming."

"We'll have to pull him into line. Would you be best handling that, Cathal?"

Terry's heart panicked in his chest. "Couldn't you just warn him, tell him to give himself up? He's a sound man, Mr. Grady, no matter what he's done."

"Hold your horses. We haven't decided if Cathal will deal with it."

"But he's a nice man, and he's been great for the organization ...."

"I'm not going to kill him," Cathal said with a smile. "He's my nephew."

"Your what?"

"His mother was my sister."

Grady chuckled from across the table.

"Do the police know that?" Terry asked.

"I'd say they might figure it out eventually."

"Your nephew?"

"Of course he is. Why else would I have taken a young lad in, when I had the fighting for Ireland to be worrying about?" And Cathal downed his pint in one go.

43. Meeting Kieran

Suzanne brought her son into me the next day, and I was happy to see them both. I'd phoned her after she'd left my house, apologizing for acting like an idiot. I was stressed at work, I said, and I convinced her to let me try and help the young man. But she still seemed worried when they arrived in reception, and I reassured her that the session would be of some benefit, at least. Kieran followed me into my office, his shoulders bent. He looked at me long enough to see where I was sitting.

"We have to get the big thing out of the way, Kieran, and that's the food. I know you know food is important. Are you taking vitamin supplements?"

He said he thought his mother tried to mix them in with the spaghetti hoops.

"The thing is, your insides can be affected in the future if you don't get certain things. And it would be nice to have strong muscles, what do you think?"

"They said all this to me before."

"You saw a nutritionist? That's great." I screwed up my face like a conspirator. "Was there anything helpful?"

"Nah."

The kid-gloves weren't going to work with this one, no matter how gently I spoke. I swiveled my chair around and stared out the window. I could half-see the boy while I gazed into the car park, with its lining of thick green shrubs and bushes. We weren't far from the city center, yet we couldn't keep the green down. How could anyone starve to death in this country? A country of rain and green and life. And it occurred to me what I had to say.

I had moved so far from professional ethics in recent months that I doubt I would have recognized them again. And now I was going to move further, to help a boy at the start of his life, to share with him something I should never have told any patient. But after thirty years of fixing broken souls, I believed it would work.

"My mother died from starvation," I said, still looking out the window. "And it was my father who killed her."

I turned back around to face him. "He was the only person who could help her by then. She was sick, covered in cancer."

I held out my arms wide, as if trying to fit a full-length woman between them. "That much of her. All of her." I gave a weak smile.

"The stomach problems were the worst, because she couldn't keep anything down, but the blockage in her body meant it couldn't go through either, so everything came back up. Food, puke, and shit.

"The doctors gave her packets of powder to mix with water. It'd bulk her up and give her protein and that, but all she wanted was one pill and to say goodbye. But they didn't do that back then; they hardly do it now. So my father took her home and made up a beautiful bed for her. The first bed he made in his life, I think, and she stayed in it for a couple of months."

Kieran's eyes were fixed on me.

"She'd cry when he tried to feed her. And then he'd cry, saying that she was killing him. And then they came to a deal, I think that's what you'd call it. Dad wouldn't give her the powders anymore, and she'd pass away in peace.

"It was better going in to see her from then on, her face changed. It was like the decision was made and she was happy. But damn me anyway, I couldn't touch her. Cancer wasn't a good thing to hear. And when my teacher told everyone in the school, to be nice to me I suppose, it may as well have been the plague to the lads I hung round with. And that got into my head and stuck there.

"And Dad saw that I wasn't giving Mam the usual hug when I went in. So the one time he made me hug her, I touched her arm and I fucking nearly screamed. I knew I'd gotten cancer, right there, my mother had given me cancer. I ran out of the room and never went back. And she died two days later. I never got to see her again."

I paused, but it wasn't for Kieran's sake. "I made a dreadful mistake."

Kieran Murray was on fire with fright and excitement. This was the greatest, worst story he had ever heard in his life.

"I don't know what all this means for you, Kieran. I just wanted to tell you about it before we start the sessions. Everyone has some crappy shit they go through as a child; it's poxy and it's not our fault. I lost my mother when I was young. Now you didn't lose your dad exactly, but he wasn't there when I'm sure it would have been nice if he was. All the other lads have their dads. But I'll tell you something – some of those dads are crap. Sometimes they have it all wrong. Like your dad, he had it all wrong when he left.

"My dad loved my mam to bits but he stopped feeding her, because it was the best thing for her. He loved her so much that he killed her. And your mam, she knows all you like is spaghetti hoops and she'd give you every spaghetti hoop in the world if she could, but it's not good for you and it'll rot your body. That's how much she loves you. She wants you to be happy, but only eating spaghetti hoops will keep you small, you won't grow and be able to beat the heads off the other fellas, the lads who are mean and have crappy dads. Can you help your mum out and take a vitamin tablet, one each day? Maybe try an apple? Nah, they're crap. Something like Cheerios? Would that be alright?"

And to my surprise, Kieran said that maybe it would.

"Now," I continued, "if you get to choose whatever you want, and you can eat as much or as little as anything, would you like to go to McDonalds? I can take you there now."

I swear to god I would have been happy if that child ate just one chip.

"Nah."

And that was okay. The rest of the session was slightly more orthodox, on my side at least. It may have been novel for

Kieran to open up, I don't know, but he certainly told me about some of the things that were troubling him. At the end of the hour, I watched the skinny little lad pull open the huge wooden door of my office and go out to his mother. She gave him a hug and waved a thank you at me. A starving woman might save him. A woman who had been beautiful and strong before she was eaten away. I was trying to remember her face when I noticed Suzanne standing by my desk.

"He's a clever man," I whispered.

"Will he be okay?"

"He will, but I don't know how long it'll take. I'll have to steer him to the place where he can make the decision to eat on his own. Bring him in every day next week, and then make appointments with Deirdre, the receptionist, for regular sessions, as often as you like. We'll ease him into eating, ease him into himself."

"I'll pay you."

"I won't see him again if you do."

I expected a smile, but she looked anxious.

"Is something wrong?"

"I don't want to dump more stuff on you."

"What is it?"

She hesitated, then she walked back to reception and told Kieran to wait there. She returned to the office and closed the door after her.

"When I was walking home from your house last night, I thought a car was following me. I was probably totally wrong, but it gave me a fright. I want you to tell me I'm being paranoid."

"How long were they behind you?"

"All the way into Sandymount village."

I suddenly wondered if it had anything to do with me.

"Did you call the police?"

"No, I jumped on a bus."

"Ring them immediately if it happens again. Or ring me."

She looked at me in surprise. "You're very good, but maybe I imagined it."

"Can you move out for a while?"

"Move out?"

"Just to be safe."

"No."

"You should get out, Suzanne."

"What?"

"I see a lot of mixed up people in here."

"What are you talking about? Is it something to do with you? And why would they be following me?"

"I've a bad feeling about it. It'd be best to move out."

"Definitely not."

"Well, drop over to me then, all of you, if it happens again. There's a key under a pot around the side, so let yourself in ..."

"Michael, don't take this the wrong way, and I'd give you the world for seeing Kieran today, but I hardly know you. And we're not moving anywhere. We'll bolt the doors, lock the windows, get a dog. I'm a fairly hardy soul."

She made a move for the door, and I went over to my desk and opened the drawer. I lifted up the false panel and put my fingers on the Glock. But I only moved it up to rest in the now-empty drawer above it.

"If you think that's enough," I said, closing the drawer.

"Don't forget my grandfather was a murderer," she said lightheartedly before leaving the room. When I heard shouts in reception ten minutes later, I wished I'd left too.

44. Next Patients

The shouts burst through my door, and it was Deirdre who was making them.

"I told them they can't come in!"

Two men, one of them pushing her out the door and banging it closed.

"Buzz her and tell her not to ring the police," the other said, a redhead.

"I'm not..."

"Do it or she'll die."

I buzzed her and told her that everything was fine. But when I heard a door close outside in the car park, I was sure it was her. My neighbor next door was away from his surgery, so I was glad she had the sense to leave.

The redhead took a small black stick from his pocket. He jerked his arm and the stick extended into a baton. I'd begun to speak when he came over and, hearing only a whoosh, I got a belt in the face that felt like my cheek bone had been split into the side of me. A whack to my leg and I felt the sting, then one grab at my hair and my head pulled backwards. I fell, my legs twisted under me.

Another smack with the baton nearly took off my fingers. Throbbing pain, red split skin. I pushed myself back towards the wall, back beside a plant, and held my fingers tight to my chest.

"What do you fucking want!"

They stood looking at the adult man on the floor, at the books on the shelves. The monkey heads, then back at me. The redhead grabbed me, pulling me up by the shirt. He flung me into the patient seat and I wasn't there a second before the other man hit me on the left side of the head. Both sides now throbbing, my eyes watering, and a deadly fear within me. I was going to die if I couldn't get to the gun.

"That's enough, Redser," a voice came in through the door.

A man walked by me and sat in my swivel chair, swinging it once to each side. I didn't know whether I was in a better position, or worse.

"Mr. Grady," I squawked.

"This is an awful situation, Michael. I'm shocked at what you've done."

He was sitting with his back to the light and I couldn't see his face. My eyes were speckling but it wasn't a migraine.

"You're a one-man war, Michael."

A towel appeared beside me, taken from the patient bathroom. It was wet and used but I held it to my head, the pressure giving some relief from the pain.

"It's not yours," I said.

"What's not mine?"

"History."

"Of course it's not. What are you talking about?"

"I had my own thing to do."

"It's flowed over to us." Grady stood up and came over to me, perching himself on the desk.

"We were making headway, Michael. Can you hear me? Real progress. I put up with being stuck between the idiots on both sides of the water, because things were moving along. And now I'm in a difficult position."

"You'll be grand. You're in the civil service."

"Do you think I'd still be Special Advisor if I was linked to a murder? Even a whiff of that, and I'd be out. But more than that, it's all gone to pieces in Belfast. Bringing those men out of the past stirred things up. And now with the walls down, they're busting the heads off each other. What have you to say about that? Did it all go according to plan?"

"It did."

He grabbed hold of my stinging face with two slaps from his palms and shouted at me, "You should have left it alone!"

He threw my head back and a baton came into my forehead from the right. I tried to stand up to face them, but I only managed to lean on the desk. I noticed then that there was someone else in the room, off to my right. Terry.

"You're going to the police," Grady said. "And your tool will go with you."

"My what?"

"The ghost who did it for you. No names with him."

"He's going nowhere."

"They won't believe you did it on your own. He's with you or he's dead. Your shit little plan was not his job to do."

"You'll only have me."

Another baton came down and I stopped it, grabbing Redser's wrist and punching him in the stomach. I grabbed his neck and wrenched him to the ground, my fingers tightening around his throat, squeezing until he'd be dead. A strike to my back, and another, and the flashes of pain that came with them, but Redser's eyes were wide and his tongue was out and the spit was flooding from his mouth. The baton kept hitting my back, my shoulders, but I knew this man was going to die.

"Stop Michael, for fuck's sake stop!" Terry's voice behind me, the baton in his hand.

"I'll kill him."

"Don't, Michael, there's no need."

The first sound of sense, and I let my hands loose, my fingers sore from gripping. Redser coughed for his life.

"You might have it in you after all," Grady mocked.

Everything in pain but I stood up. I limped around to my swivel chair.

"You're out of it, Grady. You've nothing to say."

"I've too much to say. And I'm telling you you're going to the police."

"That was the whole fucking plan. It's all set up so it points to me. Plane tickets, ferry tickets, bloody restaurant receipts. Even my head on the telly. I knew it'd click with you sometime. Working that out is my bloody job, remember. I'll take the punishment for what I've done, but 'my tool' is not going with me."

"Why not?" Grady asked in pure wonder.

"Why do you think?"

"You're a mystery to me. Cold as stone but with a heart of jelly." The anger came into his eyes. "But it stops now. You'll go to the police because we have a little profile on your lady friend and by god it won't be hard to go through everyone else you know. You'll see sense with one of them."

"You won't touch any of them!" I opened the drawer and pulled out the Glock before Redser had gotten his breath back, before Grady remembered I owned one. But not quick enough for Terry. The black line of the baton came down and cracked me in the wrist, banging my hand to the desk. He grabbed the weapon before I did.

"No more of this fucking nonsense." Grady pointed his finger in my face. "You'd be dead now if it wasn't for Cathal. But he's only given you one chance. You're off to the police."

I belted his hand away from me, and another swipe of the baton came down. With a look of disgust, Grady moved towards the door, then he stopped to add his few little fucking words:

"I'm struggling, Michael. I'm struggling to keep the peace going. I tried to keep the walls up, the violence down. And I'm struggling to stop myself shooting the lot of you! Your father didn't follow orders and he was snapped back into line."

He headed out the door, followed by Redser and the other man, and I hobbled after them, shouting.

"What about my father? What are you talking about!"

Terry's forearm came up like a wall to my chest and I almost fell back to the floor. I was in too much pain to do anything except slump into the nearest chair.

"What are you doing with him?" I spat out.

"This is a warning. Only a warning."

"I don't need a fucking warning."

Sirens in the distance. Deirdre must have done what anyone would have and called the police.

"I spoke to your uncle a few days back," Terry said.

"How's he doing up in his ditch?"

"I don't know about that."

"There's not much you do know."

I almost jumped when he shouted at me: "Everyone thinks they know everything! Grady, you, Cathal, even Redser has something to say."

"And what do you say? Or have you said enough?"

"I say if we don't get the North back, this shit will continue for another hundred years. I'm tired of wanting to run away from it every day and then remembering why I'm here in the first place, remembering all the people who've died and all the Cromwells and Trevelyans and the other bastards who kicked a neighboring country who was just minding her own business."

"I'm not finished with what I have to do."

He lowered his voice. "Finish it, but do it quickly. Grady's tied up with the walls, but you don't have much more than a week. Do it and then give yourself up."

"And what about Suzanne?"

"They'll find her, wherever she goes."

"That would be the end." I put my elbows on the desk, my head in my hands. To stay in this moment forever and do nothing. She'd be safe if I didn't move. She and her family would be safe.

"I'll watch her," he said.

"You'll what?"

"I'll look out for her. Nothing will happen."

"There aren't many people who could have told Grady what I was up to. I know it wasn't me and I'm even more certain it wasn't the man working for me. So that leaves you. And I saw my little note was gone from my desk. I don't blame you for doing it; the organization's fucking toxic. But what in god's name makes you think I'd let you look after Suzanne?"

"It was me, I showed him that paper. I told him what I saw. But I'm not sorry I did, and I'd do it again. I told him because after I talked to you, I knew what I had to do. I *have* chosen the right life, but they're not on the right path, and I'm not sure you are. But none of that matters. Grady was already watching you, they would have found out soon enough, and they had reason not to be sure of me. I have to be secure now, they have to think I'm in. But unlike you, I'll be damned to hell if I see another innocent person being hurt. I'll watch your lady's house, I'll make sure nothing happens. And I'll call off anyone who's sent over to harm her."

"You can do this now? You have this power now because you sold me out to Grady?"

"I have this power because I've got the support of the men on the ground. I always have. They trust me like no one else, not even Grady. I haven't spent years building relationships for nothing. You're a psychiatrist, Dr. Gleeson – you can tell me now if I'm lying."

He stood for a second and then walked out the door, and I wasn't sure whether he was the fool or I was. I heard the police sirens moving down Ailesbury Road, in through the car park as Grady and his men drove out. I tried to seem as normal as possible when they came into the office, two policemen checking on trouble. There was a slight robbery and I hurt my wrist. I can give you descriptions but it all happened so quickly. They took the few euro that I had in my wallet, but there was nothing else in here that they liked. I certainly did get a shock, and it was a dreadful thing, but it so rarely happens, and thank you again, officers. I have an important young patient to see next week, but then I will indeed take some time off. And I'll call you if I see any suspicious behavior in the future.

45. One Y

"The results are back, Maggie. You look wrecked," Alex had a sheet of paper with him as he stood before her desk, staring at the wet towel she was holding to her head.

"I was out last night. Did you find anything?"

"Lots of things, lots of individual samples. Lucan, Lady Lucan, Sandra Rivett. It was only a rug you asked me to look at, but there were at least ten other people who had walked on it over a short space of time. I found the DNA of three policemen who worked on the scene. None of the other genetic material matches anyone in the database."

She had to say thank you without looking disappointed.

"You didn't find a boy?" she asked resignedly.

"DNA doesn't tell age, you have the same DNA for life."

"I know. I'm tired and just chancing my arm."

"But I did find two Ys." Alex looked at his sheet. "Not two exactly, one. They were easy to get because there were a lot of skin cells, in the most recent layer of debris at the top of the rug. They were cells from two different individuals, but the computer flagged them because the Y-chromosomes were the same."

"Are you serious? Do you know when they were shed?"

"No. In relative terms, it would have been recent."

"That won't be enough for Booth."

"Sit on it if you're not sure."

She asked for the sheet and thought for a second, then she went to Booth's office, knowing she should turn around with each step. When an officer came out, she went in.

"I couldn't let the Lucan case go, sir," she said quietly.

Booth sat back from his desk. "Why am I not surprised?"

"Before you told me to drop it, I asked Alex to do a DNA analysis on the rug that's held in evidence from the Lucan household. He found two identical Y-chromosomes from two separate individuals. That could mean non-identical male twins, but it's more likely to have been a father and son."

"They were there on the night of the attack?"

"The analysis can't say when, just that they had been there recent to when the rug was taken as evidence."

Booth stared at her as if he had never seen her before. "Why do you keep chasing after a ghost from forty years ago? We've too many cases for individuals to wander off on their own."

"Lucan is central to everything, I know he is. The attack, his disappearance, and then his murder can't be a coincidence."

"He's just one among many, and that many is getting larger. We're overwhelmed with these cases, and if we don't get a break soon, another head will turn up on a railing. I'm under so much pressure from on high to find leads that tie the cases together that I can't have one of my detectives distracted. If I told them you were running after someone who nobody believes exists, we'd both be out of a job."

"I can't let this go, sir."

Her words startled them both.

"Then all I can say is that your time here is due to run out in a few weeks. I hope the experience was a good one."

Her heart pounded the front of her body. If she was making a mistake with Lucan, there'd be no recommendation from Scotland Yard, and a negative report might be sent back to Dublin. She'd be known as someone who couldn't be trusted, an officer who baulked under orders. It'd be the end of the SDU, certainly the end of any future in London.

But that couldn't be helped.

"I can't let it go. Someone found Lucan, when the UK police and Interpol never could. Even Europol had an open file on him, and with all the technology they have today, they still had no idea he was alive. Somebody found him, and the only organization that could have done that was the IRA. They're everywhere."

"They're not everywhere, they're gone." Tired and infuriated, Booth couldn't keep his voice down any longer. "What do you want to do? I have to weigh up your paycheck and your desk space with your contribution and, at the moment, it seems like you're working in a different department."

Booth stopped, keeping his eyes on her. He took the time to calm his temper.

"What do you want to do?" he said again, and she knew she couldn't go any further.

"I'll drop it."

The tears in her eyes as she walked back to her desk were more from embarrassment than anger. She felt like a fool. She wanted to sit for the next few minutes without speaking to anyone, to assess how much damage she'd done to herself. But as soon as she sat down, her phone rang, and Paul Priestley's worried voice came on the other end. Maggie's head spun, and she needed to think, but Paul just kept talking, talking, and wouldn't be interrupted. They'd found out about the missing drink during stock-taking, he said, and he didn't know what to do. Could she come in and smooth things over with Griffiths, seeing as he'd helped them with their investigation? Maggie promised to do what she could, though it couldn't be much. And just as she was about to hang up, when she realized she had nothing left to lose, she said,

"Paul, answer me straight, did Joseph Gleeson tell you he went after Lucan in 1974?"

"I'm sure he would have said something. We'd been good friends, working in Blackwell's garage in Woolwich. Maybe after that nanny got murdered, he might not have liked to mention the night to anyone. She was a lovely girl, and it was a terrible shame."

"If Joey said anything, you have to tell me now."

"Everybody's dead, Officer, there'll never be a trial."

"The investigation won't be dropped because of that. We still have to find out who did it. Sandra Rivett was forgotten in this whole thing over the years. She was going to get married and start a new life."

"With that Australian fella? I remember reading about it in the papers. It was very sad."

"She hasn't found justice yet, and that's what's killing me. Lucan's dead, and Joseph Gleeson probably is, but we could do something good for Sandra."

"I saw her face in the papers. She was lovely, that girl, with her long red hair."

"Was it Joey, Paul?"

There was silence at the end of phone, and Maggie was too drained to press him any further.

"Okay, I'll drop into Griffiths next week, and if you remember anything else, please let me know."

When she hung up, Maggie felt sorry that she'd had to badger him. She suddenly needed to see the face that she was doing it for. She brought up a page of images on Google, all of them showing a young woman looking glamorous for the camera. Sandra Rivett was beautiful, and she had her head smashed in. Someone kept beating her until they knew she was dead. If it really was Lucan, Maggie thought, he must have been in some rage to keep going and not recognize that she wasn't his wife. And if it was Joey Gleeson, he must have been so cold as to have had to be certain that he finished the job. Beautiful Sandra Rivett in the seventies' style, with her long, dark hair in all of the photos. All of the photos showed that dark hair, because most of the photos were black and white.

Maggie saw one color photo of Sandra sitting in front of a fire, but her hair looked black in that too because of the color-tinted camera film of the time. Beautiful long dark hair, and her eyes looking hopeful toward the camera. *So why the fuck did Paul Priestley describe her as a redhead?*

46. Michael's Trip to London

"Fuck off" was the first thing Linda Hograve said to me. It shouldn't have been a surprise. Ms. Hograve had celebrated more Christmases with prison guards than with her own family, a pair of half-formed children whose mother couldn't care less about them. She'd attacked a police officer and broken the eye socket of a social worker when they called to check up on disturbances in the home. Not only was her picture and details in the local news section of the *Croydon Weekly,* but the fact that she never married meant I found her with ease.

I had landed in Heathrow on the Friday, a freezing cold day at the start of December. I checked into the Connaught Hotel, for the comfort as much as the name. The blazing fire in the lobby held me for too long, as did the sight of the teak staircase in reception, a magnificent square structure that rose around itself to take guests seven stories up. I eventually pulled myself away and took the Tube to Croydon, where I walked around the littered streets, wrapped up and well-concealed.

On the Saturday, I strolled up and down outside Hograve's block of flats and hung around outside a local drug rehab clinic for an unreasonable length of time. I couldn't work out how Turlough did it. How he could spot faces among hundreds without being seen. He told me once he would think about cooking, but I only half-remembered what he'd said. I sat in a local bar and thought about French toast for as long as I could, until the sour ale tasted better and the noise of the place didn't seem like English at all, but like a foreign drowning language. And when I left the pub in the evening to return to the hotel, I walked into Ms. Hograve on her way in the pub door. I apologized to the back of her head, and then I seized my chance.

"Miss Hograve?"

And that was when she spoke those first words.

"Are you Linda Hograve?" I asked, and those first words came again.

She went into the bar, and I stood outside. Then I walked back to the Tube station, phoning Turlough on the way.

"I think I've just met Linda Hograve."

"I'm out of the country."

"Which one?"

"All of them."

"Can I ask your advice?"

"I'll meet you tomorrow."

I'd barely told him where I was staying when he hung up. I carried on for the train station, wondering what to do. I was tall and solidly built, but so many things could go wrong. And I had serious doubts. Ms. Hograve had reached this point in her life when she never meant to, when her life had been battered down, right from the start. I'd chosen her because of what she turned out to be, but it wasn't her fault. Was it the fault of any of them?

What will I do, Honoria, tell me what I'll do now.

I took the train back to the city center, in a carriage filled with whispers and draughts. I checked my emails, updated my apps. And on the tiny screen of my phone, I read a story about a walk through the mountains of Mayo in March 1849.

47. The Doolough Walk (1849)

Louisburgh. It wasn't even an Irish name, long changed by the English. *Cluain Cearbán* was the real name, meadow of buttercups. And they were already out across the fields, a sight of yellow stretching to the hills around us. But when some of the others grabbed handfuls of the flowers along the road, tipping the heads and stalks into their mouths with their fingers, it wasn't long before everything dripped out of them. Their stomachs weren't filled, but whatever was there came down their legs. And they didn't care.

It was spring and the weather should have been turning, but it remained foul. We were told that the Indian corn would be given to all who needed it, and I couldn't have named a soul who didn't by then. It scraped the gullet going down, but there was nothing else to keep us alive. There were the buttercups, of course.

The path out of town was black with everyone I knew who was still with us. There were others from Westport and Knappagh, and all the places in between. We joined them when they inched through Muraisc. I had Katie by the hand, and God love her she made no sound. I thought we would stop if we moved any slower. Six hundred on the way to Louisburgh for the outdoor relief or a pass to the workhouse. Six hundred lengths of bones with no thought but walking.

I had no strength to hate anyone when we reached the workhouse at Louisburgh. With tears on his face, the officer shouted that he had nothing to give us, that we had to ask Colonel Hograve and Mr. Lecky, they were in charge of it all. Where were they? We'll have to ask them. It would be tomorrow, and they were meeting at Delphi Lodge, twelve miles down the road. Twelve miles and through the Doolough Pass, between the Sheffry Hills and the Mweelrea Mountains.

All of us said we'd go and all of us slept on the street at Louisburg. There were few houses left, even fewer left occupied. And when we opened our eyes the next day and stood to walk again, one hundred didn't stand at all. And some of them were to have the company of their kin, who stayed to join them soon enough.

Five hundred sticks walked in the rain along the goat path toward Delphi Lodge. The goats were long gone, we didn't see one. We crossed the high Glankeen River and I held Katie's hand as if she would be pulled under.

The men were eating when we came at the lodge and they would not be disturbed. While we waited outside, I had Katie's head in my lap, and oh, she was light by then. My beautiful sister, who made me never lonely. I was watching her fair hair when Hograve and Lecky came out. They looked at us with not a fright and said they would give us nothing, that it was back to Louisburgh for us. They never told us why before telling us to move off. We could not even be angry, it was enough to keep the hearts beating in our chests. As I stood to take Katie back the way we came, I saw she made no move and fell a little from my legs. I put a hand on her and she was as cold as the wind.

Ten years was what she had seen. I kissed her head and left her and knew that I'd be meeting her somewhere down the track, she wouldn't be alone for long.

The freezing rain. It would have made us laugh to think there could be worse to come and then the drops of them happened along the way, the falls of the dead as the mass of us got lesser still. And whoever was family let out one cry and touched their people on the face and walked again, away. And then to Stroppabue, with the cliff looking onto the lake of Doolough. And a storm of ice wind ran at us and pushed many in, down to the black waters and the end, I think, and some went after them without having to, but for having had enough of this life.

There were so few of us left that made it home. The path behind me was a path of the dead, so many you would have trouble in walking through. I, into Muraisc, not knowing if I was still alive from the feeding I had before the time of the bad life or because of the sight of God in heaven. But I know it was Peigín O'Gliasáin who found me, the one who saw me first in the world and who was to give me life again. She had one child out of seven remaining and now another half-dead to feed, and when I got over to America, I could do no less than send her the money I could, wishing I had the world entire to give her.

I never spoke of Doolough to anyone, though it sat in my heart as if it would burst out. But when I prayed to the Lord each night and early morning, I sent him a plea to take my soul if he wasn't going to punish those men Hograve and

Lecky. Or if it not be Him, let it be some man down the years who will take the sharpest hands and pull the tongues from them. And then burn their bodies black.

(Honoria Gleeson, New York, 1858)

*****

I took the first train back to Croydon, knowing what I had to do.

48. You Try Your Hardest

Ms. Hograve was leaving the pub by the time I reached it. I followed a distance after her, but she only noticed the ground. A mile to the block of flats, with its smashed glass entrance and lift that didn't work. Graffiti and urine took me up to the fourth floor. She was lighting a cigarette at her door when I came up the stairs and into the passageway outside her flat. A meter-high brick wall ran the length of the passageway, but the wind came over it, and Hograve cursed her sputtering lighter. She saw me, and I walked up and said hello.

"Are you the cunt from before?"

"I am. Well, I'm not sure if I'm that."

She opened her door to go in.

"Ms. Hograve, I just want to ask you something."

"Get the fuck away," she shouted, likely alarming any neighbors within range.

"It's about your family."

"You're here about my fucking kids again?"

"No, I mean your great-grandfather."

"He fought in the war. Don't say a fucking thing about him."

"I mean the one before."

She pushed open the door and went in, and I hesitated. I heard voices inside, one of them loud, and I figured there must be a man and I started to turn away. But Hograve was back at the door, with two small faces behind her, one red in the eyes and the other sporting a dark bruise on her forehead. The loud voice was Hograve's.

"I have a picture of my grandfather and here it is," she said, and a wooden bat came down before I could see it. It smashed into my temple and I doubled over as it went up again for another blow. Down it came, but the shock of the pain was gone and I bounced the bat off my arm. I grabbed it and pulled her out towards me.

She wrenched the bat away and I let her, lunging for the door and banging it shut, closing the faces away. I punched Hograve so hard that she hit her head off the doorframe. Her hand went near the ground and she dropped slowly down. I shook, I couldn't move with anger. I couldn't move with wanting to take this monster's head off her shoulders.

I wasn't ready for it. A knife appeared and stabbed me in the shin. I yanked my leg back to rip it free. I kicked her wrist so hard that the knife flew out and she fell back, yelping with the pain.

Footsteps behind me and I turned to see a neon vest, a policeman. I was ready for his arms to grab me but instead I saw a black gun in his hand. I dived into his shoulder and sent us both back to the ground. The police hat came off and in the dim yellow light of the passage, red hair stood out in the dark.

Hograve shouted at him, "That cunt attacked me!"

Redser raised the gun and I was up and kicking at his hand, but it stayed in.

"You were warned, Michael!"

I ran. I ran by Hograve on the ground, I ran as far as I could before a bullet snapped near the side of me, into the brick wall. I turned into the stairwell and saw the stairs, and a ceiling light was shot to shards above me. I took five steps at once, down four levels to the ground, and shouts rang out before I burst through the entrance doors. I ran along the side of the building, and I heard the sound of another shot before running out onto the road.

*****

A policeman was in the hotel lobby the following morning. As soon as the lift doors opened, I saw him, standing by the entrance with an electronic device in his hand. Likely compiling the identities of everyone who was checked in the night before, taking details of unusual activity seen by staff or guests. I had been a fool. I shouldn't have taken a taxi back from Linda Hograve's but I wasn't thinking five minutes ahead. Now I just had to get out of this hotel. I was going to be caught or I was going to die, and I wasn't sure which would come first. Hograve had heard my name. The taxi driver would have given a description. A panting man in the back of his cab, holding his leg and not able to sit still, popping painkillers until they nearly choked him.

I pressed the lift button to go back up, but the officer looked straight at me. *Act now or be caught upstairs.* I walked out of the lift. I could run to the door. What did Turlough say about sausages? My cheeks flushed hot. *Act now*. He said to think about what you're cooking for dinner, that you live here, that you own this place. *Act*. This is where I'm meant to be, this is mine. If I go out the front doors, I go now. I took one step forward, then another, then I turned and walked over to reception. A smile from the receptionist, and my mind went blank.

"I live here," I said.

"Sorry?"

"I feel like I live here, like it's home. I had a lovely stay."

"You're checking out?"

"Not yet. You know, the park over there is very well maintained." I casually pointed in the direction of where I thought Hyde Park would be. "Does the local government look after it?"

She put up with a brief conversation about gardening, and I said goodbye and turned towards the main doors. The sweat on my back was soaking my shirt. The officer's body swayed as he watched me. I walked towards him, I didn't look. *Sausages. I live here.* I felt the breeze of the door. *Eggs and things.* I walked by him, I walked out. And what he saw walk into the street was a middle-aged man in a cheerful tweed coat, red scarf, and reading glasses. A guy who looked like he owned the place, a guy who got into a taxi outside. Someone who asked politely to be taken to Portsmouth, in order to meet a man his father used to know, a man his father used to call the Novice.

49. Just Dropping By

I took the chance, because I might never have got the chance again. The headaches were worse than ever, not helped by a bat to the head, and doubling my painkiller dose was having no effect. There was one more name on my list and then I'd be finished, one way or the other.

The British tabloids had mentioned the Novice, a mini-celebrity who was familiar with the criminal underworld in London in the seventies. He was happy to be interviewed about his memories of Lord Lucan, delighted to be photographed outside the distribution depot he worked at. And it was through the revolving doors of that depot, a place called Griffiths, that I now breezed to get my man.

"Does Paul Priestley work here?" I asked the receptionists.

"He's not talking to any more reporters."

I smiled at the sullen ladies, thinking of my next question. And with that, a man came out of a door to the right and the women's eyes followed him for too long.

"Mr. Priestley?" I called, jogging after him.

He turned and looked down at my hands. "I've had enough of the press."

"I'm not the press."

"Who are you?"

"I'm Andrew Goodwin. I'm a doctor."

"I know who you are."

I didn't know what to say.

"Come with me," he ordered, and I followed him through the revolving doors and out toward the side of the building, where wooden pallets were stocked as high as houses and mini forklifts were quietly beeping around the yard. When he turned the corner, I suddenly thought he might run.

Instead he frightened me out of my skin. He grabbed my hand and almost pulled it out of the socket, shaking it with happiness.

"You're Joey Gleeson's son."

"I am, sorry."

"For what?"

"I'm not Goodwin."

"That's okay. You have to be careful."

He hugged me out of the blue. "I never thought I'd see Joey's son again."

"How did you know it was me?"

"You're as tall as him, that's for sure. But I'd never forget your face. You could say it's imprinted on my brain. The last time I saw you, I was teaching you to box, and it was quite a day for me. But never mind that."

"I remember you Paul, I remember you worked in a garage."

"That's right, with your dad. I suppose he's long in the grave now?"

"He is. And I'm here because of him. I'd like to ask you about him. Can we go somewhere to talk?"

"This is it, I'm afraid. I don't want you near me."

"How do you mean?"

"I'm sorry, but I can't be seen talking to you. What with all this Lucan business. I'll tell you what I know, but then I have to leave."

I didn't hesitate. "You remember the 1974 attack?"

His head and chest rose up indignantly. "I can't talk about that."

"No, I'm sorry. I was there anyway."

"You were?"

"He had to take me."

"Christ, what a sight it must have been. He asked some of us to mind you, but we were all going out. We were young lads back then, and hanging onto a kid was the last thing we needed. I guess your mam was sick at the time."

"She was. The cancer had started."

"And he took you all back to Ireland. Though I don't think he wanted to go."

"He liked London?"

"It was more about what he was returning to. "Back to the bleeding streets," he said, though I didn't rightly know what he meant."

"I hardly remember him. He and my mother died a few years later, and he never said a lot before he passed away, he never spoke that often."

Priestley snapped out a laugh. "I'm awfully sorry. Don't think me heartless, but your dad never said much here either.

I had to pull the gossip out of him. Very quiet man, very quiet." He shook his head, remembering.

"He wasn't a talker?"

"It was more like he didn't feel the need than he didn't know what to say. But where does it say we all have to be rattling around making noise? In any case, he always got the job done."

"And the Lucan job. Was Dad ever angry that Lucan got away?"

"Your dad scared the soul out of him, I think that was enough."

"You never heard him complain about it?"

"Look, lad..."

"Please Mr. Priestley, anything you know."

"I never saw him afterwards."

"Paul, did he do that job because he was a Republican? Getting back for Ireland and all that? My uncle told me that could have been the reason."

"I don't know about them kind of things, son."

"I remember him taking me, I just don't know why he was there. I wish I could be sure." I put my hands in my pockets and spoke so softly that I didn't know if he heard my words. "Would he have been proud of me, Mr. Priestley?"

"Of course he would," he said in earnest. "He loved you more than anything. He did everything to keep you safe."

"From who?"

"A bad man. A very bad Blackwell. The man who stopped you laughing."

"Outside the church?" I hadn't brought up the memory in forty years.

"That's it. Maybe you remember. Maybe it's better to forget. Listen, lad. The police had me in, asked me a few questions. I had to tell them about people from back then, and your dad's name came up. I'm sorry I had to mention him, if it'll get you into trouble."

"They were asking about Lucan?"

"They were. But I think they were more after who killed him, down in Africa. And that couldn't have been your dad, unless he's a ghost."

We stood nodding our heads, listening to the beeping machines in the yard. Then he made a move to go. I asked him if I could give him anything for speaking to me.

"I'm only too glad to see you, son. Joey saved my life, on more than one occasion. He was a good pal of mine. And I'll tell you something else – he found my wife for me, introduced us. Though she turned out to be a bitch. But he wasn't to know." He laughed.

"If you remember anything more, can you give me a ring?" and I started looking in my bag for a card to give him.

His two hands came up to cover mine. "No, listen son, you won't be hearing from me. It's nice to have been a bit of a celebrity, finally telling people about all those high times we had. My wife couldn't stop me when it was the police doing the asking, and she wouldn't stop me when the newspapers started giving me a few bob. But I've had enough of this Lucan thing. I'll just have to wish you well." He winked and turned and headed for the yard.

I left the depot for the nearest main road to find a taxi, so distracted that I barely noticed where I was going. I wasn't sure whether Mr. Priestley had helped me at all, and I didn't know what I needed help with.

50. Police on Michael

"Who the hell is that?" Maggie said to Liam. They were in an unmarked police car outside Griffiths, about to visit Paul Priestley. Maggie had told him they'd try and help him out with his bosses, but she was really hoping he'd let something else slip out. How did Priestley know that Sandra Rivett had red hair? Maybe he'd met her or, more likely, he'd heard Joseph Gleeson talk about how he'd mixed up her hair with Lady Lucan's blonde in the darkness.

But all that went out of Maggie's head now that she and Liam were watching Priestley with another man, a younger man he seemed very warm towards. That man was wearing a suit and a grey tweed overcoat, out of place among the pallet movers.

"He looks like a doctor," Liam said, "or a bird watcher."

"Would he be a reporter?"

"Would you hug a reporter?"

The man headed toward the side gate of the depot. The officers took their eyes off him when they saw Priestley return to the corner of the building to watch his acquaintance walk away.

"Do me a favor, Liam."

"Do what?"

"Follow him."

"It could be his boss."

"It could be the man on the CCTV."

"Outside Westminster?"

"What do you think?"

"I don't think Booth will be happy."

Liam spun the car round, and they followed the man as he reached the main road and hailed a taxi. They followed the taxi, as it drove out of Portsmouth and hooked up to the A3, the motorway leading towards London. They followed it into the city.

They drove to the Connaught Hotel in Mayfair. The taxi stopped at the busy entrance, and the man got out and went through the doors. The police car pulled up behind.

"We'll need a warrant, Maggie, if we want to search the rooms. The Yard is only ten minutes away if we hurry."

"We don't have time. And Booth would never get us one."

"What do you want to do?"

"We have to hope the man is Gleeson, and we have to hope he tries to run when he sees us."

The officers went through the entrance. Maggie scanned every individual in the lobby, while Liam went to reception and asked who the individual was who just came in. The receptionist needed more details. Did the officer have a name? Was this the same investigation from this morning?

"What investigation?"

"A policeman was in here looking for someone who may have been dropped off last night. You haven't found them yet?"

The concierge appeared from nowhere.

"This is the Connaught Hotel, officers. We don't usually have the police walking in and out."

"We're looking for a man who just came in. A tall man in a heavy grey coat."

"He doesn't seem to be here," the concierge said without looking around.

"Have you got a list of everyone who's checked in at the moment?"

"Of course I have. And have you got your ID and a search warrant? We protect our guests like family, Officer, family we actually get on with."

Liam took out his ID, not sure what he was going to do next. Maggie moved to the right of reception and stared at the huge teak staircase. It rose several floors to the roof, and she could see all the way up. Which floor was he on? Was he up there at all? Was she wasting...

A hand grabbed the handrail three floors up. Enough to see the cuff of a heavy coat. Maggie's heart raced as she went slowly up the stairs, as if she was just looking around. When she was out of sight on the first landing, she flew up the stairs three steps at a time.

"Where is she going?" the concierge asked, then he continued to educate Liam. "He might be in his room or he might have left. What people do outside the hotel is their own business."

But Michael Gleeson hadn't left. He was opening the door of Room 301, to collect his belongings before checking out. He noticed a young woman in a dark suit turn the corner onto his corridor. Her hand was covering something on her hip, and she was looking at nothing else but him.

51. Turn Around

"Are you Joseph Gleeson?" the woman asked me, and my heart stopped with my father's name. She had the confidence of a police officer, and I wasn't prepared. I said the first thing that came into my mind:

"Is that a gun?"

"I'm Detective O'Malley from Scotland Yard. Are you Joseph Gleeson?"

"Will I put my hands up?"

"Keep them down. How do you know Paul Priestley?"

"Eh..."

"How do you know him!"

"He taught me to box." My own words shocked me.

I saw it on her face – one second of thinking, one second of revelation, then her eyes opened wide and she shouted in certainty: "Turn around and face the wall! I'm arresting you in connection with the murder of Barney Hutchinson!"

I wouldn't turn around. Her gun came out, but I couldn't turn around. I had a few seconds to do something, anything, and I had no idea what it would be. She clicked on the device at her chest and radioed that she was arresting me outside Room 301. An answer came back, someone else was on the way.

"Turn to the wall with your hands behind you."

I was taller than her and had strength, but she was younger and had a weapon. A few seconds to do anything, something.

"Turn around!"

I could have run and be shot in the back. Paralyzed for life without finishing the fifth name. I turned to the wall but kept my hands in front of me.

I heard her holster her weapon, and the order came again to get my hands behind my back. I put one behind, and then the other as slowly as I could. I'd have to swing around quickly before she'd tie my wrists.

Movement caught my eye, a man turning the corner onto our corridor. I had to let her bind my wrists. She locked one cable tie around them, then started on another.

"Don't think about running."

I swung around to face her, saying, "Who do you think I am?"

She stepped back and took the gun from her side.

"Face the wall!"

"Who do you think I am?"

"Face the wall!"

"I'll be seeing you..."

I looked at the man behind her while she kept her eyes on me.

"...but not today," and I saw her give the slightest frown before the butt of a pistol smashed into her head. She fell without a sound, she didn't feel a thing.

Turlough grabbed my briefcase and rushed down the internal fire escape without checking whether I was behind him. When he stopped on the stairs to pull my cable ties apart, he complained that I should have been more careful.

We left through the hotel delivery door and crossed the road to Hyde Park, hearing a siren in the distance. I was itching to run, but he forced me to stroll, and we headed for a taxi rank on the other side of the park. We stopped before exiting the black gates.

"Get home," he said. "And stay there."

"I don't have long left."

"This was a mistake, Dr. Gleeson. You could have been caught." He didn't pause to gather his thoughts. "But I have to tell you something, something I've been thinking about, and I might not get the chance again. You know I've been a Republican all my life, and I've seen the men at the top make decisions for a lot of people. Good decisions, sometimes bad. But your plan, Dr. Gleeson, your plan means more than anything they've ever done in their lives. I know the names you've been going after, and I know why you're after them. You're putting an end to all that history. You're saying it can't ever happen again."

"I'm glad I did this," he continued, "and even if I were never to see Ireland again, I could finally say I did some good for the country."

He didn't let me reply.

"You've one more to do? I'm off to Denmark for a few days. I have to go." He was almost apologetic. "It's a job for enough money that I'll never have to do this again."

"You'd give it all up?"

"Of course I would. It's not a pleasure what I do. You'd want to be mad to enjoy this. And because of you, I'm not mad anymore."

And off he went, off he disappeared. I didn't know what he was up to, what shit he was about to wade into. All I knew was that he was a good man, a dreadful human, and someone I could never hurt in my life. I took a taxi to Heathrow armed with a very shiny passport in the name of someone called Xavier, one of the perks of knowing the people I knew. And as the plane lifted off to take me home – my old home, that is, in Monaghan – I had one creeping thought: I couldn't get my friend to go after anyone else again.

52. All Ports Call

"Can you hear me, Maggie?" Maggie heard as she opened her eyes. She was lying on a floor with Booth kneeling beside her, and what seemed like someone kicking her head.

"Was it Joseph Gleeson?" he asked.

"It was his son," she said through the pain, doubling over and holding her head. "How long was I out?"

"About fifteen minutes. How do you know it was his son?"

"He talked about the boxing."

"The boxing?"

"And I've seen his fucking face a million times. Now I know what he looks like as a man."

"Did he hit you?"

"It wasn't him. I thought it was Liam."

"You were on the ground when I came up," a white-faced Liam said, kneeling on the other side of her.

"I had the cable ties on him," Maggie managed, before a third person, a paramedic, knelt down to check her head.

"We think his name is Michael," Booth said. "Linda Hograve's neighbors heard that name the night she was attacked, and we're getting Paul Priestley back in to confirm it. We're matching the CCTV from Griffiths with the Westminster footage."

Maggie stood up, despite the hammering in her head and the protests of the paramedic. "I should have been more careful."

"If he's working with someone else, you couldn't have done anything."

"Could it be his father?"

"We've no idea. We can't even find any taxi drivers who remember him as a passenger. He must look so harmless that he doesn't stand out."

"The son of Joseph Gleeson," she said quietly. "The little boy didn't turn out that well after all."

"You'll have to be monitored for the next few hours."

"I'm not going home, not when he's this near. He could be right in front of us, and I'd be the only one to recognize him."

"I'll take you back to the station. We're checking every Lecky in the country, and now we'll have to put out an all-ports call."

Liam and the paramedic went ahead of them down the stairs, while Booth held Maggie back.

"I'm sorry this had to happen, Detective, to confirm what you told me. You could have been seriously injured or worse."

Maggie slumped down at the top of the stairs. She held her throbbing head, and her eyes began to water.

Booth dropped down beside her.

"I should have had him. I did have him!" She startled him with her anger. "Christ, I should have looked behind."

"You should have waited for Liam."

"I'm a fool."

"It's not your fault. He's a madman."

"I have to be better than him."

"What do you mean?"

"I could have caught them…"

"We'll find Gleeson and whoever he's working with."

"Gleeson?" Maggie said, before she blacked out.

53. An Essay on Eviction

I was seventeen and trying to learn twenty-five essays by heart when he broke my concentration. At any other time, I would have been glad of the interruption, but I only knew three essays well and hadn't looked at the others. I told him all this, I said I'd only a few days before the exam, but Michael, he said, by the fourth year of the famine, the people couldn't even die in their homes. And those are words of a story you can't help hearing.

"Some of the men who were still strong enough boarded up the doors of their homes to let themselves and their families die in peace, as they had done for any of their neighbors who had breath enough left to ask. But the earl always found his tenants, and he swept his men in to crack down the boards and pull out the lines of skeletons. Set them outside at first, where they could see the door of their home but couldn't get back in, lacking the strength to crawl. It didn't matter that it was bitterly cold and they only had slips of clothes on. They and their children would die without dignity. And if it looked like any could pull themselves back inside, the roof would be torn off the house and the bricks kicked in, collapsing everything onto itself. And sometimes there'd be someone still in there, and neither they nor the bailiffs would care.

"And if they didn't die then, they'd be pulled along the ground, out to the edge of the land. It mattered to no one where they were moved. When it came time to pass on, they should have had the name of God on their lips, the names of their parents or children. Beautiful names to them, when words were the only thing they had left. But they also spoke the name of Lucan or whatever landlord had claimed the Irish land they lived on. A thousand names went up to the air, a million curses. Cursing the landlords and the government and the English for telling them what to grow, banning them from finding food on their own land, sending that food away when the blight came, and blaming the Irish themselves for it all. The curses that hung in the air were loud and heavy and the generations that came afterwards could do nothing but hear them."

I heard the curses when I was a young man at the turning point of my life, from a voice that was the only sound for miles around.

And now the only sound in the farmhouse was an angry chicken. Cathal was trying to spray her with whatever pesticide he had found in a shed. The place was as bleak as ever, as quiet as the dead.

"I get new chickens and I get new mites. I'm sick of the lot of them," he said.

"Is that stuff poisonous?"

"To the mites, yeah. To the chickens, I don't know."

He didn't wash his hands before making me tea, but poison was the least of my worries. He attacked me immediately.

"What the hell are you up to?"

"It's not a surprise."

We sat looking at each other across the kitchen table.

"Before you lay into me, I want to ask you something." I didn't have much time, and he wasn't in a position to act as my judge. "The same as usual, Cathal, but it's important now."

"Your father?"

"I heard so many different things. And now someone's said he was snapped into line."

"Sometimes Grady gets things wrong."

"How do you know it was Grady?"

"These things come out. Have you seen today's papers? You know all that stuff about Lucan has come out too?"

"Stick with Dad for now, Cathal."

"It's all the same. I'll get you some biscuits with that," and he shuffled over to the cupboard and took out a tin of biscuits that had started to rust.

"Does Grady know how my father died? I was told about the steps, but the medical records could have said anything back then. And you always said it was internment."

"I always said I thought it was internment."

"But you saw it yourself, your friends being lifted off the streets and thrown in cells. Never seeing the outside again, let alone the inside of a courtroom. Christ, I was grabbed myself. I didn't see a prison, but I had one hell of a vision at 4,000 feet. Is that what happened to Dad? Was he arrested and tortured?"

"Maybe he was. Maybe we should stick to what you're up to."

"Ah, Cathal. I'll be asking about it for the rest of my life. And I don't have much time left."

"Not if you continue what you're doing."

"Let me worry about that."

"It might have been the Brits, I don't know. I just know he was found at the bottom of steps at a pub on the Falls Road. He might have had a few pints on him."

"He wasn't much of a drinker."

"Maybe London changed him. Maybe he took your mother's death too hard. Maybe he took that other girl's death too hard."

"He had a lot to deal with."

"A lot to deal with? He beat that nanny to a pulp."

"We still don't know that, Cathal."

"You were there! You saw what he did."

"I never saw anything. We couldn't have been there that long."

"He was going after Lucan, you know he was. Your father wasn't happy unless he had blood on his hands."

"That's not true."

Cathal gave me a gruff look but said nothing.

"You told me he did it for Ireland."

"I don't know what you picked up from me, but I'm just as much a fool as you are. And he was the biggest fool of all."

"How did he die, Cathal?"

"Forget about it. It would have happened anyway."

"What do you mean?"

"Irishmen never lasted long up north, especially ones like your father."

"Republicans? But he didn't do much after…"

"Stop, Michael! Just leave it alone. It won't do any good."

"Why, Cathal? I have to know. He had such a tough life, his whole life, himself getting a rubber bullet to the chest and me getting battered. Mam dying. And all the bloody shit in Belfast. He was a good man."

Cathal reached into the biscuit tin and pulled out something that shouldn't have been there. It was a handgun and he pointed it at me.

"What the hell?"

"Calm down, Michael, but keep sitting there. This is just insurance, son."

"What the fuck are you doing?"

"Your father died of a broken neck. It was quick and he never felt a thing. But now we have to talk about you. Your historical work is over."

Fuck him and his gun. I lunged over the table and slapped the gun out of his hand.

"That historical shit was all I heard from you, Cathal! You're going to shoot me after making me like this? You told me to get them all!"

My arm came up to punch him in the face and he winced, but two hard knocks on the door stopped me moving. I took my arm back and walked away from the table as Cathal got up and went over to the door. I kicked the gun under a dresser by the time he opened it, him muttering something about why they couldn't use the bell. Two uniformed Gardaí stood outside, one more on the driveway behind them.

"Hiya, Cathal. Just a quick check."

"Again?" and he walked out with the officer.

The other officer asked me if everything was okay, and I replied that it was.

"Would you step out for a minute, sir?"

I thought about my breathing, about sausages, about the weather. I thought about being arrested and thrown in a police van. The sweat came out of my skin.

"It's a routine check," the officer said as I walked into the sunlight.

"It's a lovely day for it." I sounded like an eejit.

Cathal and the other officer went into a shed.

"Is it cattle you're after?" I asked.

"Cattle?"

"Rustlers, like in the wild west."

"We're just making sure everything's okay. Are you a relative?"

"I am," I said, hoping a plane would fall out of the sky.

"A son?"

"Cousin."

Cathal appeared from the shed with the officer behind him. When he reached us he said, "Have you met my nephew?"

"You said you were his cousin."

"Both." I wondered if it were possible.

Two officers went over to their vehicle to talk, looking back at me once or twice. The other officer walked all the way around the house.

"It's okay. All gone," Cathal said to me, though I didn't know or care what he was on about. One of the officers joined us.

"Can I check your ID?"

"Of course," and I brought out my wallet. No false passport with me, why would I have brought one?

"Michael Gleeson," he read off my license.

"My nephew's just leaving," Cathal interrupted. "So I'll say goodbye, Michael. I've the chickens to do." He shook my hand and I wanted a second of invisibility to squeeze the life out of his.

I got into my car and drove down the driveway with the squad car behind me. I thought about finding somewhere to turn around and go back up, but Cathal might have the gun in front of me when he'd open the door, or I might kill him with my name still on a policeman's lips. I drove back down to Dublin trying to understand why the gun had appeared and, with the anger in me, wondering how I was doing it without crashing. I went over all of Cathal's words in my head – while I was driving, while I was parking, while I was stopped at a garage to pick up the newspapers. And when I read what was in them, I wished I had crashed.

54. The Irish Link

After a day of rest, Maggie was in Booth's office telling him that one day of rest was all she could handle. She *had* been right all along, and he hadn't listened to her. Now she was going to get what she wanted.

"I'm not taking temporary absence. I've had bangs on the head before, and I'll get them again in the future."

"Do you remember blacking out?"

She hadn't expected the question.

"You were talking about someone," Booth continued. "You said you had to be better than them."

"That might have been the blow to the head, sir."

"Maggie, police officers' lives are not the most calm, and the best officers are often the ones who come from the least boring backgrounds. But we have to be able to control our past, use it in positive ways. We have counselors to help with that."

"I'll let you know if anything comes up." She didn't meet his eyes.

"Sit down," he said, exasperated. "I spoke to Superintendent Foster about you. Don't look worried. We agreed that if you were to apply for a position over here, you might not have trouble getting in."

"Jesus. Thank you, sir."

"Would you be interested in it?"

She thought for a second. "I've never experienced anything like this place. You have so many types of cases, so many coming through all the time."

Booth's eyes narrowed. "Is that a good thing?"

"No, but I've chosen this job, and I could be effective here. And if I could get into counter-terrorism ..."

"Don't jump ahead. You have to appreciate that the cases never end. You have to keep yourself buoyed up by something other than satisfaction in finding criminals. Because sometimes we don't find them, and sometimes we find the worst of them and they walk free."

"I understand."

"If you have any issues, you have to confront them."

"Is there anything in particular you want to know? We all have issues, and I did spend some time examining my own, until I realized they're not even mine. If I got a bang on the head and started rambling about having to fix somebody else's slip-ups, you can disregard it."

"If you ..."

Maggie's mobile rang in her pocket, and she was more than a little relieved. When she saw who it was, she put them on speakerphone, and Booth's conversation was forced out of her head.

"Your man has appeared," Foster said.

"Which one?"

"Michael Gleeson. We were asked to keep an eye out."

"Is it the right one?"

"Well, it's a Michael Gleeson. He turned up yesterday in a police report from Monaghan. He was at a farmhouse owned by another man, someone who's wanted for questioning."

"Who's that person?" Booth interjected.

"It's Cathal McConnell, William. You probably know the name. He served time in Belmarsh for low-level activity in the eighties, though we think he was nearer the top. We've had our eye on him for years, and he's always covered his tracks. It used to be weapons, and now it's fuel smuggled over the border. The officers became suspicious during yesterday's check and we arrived today to test the premises."

"Did you find anything?" Maggie asked.

"Everything. Accelerants, residues, shell casings. He's gone, and he didn't bother cleaning his sheds."

"How is Gleeson connected to him?"

"The report says Gleeson's either a cousin, a nephew, or both. But he could be none of those things. He confused an officer enough to write it up. I saw that report yesterday, and I've just received Superintendent Booth's all-ports call. We'll start a house-to-house."

"We'll send you the details we have on him," Booth said. "Most of the information comes from a witness who knew his father, a man named Paul Priestley. Michael Gleeson was a boy when he lived in London in the seventies, he returned to Belfast with his family, and his mother had been ill. He started secondary school in London, so he's probably between fifty-two and fifty-four years of age today. And so far, we have a few grainy images of someone we think is him."

"We'll get all the Michael Gleesons over here out of the way."

"I ran into Gleeson myself, ma'am."

"Are you okay? Did anything happen?"

"Not enough, but I got a good look at him. I'll send the facial composite over. He's tall, well-built, dark hair going grey. A middle-aged bloke who might be too fond of his food and drink. My colleague thought he looked like a bird watcher when he saw him. You know the type?"

"A bird watcher is causing all the trouble up north?"

"What do you mean?"

"Bringing up the names from the past agitated everyone. The British troops are spreading onto the streets, and the Republican crackpots haven't died out yet."

"Are the weapons appearing?" Booth asked.

"Not yet, but the arrests are mounting. The singing in the pubs is getting louder. When you have fifty drunk people belting out rebel songs, it doesn't take long before the old grievances emerge."

"Hopefully they'll have the sense not to do anything stupid."

"Hopefully they will. With the peace walls down, there's little to stop them. If another killing appears in the papers, it could be the end of everything."

55. News to Michael

I couldn't rock the energy out of me. Rocking on my living room floor as soon as I got home. Anything for comfort now with all this information. The details of Lucan's disappearance, why he ran, how much he owed, and who had the cord around his ex-wife's neck. My father's name in print.

I tried to rock away forty years. *Dad, you stupid man. All this for a gambling debt?* You didn't beat that woman to death, half-kill the wife, and set me on a road to so many deaths in the name of Ireland. It wasn't fighting for freedom and all that shit – that shit! – you and Cathal poured into my ears. The papers said you were hired to get Lucan, you killed because of money. My honorable father, whose image I held like a mountain in my heart. *You stupid man.* And the other stupid man, sitting in his ditch in Monaghan. Telling me about the cause, telling me nonsense. Holding a gun to my chest. Two men, starving for sense. And me along with them.

A few hours later and I was sitting in a chair. One leg crossed over the other and shaking, wanting to run me away from myself. My phone and its constant ringing.

I laughed to a cry. Money. He did it for money. I had so much money now, and it meant nothing to me.

Minute after minute. And during one of those minutes, the doorbell rang. And a minute later, it rang again, piercing the house. I ran to the door, ready to murder whoever was there. It was Suzanne, and I held the curses back.

I don't know what she said, but she was in the house now. I went into the living room, papers all over the floor, and I sat on top of them. She must have followed me, because when I looked up, she was sitting there.

"You look bad, Michael."

"I am."

"I mean it, you don't look well."

"Telling me won't help. Are you here to check up on me?"

I went back to staring at the floor.

"Listen, Michael. I don't know what to say."

"How can I hear you, if you say nothing?"

She was beside me now.

"Kieran's come out of it. He's eating everything. I can't say thank you, I don't know how."

"Sometimes they fall back."

"But eating's not the terrible thing he thought it was." She moved in, she hugged me.

"It's okay, it's fine. Nothing."

She hugged for too long. I couldn't get back to my thoughts. One more squeeze and she returned to her chair, and the air went cold around me.

"I'm glad," I said without energy.

The newspapers with the wreck of my life on the pages. My father's lies pressing on the floor.

"You look like it's the end," she said.

"It is."

"Why?"

"Nothing, it doesn't matter."

"Is it something to do with your patients? Because I did hear you speaking to Ken on the stairs."

I stared up at her. "What did you hear?"

"I heard a man in difficulty because he couldn't help his patients. And I heard that those patients were in the IRA."

"You'll have to keep your mouth shut about that."

"Don't threaten me, because it won't work. I've one goal in my life, and anything else is nonsense."

"And I've one goal too."

"Is yours to make your child strong enough to survive? Knowing he'd be weak forever if you couldn't get help for him. That's why, no matter what you do or who you really are, I'll always think you're the finest man on earth. You gave Kieran a future."

In her head, she had twisted me into a good man, and it made me sick to my stomach.

"I've done terrible things, Suzanne. I don't know how to get to the end."

"What have you done?"

"I got mixed up. I heard words from my father, and I thought they meant one thing, but they must have meant something else, something I don't know. I don't know what he believed. I don't know who he was."

"But you're a good man, Michael."

"That's wrong, Suzanne, that's not true at all."

Did I feel safe enough to let my treasure chest open? It didn't matter how I felt, because it opened on its own.

"Lucan, Trevelyan, and the builder Barney Hutchinson," I whispered.

"What about them?"

"I thought it was what my father wanted. And he wasn't that type of man at all."

"What did you do?"

"I killed them."

"What are you talking about?"

"I killed them, Suzanne."

She didn't flinch. "It was the IRA, Michael. The papers said it was."

"I work for them, but it wasn't them. I planned those deaths."

"What? For what?"

"To get them in the news, to get people to remember who they were and what they did."

"But Trevelyan was a TV host. Hutchinson was a builder? What did they do?"

"Nothing. It was their ancestors."

"You're stressed, Michael..."

"Of course I am."

"Do you take medication?"

"Painkillers, but they don't help me anymore." I gazed out the window from the floor.

She was saying something to me, but I could only whisper out loud. "I did that, I did them all. Christ, that was me." There was a head on a spike, a woman with two children, a woman on the floor in the basement. A bang against a wall. *Sing songs in your head.*

"Can you prove it?" someone was saying.

"What?"

"It's hard for me to believe."

"Come with me." I stood up, but she didn't move. "Please come with me. I'll show you."

"You're scaring me."

"So leave."

She stood up but waited on the spot. I walked out of the room and she followed. I went up the stairs to my bedroom and she was after me. I unlocked the safe at the head of my bed and I pulled the door open to reveal a four-foot-long Arctic Warfare Magnum, not wrapped or boxed or covered. Her hand came up to her mouth. She didn't need to ask me if I was lying or joking or gone insane.

"I can't be here," she said.

"Go then," I said.

She looked at me in terror, and she left.

*****

I went into the kitchen sometime that evening. A musty smell came from the sink. It was from the bin in the cupboard below, filled with the wet shriveled potatoes of the last dinner party. Twenty wet and cold black heads looking up at me. How many nights old now, two? Ten? I dug my hands into them and felt their round bodies, like gentle stones. Useless. And I did it again, lifting them up from the bin and letting them fall through my fingers. Hard and wet and cold, dripping their old liquid into the bin. One stayed in my hand, and I looked at the black thing. I lifted it to my mouth and tasted it. Hard skin with the softer mush inside, and I swallowed a bite and a bite and another and I ate it all. Back into the bin for a second, and I didn't leave the sink. I felt with each swallow that they'd come back up, but I kept going until they were all gone. And then I took three sleeping tablets and went to bed with my nightmares.

56. A Bit Peaky

"I can't do those extra things, Dr. Gleeson."

I would have laughed down the phone if I wasn't sick to my stomach. Turlough's words weren't a surprise. Neither was the fact that I had gastritis and was laid up in bed for two days. I couldn't put anything into my mouth that didn't come back up. My ribs ached from vomiting and I didn't know how my body pumped the sweat out of me because not even water was staying down.

I told him not to worry, that I just wanted to see what he thought. What I really wanted was for it to be a few days in the future, when I would be feeling better.

"I can do the job, but not the method. That's not me."

He was almost embarrassed that he couldn't tie a person to a bed, starve them for a month, take their clothes off, and roll them into a ditch. He was the coldest person I'd ever met when it came to shooting or knifing, but get a bit imaginative, and he backed out. He took Barney Hutchinson's head off its shoulders easy enough, but he recoiled at anything further. It was me who did the crockpot roasting for two weeks. It was me who had to drive into London with the head in my trunk, me who had to stick the shriveled thing on the spike. And it was me who had to walk up and down the street in front of it, just so it was me who would be seen. I couldn't blame Turlough for anything.

"Don't worry, I'll do..." I didn't finish the sentence and hung up.

Falling back on my pillow, the smell of sick wafted around me. I must have seemed just as foul to Suzanne when she ran out the door.

By the third day, I wasn't hungry, all I wanted was sleep. I kept some water down, but diarrhea flowed out of me whether I noticed it or not. My sick-smelling, shitty, warm little bed. You were clean when you died, Alastair.

Day four, and there was a pair of cheekbones that hadn't been there in years. My chest rose and fell, quicker when I noticed it.

The evening, maybe day five. How long did you last in your bed, Carmel? Was it a month before all the meals that you'd had went from your stomach and your muscles and your breasts? What did you look like to Dad, when he knew he could stop it? Your blue grey face, your lips double the size from cracking. A bony animal, the bedsheets covering you in a long single line. Was leaving us easier than staying, Mam?

I don't know the day. My throat is stuck together. I can't get the air into me, quick and short and my heart hammering my ribs.

A bang at the door. Here, I'm here.

Stay out. I'm almost with her.

Here I am, still.

"You'll have to drink something, otherwise you'll be in trouble." My mother was speaking to me. "Here's water, you eejit." My mother never said that.

If I opened my eyes I'd see her. One lid opened as much as it could, to see a figure standing there. Dark clothes and tall. A uniform. A policeman looking down at me.

57. A Call from Quinn

"What do I have to do?"

"Find some Gleesons," Superintendent Foster told him.

"In Dublin?"

"I think they mean the whole country."

Officer Quinn's heart sank when he realized the job ahead of him, then it rose when he found only forty-three men matching the age profile in the Greater Dublin Area. If he could get to ten of them a day, it wouldn't take too long. But what was he looking for?

"Someone shifty," was Foster's advice. "Someone who's not too happy about you standing at their door. And keep in mind O'Malley's description of Gleeson. I'd send more officers with you except there's no one to spare. The PSNI is asking us about personnel exchanges, but I've a feeling it's all going to be one way. And I'm not too keen on my officers spending time in a war zone."

"Is it that bad already?"

"Not yet, but it's getting there."

*****

Two retirees, two company directors, one teacher, and a handful of unemployed individuals were the first batch of Gleesons that Quinn had to cover. None of them liked to see him knocking at their door, but all of them were chatting away without end by the time he left. On day two, there was a priest, a psychiatrist, a pub owner, and two lawyers. The priest offered tea and told him he had two cousins who went by the same name as him, all Michael Gleesons, fellas who never stopped beating the heads off each other until one of them was trampled by a cow. Both were long dead. The psychiatrist was next.

An old woman opened the door of a huge house in Sandymount. Quinn introduced himself and showed her his ID. She looked worried.

"We're trying to find a man named Michael Gleeson and we're narrowing down the list. Someone of that name owns this house?"

The woman stood like a statute, as if she knew that a spider was crawling up her neck. Then she animated, keeping her voice down low.

"He does. Do you want to see him?"

"Would he be able to come to the door?"

"No. And that's the thing. He's in bed." She shook her head as if the world had ended. "He's not well. But you have your work to do, and you're more than welcome to come in."

Quinn scribbled in his notes about the sick Michael Gleeson he'd found. "What's wrong with him?"

"Colitis. It's nasty and gets worse with each bout."

"Can he talk?"

"No."

"Will he know I'm here?"

"Not likely."

"I'll come in, so," and Quinn made a step toward the door. The woman paused before opening it.

Quinn entered a dark hall almost as big as his own flat, square and fitted with a soft, thick carpet. A wide staircase up and one going down, reception rooms on either side.

"What's this your name is?" he asked her as he followed her up the stairs.

"Teresa Canavan."

"Are you his mother?"

"What? I'm only sixty-eight."

They stopped at the top of the stairs, where the whispering continued.

"The church sends me over to him when he gets the colitis. I try to keep everything clean, so he doesn't catch that MRSA thing you can't get rid of. But I'll have to stop soon – the arthritis."

She waved her fingers as if playing the piano, then she opened the door of a bedroom, saying, "If he's awake, he'll want to shake your hand. Just go along with it."

The dark hall, the heavy air, an arthritic woman in a house of colitis. And a deathly pale man asleep in the bed, snoring so loudly you couldn't have talked over it. Quinn wasn't comfortable.

He walked over to the man and studied him. He saw the thin face and white skin, the uncombed hair. He bent closer, and the man stirred in his sleep.

"Has he been out lately?" the officer asked.

"Out? I've trouble getting him to the bathroom."

Quinn opened his notebook again, and the woman lifted something up from under the bed. A portable commode, filled with dark urine.

"This is what I spend my days doing. If you want, I'll wake him and we can get him to the toilet together."

The officer took another look at the patient. Any moment now, he'd wake up and want to shake hands. Any moment now, though he looked half-dead.

"Ah no, don't worry," he said, fearing any loud noises. "Maybe it's better to let him sleep."

"Are you sure? He'd love some company."

One of the man's eyes tried to open. It was now or never. Quinn made his move and, smiling at the woman, he backed out of the room. He reversed out the door, and if there was a prize for the quietest tip-toeing down a stairs, he would have won, though he wouldn't have stayed to collect. The heavy smell tried to hold onto him but he reached the front door, and the woman, like a phantom, was there behind him. She let him out, they said goodbye, and Quinn breathed the air of life outside. *It most definitely couldn't be him.*

58. That's Better

I woke to the sound of the bedroom door closing and someone coming in.

"What are you doing?" I whispered.

"What did you say?"

"What are you doing here?"

"Don't start that again. You wouldn't answer your phone. I knew where the key was and came over."

Suzanne was wearing yellow.

"I didn't know if I'd find you alive. You hadn't eaten in a while, but I was able to drown you with water."

I closed my eyes and felt her holding my hand. But then I heard the door open again, and I looked up to see an older woman in the room.

"This is my mam, Michael. She used to be a nurse, and I didn't want to come on my own."

The woman had a cloth and one of my vases in her hands.

"Hello Mrs....?"

"Canavan."

I heard Suzanne say, "Mam thought we couldn't take you to a hospital, Michael. Did we do the right thing?" before I fell asleep.

Suzanne stayed with me for two more days. Her mother came in and out, talking about Ireland in the twenties as if she had been there, talking about her father as if I was him. The color came back to my cheeks, and those cheeks filled up. I began to feel better than I ever had, a funny thing after a slow dance with death.

"There was a policeman here, and he was looking for you," Suzanne told me the day they left.

"Did he find me?"

"I doubt if he knew what he found. He found Mam."

I asked her what her mother had said to him, and there was nothing that couldn't be disproved in the future, nothing I couldn't confirm, should it ever come to that. But Suzanne still skirted around the big issue, the one about what I had done.

"Something's snapped in the country," she said. "People are talking about all those men from the past."

"What are they saying about the North?"

Her face turned grave. "The South wants it back."

I lay on the pillow and closed my eyes. This was the feeling, this was what I wanted to feel, and I only realized it now. If I never felt anything again in my life, this would be enough. My father's words didn't matter anymore, Cathal's stories faded into the air. This was the right way, the good thing, the only good thing. I would see it to the end.

"The British army's moved in," Suzanne said. "There used to be walls that kept the sides apart, but someone thought it was a good idea to get rid of them."

"The walls are down? My little name must be gone."

"Your name?"

"You have to get away from here, Suzanne. You saved my life, and I can't ask you to get into trouble for me."

"And you saved my son. You brought him out of a pit when no one else could, and that's the most important thing anyone's ever done for me. But he's the most important thing in my life, and I know we have to go.

"Mam thinks you're a hero, and she's told me to go easy on you. I know the stories about what her father did, fighting for the country. I wish I was more like him, but I'm not. I'm sorry for lying to you."

"You wanted help for Kieran, I would have done the same."

"It's more than that. I'm not a good person, which is probably why I'm here. I never had back problems. I don't work in Tesco because I was sick. I've a record, and you don't get many companies who hire people with those."

"A criminal record?"

"Shoplifting. A few years ago. They caught me eventually, when they realized a well-dressed woman can have itchy fingers. But my marriage had fallen apart and I know I was only trying to get some control in my life. It's not important anyway."

"You lied to me?"

"I did, I'm sorry."

"No, I mean, you lied to me."

"I did. Sorry?"

"I could always spot a liar up to now. Come closer."

I sat up in the bed. Any politeness in me had gone and I held her upper arms.

"You don't blush or twitch or blink too many times when you're lying?"

"Is that a bad thing?"

"Pathological. Tell me a lie, I want to see it."

She thought for a moment and said, "I don't want to be here."

Her pupils dilated, black circles taking the whole of me in.

"And I love mashed potatoes."

"You don't?"

"Can't stand them."

She brought my two hands up to her chest and kissed them. She must have seen something in me, she must have thought that I was in some way a good man. Because she sat with me for so long that it seemed like she never wanted to leave. And I told her everything.

But the thought of her or her family being damaged by what I was doing would have crushed me. She'd go back home and get on with her life, not knowing that Terry was protecting her. And I had to get away too, not because the police had been knocking and anywhere else in the world would have been safer, but because of the final name on the list that had to be ticked off. I thought about that name as I lay in the bed, as I heard Suzanne and her mother leave the house. I thought about it for hours, as the light in the room dimmed to black.

59. Which Flavor

"There are sixteen possible Lecky targets, and at least two officers will be on each of them from today. It'll be full uniform," Booth explained to a packed briefing room.

"That might put us at risk," Liam said.

"It's part of the visible policing scheme. You'll be watching several members of the public, and if one of those individuals were to be targeted and taken out, we'd be blamed for using them as bait. Full uniform. How far are we with the Gleesons?"

"A Joseph Gleeson from Belfast is a possible suspect in the 1974 incident in Lucan's home. But it's Michael Gleeson, probably his son, who's the lead suspect in the current homicides. His name has been confirmed by Paul Priestley, and he's been linked to a known Provisional IRA member in the Republic of Ireland."

"The PSNI and the Irish police are interviewing every man of that name," Maggie contributed, "but it's a common name and if there were paramilitary links, he could have disappeared."

"Then we're right to focus on the target," Booth said, and he handed the floor to an intelligence officer standing at a whiteboard in the center of the room.

"This is a list of sixteen adults in the U.K. with Lecky as a surname, middle name, or maiden name. The number of Leckys started out at over a thousand and has been narrowed down to direct descendants only, focusing on individuals who are in some way similar to the previous victims."

"We have to decide what type of Lecky the killer is after," Booth said. He stared at the names on the list, their addresses and occupations beside them.

"There's an Andrew Lecky in Edinburgh who's a journalist," Maggie said. "And Evan Scott Trevelyan was a journalist."

"Andrew Lecky covers science news for an American journal and is out of the country for most of the year," the intelligence officer replied, "so we feel he would be a low-level target."

"What about that one, Rosemary Lecky?" Liam asked. "She's unemployed, like Hograve was."

"Technically she is," the officer said, "but she's also the head of the largest disabled-rights advocacy group in England. Again, an unlikely target, but we're hesitant to rule anyone out."

"There must be an obvious one, one we're not seeing," Maggie said.

"I've been following a few Leckys on Twitter to check for anything noticeable. There's one who's a politician, and his feed is interesting…"

"There's a Lecky who's a politician?" Booth shot out. "He's not on the list."

"He is on the list, but it says he sells cars. He's running for local elections."

"Where does he live?"

"In Clerkenwell, Islington."

"And his profile?"

"Fifty-eight, divorced with two sons, and he owns two showrooms. Excuse my language, sir, but he's a bit of a dickhead. He's running for reelection on an anti-immigration platform."

"O'Malley and Doran, get over to him immediately," Booth ordered, and the officers ran out of the room.

*****

The political offices of Gareth Lecky consisted of a few well-appointed rooms on top of a Chinese restaurant. It wasn't Parliament, but he knew he'd get there one day. And for now, they were his offices, his castle.

And in his castle, he wasn't alarmed when Detectives Doran and O'Malley searched the rooms and told him there'd be a police detail following him for a while, in case he should run into trouble.

"Is it to do with those killings in the papers?"

"We can't say. We just want to make you aware of the situation," Liam said. "Take someone with you if you're going anywhere."

"Do you have a name?"

"Not at this time."

Lecky puffed out his chest. "Should I carry a gun?"

"Do you own a registered firearm, Mr. Lecky?" Maggie asked.

"No. I just wondered." His chest puffed back down.

"Don't carry any guns, sir," she cautioned.

"Will this impact on my campaign?"

"In what way?"

"I can't stop going around the houses." But something occurred to him and his eyes opened wide. "And now I'm a marked man. Fighting for justice."

"Just don't go anywhere on your own, and give us a list of places you'll be visiting this evening. Tomorrow morning, call this number at Scotland Yard and outline exactly where you'll be all day."

The officers left Lecky and waited outside in the car. By the time he finished work that evening, he had a skinny man accompanying him. Maggie and Liam followed the pair to the local store for cigarettes and then to the Princess Louise for a pint, where the officers sat outside in the car for two hours.

"I like being back in uniform," Maggie said while they waited.

"I feel like a target."

"I suppose we don't really blend in with these vests. But I'm not crazy about blending in."

She remembered when she first arrived at Scotland Yard and quite fancied the idea of keeping her head down. She smiled at her own naivete.

When the officers went into the pub to check on Lecky, he was nowhere to be found. Liam radioed in the situation, but after a few minutes, word came back that Lecky wasn't answering his phone and couldn't be contacted at any of the places on the list that he'd given them. The officers radioed back for assistance, for any patrol cars in the area to help out. The only thing they could do was to check every pub in the region. It would be a full three hours by the time they pulled up outside the beautiful old-fashioned Lamb, on Lamb's Conduit Street in Bloomsbury.

60. Lovely Lecky

Turlough looked pleased when I came into the Lamb, a busy place in Bloomsbury. It was a wonderful pub, catching weary visitors to Great Ormond Street Hospital across the road, delaying travelers with suitcases on their way to Saint Pancras Station. He had two Guinness in front of him, at a high table in a small snug behind the bar. He waved when he saw me, and we well shook hands.

"How's all?" I asked.

"Not bad. One more to do?"

"One more." I didn't look excited at the prospect.

"You don't think you can find him?"

"I don't know how you do it, Turlough. I don't know where to start. I have his work address, and that's it. He wasn't there this evening."

"I've been doing this a long time."

"And now you won't have to anymore."

"I'll be able to do other things."

"Like what?"

"I've no idea. I'm good at languages, or at least I have a few."

"How many?"

"Ten more than I need."

The noise of the pub increased, and the lights came on in increments. A dark Friday night, and the place was filling up.

"I can help you with this one," he said.

"You won't. You've made a good decision, the most important of your life. Don't go back on it now."

He nodded and sipped again. "I have his home address, if you want it."

"I might take it off you."

"And I can show you where he is."

"Don't worry about ..."

Turlough's finger was pointing out of the snug and into the main area.

"He's here?"

"You'll hear him," and he took another sip.

I heard a lot of voices, men and women and laughing from both, but none stood out.

"He was at another place first," Turlough said, "but it wasn't safe for you. He had to leave when some Irishman started rambling on at him. He's not a very sympathetic politician."

"Was it you? Were you seen?"

"No one ever sees me, Dr. Gleeson. He's out with his campaigners tonight. I know all of their names by now."

I had to get a better look. I strolled to the bathroom and as I did, a man shot up from his seat and almost banged into my face. No sorry from him, but one from me. On my way back, the man was standing, shouting some funny story at listeners three tables away, letting everyone hear his words. Plates of pub food were coming out from the bar, and he swayed to let the servers reach the tables.

"That's him," Turlough said as I sat down.

We sat a little longer and discussed the traffic in London and the lighting in the pub. I told Turlough about a book I was reading, and he told me about a touch of tendonitis he had in his wrist. I took a look at it and advised him to use a topical anti-inflammatory cream and to do some strengthening exercises. And then I told him to go. Like the very first day I met him, I didn't want him around, but for very different reasons.

"I can stay an hour longer," he offered.

"This has to be just me. But if there's anything you need in the future, let me know, though I'm not sure I'll be available for a while."

"Same for me," he said warmly, and with a long shake of the hand and an embrace of my arm, he walked out of the pub and was gone.

I felt alone when he left, on my own and out of sight. I sat for a few minutes before moving to the main bar, onto one of the few empty barstools. I ordered a diet coke to keep clearheaded, a gin and tonic to make me smile.

Lecky got my full attention from then on, whether I wanted to give it or not. His talk was about some football team and how it was no good, how there were no real English players left. A nationalist, but no different from any other football fan anywhere in the world. He came up to the bar to buy a round and it was my happy fortune that he stood beside me, shaking a few pounds at the barman. I stared into the mirror above the bar to see his face. The same type of face, perhaps, as the one that stood outside Delphi Lodge before the walking dead.

"You should take your scarf off," he said to me, looking at it hanging loosely around my neck.

I turned to him. "I should, maybe I will."

"Where are you from?"

"Ireland."

He punched his lips out as if saying, oh, that's what the sound is, and he went back to looking at the bar, this time in the mirror, staring at me and stopping me from staring back.

"There's a lot of Irish over here," he began again. "I suppose they feel like it's home."

"It's a little different."

"Not really. The football players are the same. The queen is ours."

"She is. We don't have one."

"Great for tourists."

I nodded.

"I'm running now ..." He started the sentence again. "Let me ask you a question. I'm running now, for local councilor, and I want to ask you this: how do I get the Irish to vote for me? My numbers are up with everyone else. But I can't seem to shift them."

"Oh, I'm not a politician."

"What are you?"

"A counselor, like yourself, but in a different way."

"What way?"

"A shrink."

"Ouugh, a qualified man. I'll drink to you," and with the arrival of his pint, he raised his glass and toasted me. And then he left.

It was barely a minute before he called me from his seat.

"Hey, man, counselor. Counselor."

I turned around to see him gesturing. "Come over here. Sit here."

With a smile, I held up my hand to say no thanks, but he was up from his seat and at me.

"Listen, mate, we'd like you to join us."

"I'm sorry, but I have to go home."

"Ah, really? If I buy you a quick pint, will you stay for that?"

I declined again, and deep in my heart I knew I wasn't going to get Mr. Lecky. In this short time, I'd learned enough about him to know that he was a buffoon, an attention-seeker, loud and harmless. I wasn't able to finish Hograve, and I couldn't do Lecky. He was probably going to lose the local elections, and it would be because of the Irish. And that was enough for me. The Lecky of Doolough would be spinning in his grave, and it was good enough for me. And the North had started its rumblings anyway.

As Lecky went back to his seat, I stood up and took my coat from the stool. It was warm from where I'd been sitting on it, and I wrapped it comfortably around me.

And then I took it off.

Lecky had said something to his companions, and the distinct words I heard, the words I was meant to hear, were "Bloody Irish." I smiled and carried my coat and gin and tonic over to Mr. Lecky's table.

"I'd love to join you." I sat down.

"Great, good man," came from him, not in happiness but indignation. I'd finally seen sense.

His motley crew was a fabulous assortment of ballast, as the old ship's captains would say. Keeping Lecky afloat in his views but easy enough to be replaced if required. Believing in him until then, hoping his rising tide would lift their boats.

"We want to get the litter off the streets."

I figured he was speaking metaphorically.

"It sounds like a small thing, but dirty roads can bring everything down. So that's an important goal for me, getting cleaners out, maybe neighborhood groups to make the place better."

He added, "and of course, the neo-Nazis," and I wasn't sure whether he meant use them or lose them, because another man joined our table and diverted Lecky's attention.

"This guy, this guy here is another one of you. Patrick, meet Mr....what's your name again?"

"Hugh O'Neill." I stood up and shook his hand.

"This guy's great, aren't you, Paddy? He helps me with the leaflets."

"Where are you from?" the man asked me meekly, through the words of his boss.

"I'm from Dublin, just visiting."

"Ah, very good." His accent had drops of London in it, but it was still the soft Irish.

The pints came and went, with Lecky chastising me for not choosing the stronger English ale. But it was a friendly, buzzing place, and I knew I could easily get sucked into the atmosphere and have one too many for sense. When we got further into politics, however, my mind sharpened like a spike.

"That socialism is the way to go," Lecky told me. "They hate it in America, but they've got it all wrong."

"If people are unemployed, starving, you have to look after them."

He agreed with me, and then he just as quickly flipped, saying, "No, you have to help people to feed themselves. You can't give handouts to everyone, they'd never get anywhere."

"What if they couldn't feed themselves? What if there was no food left?"

"Like in Ethiopia? Then you'd have to get that Bob Geldof fella to do it," and he laughed at his own joke.

"Something must be going right in America," Patrick said, "because everyone wants to live there."

"Nah, they're all coming over here. Like you guys, the Irish, you've always come over here," Lecky told us. "And the Syrians, they're coming too. We'll have to stop them, though."

"Why?" I asked.

"The culture is too different. They'll never fit in. They get married at twelve, then it's handouts for life. It's too easy, and it breeds a bad feeling in the country. We'll take our fair share, but small enough that it isn't bad for the country."

"And when they become English?"

"Oh no, we can't be having that. The Irish knew their place, and I don't mean that in a bad way. But you brought your culture with you and it got mixed in with the English ways." He lowered his voice, "That doesn't happen with the darkies."

I needed a break from him. I went up to the bar and ordered another round. When I returned, he started again.

"So, what am I going to do about the Irish? I can't get them on my side. What do you think, Pat?"

"I don't know," he shook his head with a look of pain.

"See, he doesn't know. Nobody knows. It's the hardest problem I have. Well, there's another problem. Someone's out to get me because I'm fighting for my country, but I don't mind that."

I took a long drink, and then I brought him back. "No votes from the Irish?"

"No, and you see, they're going for this other fella, Jim Moriarty. His father was Irish or something, so they're sticking with him. I want to show them that it doesn't matter where their local councilor is from, they should just choose the right one."

"They're sticking with him because he's familiar?"

"They like to keep together. And I'm sure if I looked into my background, I'd find some Irish there, something I could use. But I won't do that, pander like that. I won't drop that low."

"Some Irishman who married into your line?"

"Yeah, I don't know about that. Maybe some Englishman who went into an Irish line," and he winked at me.

"They were too skinny to be gone into."

"What did you say?"

I gave him a neutral smile. "I heard your surname when I was a boy."

"You learned about the Leckys in school?"

"Well, my uncle never stopped talking about one of them."

"I bloody knew it. There was a Lecky in Ireland?"

"There was. A government man. He didn't marry in, though, at least I doubt it."

"He didn't like the look of the Irish women? They're not too bad. A bit weather-beaten."

"There were none left."

Lecky gave a quick snarl of disappointment. "Not to worry, but I knew my family was set apart. We've always been working for the common man." He tried to put his two hands on his chest, but it was difficult with a pint in one of them.

"Your father was Charles Lecky?"

"Charlie, yeah, that was him."

"And his father was also Charlie? It's all in the history books."

He didn't want to show any ignorance. "Yeah, Charlies. They're all Charlies, all the way back. I didn't get that name though, my brother got that."

"All the way back to William."

"Who was he?"

"One of your ancestors was called William Lecky."

"I don't think so. None of us are Williams."

"He was a Poor Law guardian, over in Mayo in the West of Ireland."

"A guardian," he said, looking chuffed.

"Six hundred people walked from their homes to see Mr. Lecky, to be given food."

"He was a great man."

"How can men feel themselves honored by the humiliation of their fellow beings?"

"What does that mean?"

"Gandhi said it. It's written on a commemorative plaque at Doolough."

"Did my fella feed him as well? What's that?"

He looked at what I was pulling out of my coat pocket, a line of rope with five knots at intervals. A fine line of rope, bigger and thicker than a washing line, like a rope you'd use on a ship if you had been a pirate many years ago. And he thought nothing of it.

"The six hundred didn't all make it, but some of them did. And Colonel Lecky and Mr. Hograve came out to look at them, both of them Poor Law guardians, both of them elected to help the poor. In a country that wasn't theirs. Eating Irish food. And without a thought, they sent everyone home. Most of the six hundred died. These represent the five I'll have in order to make up for that. And this is for Honoria Gleeson."

I swung the rope around his neck and rose up. I drew him to me. I pulled the ends and his hands came up and went for my face. I was too tall and too bent backwards to let him grab me. I was going to rip the cord through his throat before he had time to suffocate. Pulling him back, back into my stomach, gripping the cord tighter and swearing I'd pull it all the way through.

Shouts from our table and two figures stood up, but I didn't let go. Lecky was crawing, guttural sounds from his breaking throat and I took the two ends in one hand and twisted both tighter.

Arms tried to pull me, and my free hand pushed them away, and I took Lecky even further back, closer to the ground. Two men at my side trying to lift me but every second was nearing the end of this man and I didn't care that they were hitting me in the face, and the people in front were shouting, shouting at someone to ring the police, shouting at the barman, looking at Lecky's bloodshot eyes and his big open gob as his tongue came out to get the smallest bit of air. Lecky was going to die, and I didn't care if I did too. I was going to finish it.

A bang to my head sent me to the right and I let go of the rope to stop me from hitting the floor. Another bang to the back of my head and it was hard because it kept me down there, with Lecky's head near my knees and the chair gone from under him. And a smaller blow and people were dragging me away from the wheezing man, further away from his throat. Pulling me by the arms, across the carpet, screams in my ears about what the fuck was I doing.

I lurched forward to get back to him, and a knife came out between me and him. "Get the fuck back!" its owner shouted. I grabbed the arm, but the blade came up to my eyes. And then the arm jerked back with a howl, and its owner fell to the ground beside me. A foot to his jaw knocked him into a doze.

"Everyone back," someone said, but not in the frenzied squeals that had come before. Controlled, in charge. A man pointing something at the crowd. The room went quiet and the knife dropped down beside me, and I took it and bent forward to Lecky's coughing head. I slit down hard on his throat as he tried to grab my hand, squirting the blood from his neck onto himself, my coat, the table, the dark floor. I heard gasps of breath but no screams, as Lecky jerked to death, and one arm lifted me up and I got to my feet and ran out the door with Turlough.

Two cars screeched to a brake at the path, police cars with doors swinging open and we ran to the right. Shouts of "Stop!" and we heard the feet behind us and the wail of cars following after.

Turlough had his gun out and he turned and shot twice, hitting a tire of the nearest police car. The car skidded and blocked the way between us and the running police, their guns now out as well, and we ran for our lives down the street, for the corner at the top of the road.

"My car's here!" Turlough said in his sprint beside me, and I knew I could have gone on. I knew I could have got away. But I stopped in my tracks and he turned to look at me.

"Go now," I shouted. He didn't move.

"This is the plan!" I said with entire conviction, "I have to stay," and he must have believed me because he turned on his heel and ran to his car. I heard it pull away.

I was flung to the ground by two officers and two others ran by me after Turlough. Words were shouted and I was handcuffed, and the running police returned out of breath. My wrists were cuffed tight and I was covered in blood and the sound of an ambulance grew louder in a nearby street.

*****

And back in the lovely old-fashioned Lamb, the man who everyone called Paddy finished his pint as he waited for the fuss to die down, for the witnesses to get over their crying so that they could be medically assessed and have their statements taken. He gave a little chuckle that nobody saw. *At least he won't be calling me Paddy anymore*, Stephen thought to himself.

61. Seeing Stars

Liam was down on the ground, and Maggie didn't register that she was staring at him. He'd been blown two meters off his feet by what he thought was a kick to the chest. But there was no one there, and then a bang to the head took that wonder away.

"Someone's on me," he called out, but he could only see a black sky.

A scream frightened the life out of him. It sounded like Maggie; she must have been hurt. But he couldn't get up, he couldn't move his head, and someone dropped down beside him. Maggie was talking to him, and he heard the sounds but not the end of the sentence, then more sounds and not the end again. Why was she shouting, and why couldn't he get this weight off his chest?

Her hand was over him, moving across his body, but he only saw her do it, he couldn't feel the touch.

"Oh fuck, Liam, oh fuck," she said, and there were tears in her eyes and she had a runny nose, and he hoped it wasn't running onto his face. He laughed, and his chest tightened, and he wasn't going to do that again.

"Don't move. You've been shot."

"Shot?"

"Don't speak, don't move."

He tried to move.

An ambulance was there within minutes, and the paramedics checked him while he was on the ground. It was cold on the road, and the back of his head hurt. When they said he could stand, he needed Maggie's help.

Liam protested that he was fine, but he was taken by ambulance to University College Hospital, a five-minute journey that ended with him realizing he was the luckiest man alive. Maggie was with him, taking off his vest, and she got a look of horror when she pulled up his undershirt to see a screaming black bruise covering the center of his body.

"Full uniform, Maggie."

The medical staff opened the ambulance doors and asked politely if they could have him. They really should get him into the hospital as quickly as possible, they said, because they had to check his chest and head. Besides, there were other calls for them to answer that night. Maggie saw him safely inside, then she tore as fast as she could to the offices of Scotland Yard.

62. I Can Explain

The British police were very kind, partly, I think, because they couldn't quite believe it. But the truth in all its six-foot-four glory sat in front of them. At least thirty people had seen me choke and knife Gareth Lecky to death. And in a warm interrogation room in Scotland Yard, I admitted everything.

"I did it," I told a man by the name of William Booth, an Englishman with an Irishman's nose.

"We'll have to start at the beginning."

"That's what I say to my clients."

"Everything will be videotaped from now on. Who was the man with you?"

"I've no idea. I guess he saw me getting hit and came to my aid."

"You'd never seen him before?"

"Never. I barely saw him last night."

"Was he with you when Detective O'Malley was assaulted in the Connaught Hotel?"

"I saw her fall, and I hope she was okay. But I didn't see who did it. I was thinking about my own predicament."

"Did you know the man you attacked in the Lamb?"

"Gareth Lecky? Not personally, but I know of him."

"Why did you attack him?"

"His ancestor killed a lot of people."

"On the Doolough walk?"

"You know it?"

"Have you attacked anyone else recently?"

"I have. Wait, who do you mean?"

"Can you name them all for me?"

"This is a strange game, when there's no need for it. Lucan, Trevelyan, Cromwell, and Lecky."

"And a woman called Hograve?"

"Is she saying I attacked her? Because the bat that came down on my head was the first altercation between us."

"She hit you and then you shot her?"

"Shot her? I didn't shoot her at all."

"She was shot dead. Her neighbors heard the name 'Michael' being called out, and her children have described seeing a man similar to you."

"Oh." I remembered Redser. Maybe he did it because she had seen us, or maybe he did it just because he could.

"Mr. Gleeson?"

"Her children might have some type of life now."

"After their mother is murdered?"

"The loss of a parent leaves a hole that may never be filled, but it can be carried around for life. Abuse and neglect do the opposite. They touch every part, stunting yet exploding. Everything grows black. Twisted and curled."

"Mr. Gleeson, are you admitting to the deaths of Richard John Bingham, Evan Scott Trevelyan, Barnaby Cromwell Hutchinson, and Gareth James Lecky?"

"I am."

"What made you do it?"

"Historical revenge."

"I haven't heard that one before."

Booth asked me a few times if I wanted a lawyer, but I said I'd wait until later. There was no rush over anything now, seeing as Turlough had got away. I was brought coffee and chocolate, and it was a long night, though not as long as it could have been. I told Booth and his officers that I had chosen five targets, researched their backgrounds and foregrounds, and decided how they would die. Any questions they asked, I answered.

"You shot Evan Scott Trevelyan from a distance of 1600 meters. How did you do that?"

"I took lessons. Here and in Ireland."

"The shot was remarkable."

"Thank you."

"Can you prove you took it?"

"I have to prove I'm good enough to kill someone? That might self-incriminate me, and I can do that in easier ways. I have all the receipts."

"Receipts?"

"For my hours of shooting."

Booth looked dumbfounded. "Why are you telling us this?"

"I achieved what I wanted, Superintendent. It doesn't matter if I go to prison. I never thought I'd be much good at spending years on the run."

"This is bizarre," he almost laughed. "You're a clever man. All this for idealism?"

"Men have done more for less. And Ireland is twitching now. The North will be back where it belongs."

"What about the head? Did you do that too?" A familiar face came into the room.

"Hello," I said to Detective O'Malley.

She pulled over a seat without dropping a glare that told me I'd be in trouble if the table wasn't between us.

"A crockpot for several days. I was glad when it was over."

"Where did you do it?" she asked.

"In a house in Southampton. I'm still paying the rent."

"We have footage from Westminster," Booth said, "and it shows you putting the head on the spike."

"Is that a question?"

"Can you confirm it was you?"

"I can. I dropped it before putting it on. I wanted to get away quickly and the railing was rather high."

"And Lucan in South Africa? You went down there to get him?"

"Africa isn't really a 'down there' place. He was in a village outside Johannesburg."

"How did you find him?"

"One of my late patients was an aid worker in the area in the nineties. She saw some terrible things, but she also saw the beautiful Lucan. He was the first, so I was a little nervous."

"You kicked his head in."

"His family wasn't congenial."

"The previous earl?"

"I would have preferred to have got him."

"The pub goers will identify you as the person who attacked Gareth Lecky."

"And they'd be right."

"But who was the man with you?" O'Malley asked.

"I'm afraid I don't know."

"It's very strange that you choke a man to death and another man appears with a gun and pulls you to safety."

"It is very strange, but I didn't choke Lecky to death, I slit his throat, and I didn't see any gun in the pub. And it looks like I'm not very safe at the moment."

"We're going to keep looking for him. We'll find him."

"You probably will. But you can't threaten me with that because I'd say I'm in trouble enough."

"But you were a respected doctor," Booth said, "a wealthy man, and you couldn't let this lie? Couldn't you have complained about the injustice done to Ireland in the newspapers? Written a book?"

"Would a few words that nobody reads have gotten the North back? How many books have been written already? In any case, I'm guessing you know my background."

"Your father, Joseph Gleeson? And Cathal McConnell, your uncle."

"What happened was inevitable."

"It had been festering in you?"

"All my life."

"And how do you feel now?"

"I haven't had a chance to think about it, but seeing as you ask ..." I took a moment to reflect. "...I can't hear the curses anymore; the air is gone quiet. It's like I've finished an exam, and I've passed every part. I'm excited and I'm tired. And the funniest thing of all, my mind is as clear as a bell."

The witness statements were taken, and taken again. And no one knew the man who had come to my aid. He had never been seen in the pub before, and several of the witness descriptions of him didn't match. It was like he had just come up from the ground, like a ghost, one of the *Sídhe* folk in the old Irish tales, the ones who disappear.

*****

Booth was called outside at one point, and the recording was stopped. I was left in the hands of Officer O'Malley, capable or not, I didn't know. I was about to ask her which part of Ireland she came from when she did a barely perceptible thing that surprised me. She bent her head closer to the table and back up again, then down again a couple of times more. All the while humming a song that was too gentle for the circumstances or the surroundings. Her movement was self-comforting, like a polar bear stuck in a zoo with nothing to do except go quietly mad.

"I can't talk to you," she said, seeing me look at her.

"Because the equipment's turned off?"

"Because the words from your mouth make me want to cut the tongue from your head."

"They used to cut the nipples off failed Irish chieftains in the old days, so you'd almost be following a tradition."

"Stop it!" she yelled. "Stop laughing at this."

"I'm sorry, Officer. It's an unusual situation for me to be in. What's your first name again?"

"Maggie."

"And the other man is ...?"

"William Booth."

"I mean the man who got shot."

"It doesn't matter what his name is."

"Is he badly hurt?"

"He was shot. Isn't that enough?"

"It is. And he shouldn't have been."

"Do you want to kill every Englishman there is? Because there's quite a few of them. And Irish people too, when they get in the way?"

"It's the hardest thing in the world to see someone you love get hurt."

"Love? Are you talking about me or yourself?"

"You want to kill me, Maggie, so you must care very deeply for the man who got shot."

"He's my partner. Colleague." She blushed, and suspected she was more human than she'd like to admit.

"Where in the body was he shot?"

"In the chest."

She rubbed her closed fist across her mouth a few times, stopping herself from saying anything.

"The song you were humming, do you know what it is?" I asked.

"What song?"

"The song that's probably going around in your head the whole time. *Your* song."

"'The Drunken Sailor?' That's not mine."

"If you don't want it in your head anymore, you can get rid of it by singing it to the end. Then the brain knows it's finished and moves on."

"Is that so?"

"So they say. You didn't know that it's your song? The tune is from another song. A much older one. The lyrics are a bit different than shaving a drunken man's chest."

"I don't know it."

"Óró Sé do Bheatha 'Bhaile."

"I don't know what you said there."

"You've no Irish?"

"English works just fine."

I gave her the first verse of the song, half-singing and half-speaking it:

"'Sé do bheatha, a bhean ba léanmhar,
Do b' é ár gcreach tú bheith i ngéibheann,
Do dhúiche bhreá i seilbh méirleach,
Is tú díolta leis na Gallaibh."

She looked at me as if she'd never heard anything more ugly in her life.

"I won't sing again."

"What does it mean?" she asked half-heartedly.

"It says, "Welcome, lady, who faced such troubles. Your capture brought us to our ruin, with our fine land usurped by thieves and you sold to the foreigners.""

"Words from a million years ago."

"A few hundred, anyway. But you're facing troubles now, and I'm sorry for that. If your friend was shot in the chest, I hope the Kevlar did its job."

"You just look after yourself." She paused a moment. "How do you know he was wearing a vest?"

"Because you wouldn't be here if he wasn't. You'd be with him."

"Shut up now. Keep your mouth closed until the superintendent gets back."

But there was too much she wanted to know, and she soon spoke again.

"Did it seem normal to kill just for land?"

"That's what people have always done."

"Nobody cares about that fight anymore. The country's moved on."

"Which country? The Republic? Have you ever been to a football match, or a rugby game, and Ireland's playing and half the stands are filled with Irish people?"

"So what?"

"We're not the best-looking race in the world, and I count myself among that, but it doesn't matter when we're on those stands, because we turn into the most beautiful people on earth. One voice starts to sing "The Fields of Athenry," then another joins in, and the row catches the tune. And in a second, they're all singing, drowning out the stadium. Making the stands hum. Bringing tears to their eyes, and the singing can't be stopped."

"And?"

"They're usually southerners doing the singing, people from Cork and Galway and Dublin and everywhere in between. People who've never seen the fighting up north, but they have some small idea in their head that their granddad or someone way back fought for the Republic's independence. They're singing about the past, sharing something with their ancestors, thinking those ancestors might be proud of the words. But they're also lamenting the future, singing a wish that can't be spoken, something the media or their friends or their neighbors would condemn them for. Something that would turn them into what is seen as the worst thing in the world today: a Republican. But in the huge stadiums, with everyone else doing it, they can sing free. They're all Republicans.

"And you know what the funny thing is? If the six counties of the North were back in Irish hands, there'd be no singing at football matches. There'd be no reason for it, nothing to sing for, no declaration of unity against a stronger power. They wouldn't sing for the past, because that would be funny; it'd make them feel like victims who should be moving on. But they can sing now, at the football matches or in the pubs at the end of the night, when the Guinness has loosened their tongues and their hearts, and the tight barbed wire around the feeling that they're not meant to have unfurls for just a second. A part of Ireland is still missing. That's why they sing."

She didn't answer me.

"If I'm wrong in what I've done, then the old heroes of Ireland must have been wrong too. Michael Collins, Padraig Pearse, Daniel O'Connell. All the men we know and the millions we don't. The ancestors back in my line, in yours. All the Gráinne Mhaols."

"The who?"

"Gráinne Mhaol, the lady from your song. Or Gráinne Ó Máille, as she's properly known. Grace O'Malley in English, the same surname as yourself. The pirate queen of Ireland. Though I think she may have attacked as many Irish as she did English. But wasn't that our problem all along? We couldn't stick together until we couldn't stand it anymore."

"Grace O'Malley is in the song?"

"She is. The sixteenth-century chief of the O'Malley clan. The second verse of the song says that she comes over the sea, with warriors protecting her. They're Irishmen, not French or Spanish, and they'll get rid of the foreigners. So every time you think of "Drunken Sailor," think of that."

"It's a small world," she said dryly.

"For the Irish it is. And it should be bigger."

"You should have left it alone, Mr. Gleeson."

"But they still have the head of us."

"The head?"

"Northern Ireland, the top of the country. It's where the brains would be. It matters to me, and whether or not they admit it, it matters to the people singing in the stands."

Whatever I thought she was, she suddenly changed before me. Her volume shot up and her young face turned ugly, with a hatred that could have been stored for many years:

"It didn't matter to my father, when you lot destroyed him. All that mattered to him was his family and keeping the peace. Two daughters he left behind, because of your bloody love of land. Wrecking generations because you happened to be born there. I hope the North never gets back into Irish hands, because there's too much blood in the soil for it to be worth anything ever again!"

Our talk was stopped by Booth's return. Officer O'Malley used the pause to stop herself from shaking.

"Michael, I've some bad news. Your uncle Cathal McConnell, he's from Carrickmacross in County Monaghan, isn't he?"

It had been many years since I'd been interrogated about Cathal, but I felt it was fine to open up about him now. I said that he was.

"I'm afraid he's dead."

"Cathal?" I pictured the old man's face at his kitchen table.

"He was killed in Belfast."

"He's fairly old. Did you say killed?"

"I don't have the details, but it seems he was involved in an incident. You don't look well, Michael."

"Was he pushed into a ditch?"

"A ditch? No. Something happened in Belfast. I don't have further information at the moment. Was Cathal involved in anything subversive?"

"What kind of incident?"

"I don't know. Was he part of anything paramilitary?"

"I've hardly seen him in years."

Cathal was dead, and I might never find out why he'd pulled a gun on me. The little shite. Uncle Cathal, with his chickens and his sprays and Dolores and the gun. And I barely knew him, the man himself. My poor, twisted uncle Cathal. Whatever else I thought about him, I sincerely hoped that his death was easier than his life.

And then I found out that it wasn't.

63. Cuffs

"I believe your own lawyer isn't a criminal defense one?"

"I doubt it. Wills and mortgages."

"We'll see how we get on." My barrister was Alan Merriman, a man with soft hands and hints of grey. He told me he was very sorry to hear about my uncle and I asked him how he got the hopeless case.

"Yours isn't that hopeless. Not if you had motivation behind you." He fixed his cuff with one hand.

"You had to take it?"

He fixed the other cuff. "I'll do my very best for you."

It seemed like Merriman was telling me about another death in the family when he said I wouldn't have access to the Internet. And it seemed like he was telling me it was myself who had died when he said I shouldn't read the newspapers. I was being attacked in them, especially the British ones, but I had to remember that there were two sides to every story. I told him there was only one side, the side that actually happened, and only I knew about that.

That night, I wondered if the ham I'd eaten for dinner had gone off. Something was stuck in my gullet and it wouldn't come up or go down. I didn't cry about Cathal, but my throat ached. The Republican who wanted to be a farmer, the man who pulled a gun on his nephew and never explained why.

When Merriman arrived the next morning, I asked him how he was going to handle the case.

"Temporary insanity looks the best option."

"My temporary insanity lasted a long time."

"It might be our only chance. You'll be up on four charges of murder. Hograve is still being investigated. Michael, the people you chose were not the most pleasant. Was that intentional?"

"I wanted the worst of the worst blood."

"I don't think that will help in mitigation."

"Then I'll take you out of your misery, Alan. I want you to contact someone for me, and you'll have to fly him over as soon as possible. I don't think he'll mind."

For the first time, Merriman looked relieved, remembering that the man opposite him was after all a respected psychiatrist who'd committed several murders with ease, someone who might know something he didn't.

*****

Merriman was with me a few days later when a small man wheeled a large suitcase into my cell. He told the officer he didn't need any help.

"Are you the man?" Mikkel Kardonovski asked me, though undoubtedly I was, sitting in prison overalls and with handcuffs on my lap. I shook his hand as best I could.

"And this is my lawyer."

Kardonovski shook Merriman's hand briefly and sat in a chair, placing the suitcase against his legs as if he was worried that I or the barrister or the quiet standing cop would take it and run. Merriman began to speak, but Kardonovski cut him off, addressing me.

"I've read what you sent. Is it still there?"

"It is."

"And do they know about it?"

"Not over here."

"It'll have to come out."

"I think so too."

"I'm glad I can talk to you about this. I don't have to explain everything." He looked warily at Merriman.

He opened his suitcase and pulled out his laptop and papers, though there were so many it was hard to know what was important. And myself and the surgeon and the concentrating Merriman sat there for hours and discussed every detail of what was known about glioblastoma tumors.

64. Defense

"He has a medical defense."

"What?" Maggie couldn't believe what Booth was saying. She felt her stomach drop.

"He has a brain tumor and he's applying to have it taken out."

"He killed four people. He told us that."

"I know. Alan Merriman will have to show cause and effect, that the tumor directly dictated Gleeson's behavior, and Merriman is a pretty average lawyer. But be prepared, Maggie – people have been acquitted before using this defense."

She felt the acid in her mouth. "He admitted everything."

"The defense will claim that his confession will have to be struck out because he wasn't himself when he made it. I know it sounds crazy."

"It was all a waste of time?" Maggie didn't wait for an answer. She walked out of Booth's office on shaky legs. She went over to Liam's desk, hoping to get any comfort, any words that would help. He was glued to Sky News on his screen.

"There's a chance Gleeson will get off," she told him.

His eyes didn't move. "Why?"

"A brain tumor."

"Look at this, Maggie, look at it."

"Didn't you hear me?"

"He's one man. This is a country that's collapsing."

Maggie looked at the screen. She saw the rolling headlines, updates on the collapse of Belfast, details of the spread of violence to all the larger towns of Northern Ireland. Soldiers were being shipped in from Britain, a countering movement of men was coming up from the Republic.

"He caused all this, and now he might get off?" she said.

"It wasn't him. A man was caught on camera being beaten by a British soldier. He beat him to death with his gun."

As Liam spoke, footage appeared of a distressed second lieutenant being taken away in an armored Land Rover, his white face croaking that the man was going to kill his family, he knew all about his family, repeating with the look of a madman that, "they're going to kill us all."

And then there were images of cars burning on streets in the dark, men in sports tops being arrested and taken into police vans, defiant eyes not hiding their fear. Women with scarves around their faces, their hair tied back, rifles in their hands. A politician who looked tired. A police commissioner who was short-tempered in an interview with the media. Belfast was burning, and there were no fire walls to stop the spread.

And finally, the Special Intergovernmental Advisor on Northern Ireland Affairs appeared on screen. Mr. Lawrence Grady looked ill, and his black pits were bloodshot. He delayed answering each question the interviewer asked him, and most of the answers he gave were the same.

"We need to calm everyone down, everyone has to work together," he said in almost a whisper.

When the interviewer asked him how he felt about his home crumbling, Mr. Grady looked like he was about to cry.

"The peace walls should never have been touched," he managed, and then he asked for the cameras to stop filming.

65. Taken Out

The petition on medical grounds was lodged with the Crown Court, and within a matter of days, Merriman received notice that I would be assessed for a tumor in the right cerebral hemisphere and, if positive, I would bypass the waiting list for a biopsy and removal in a public hospital. I knew they couldn't justify a private facility, but apart from the food, public was just as good. The surgeons were often the same as in a private hospital and the nurses were typically excellent. And I was still a doctor, so they might be doubly nice.

A CAT scan and an MRI, a biopsy on a Monday, and six hours of a Thursday that I can't remember. I woke up in a hospital bed with a shaved head and two policemen in the room. Another two were outside the door, and several more walked up and down the corridor outside. I wasn't handcuffed, but I was dizzy and had a splitting headache, so I wasn't going anywhere. I was happy to stare at the ceiling and listen to the beeping machines.

"Hello, Michael." A whisper to my left, beside me. It was a doctor with my chart on his lap and a retinal torch in his hands. As soon as I smiled, he placed a hand on my forehead and lifted the torch to my eyes.

"Are they constricting?" I asked.

"They are, you're fine."

"No brain injury?"

"Not on first look."

"Not anymore."

"How long have you known it was in there?"

"I suspected for a while. If it wasn't a glioblastoma, it was something much worse."

"What?"

"My personality. When can I get out of bed?"

"You've a few days before the trial starts, so rest until then."

"I might sleep well now, which hasn't happened in years."

He gave a slight nod and stood up. "There are police everywhere, Michael. I'm not even allowed to bring you newspapers, so all you can do is rest. That's all you can do." And he left me alone. Me and the beeping machines and the officers watching my every move. As if I could move.

66. The Beast

On the first day of the trial, Merriman said I was looking good, though I didn't notice.

"I'll do my best for you, Michael. And if I can't get you off, I'll throw the switch myself," he said lightheartedly.

"That doesn't make me feel any better, Alan."

"You won't feel any better until you're out of here, going for a pint. Until then, here's a few letters for you."

He handed me a lot more than a few. Some of them hate mail, some of them love letters, the writers of both as extreme as each other. A postcard that made me smile, wishing me well and saying I was in their thoughts, signed by "The Novice (and wife)." And a thick envelope from a familiar address in Monaghan. I thought about ripping it up, but I wanted to see what the old man in his ditch had to say:

Hi Michael,

I hope all goes well. I spent too much time in Belmarsh myself and I know it's not the best of them, but the guards will know we're related and they should go easy enough. I've put a few names on the back of this paper, good men I used to know, and if one or two of them haven't been released yet you'll be grand.

I found the last letter written by our friend. I think it must be the last because she was very old by then. Annie and Danny and Nora – those stories kept you awake a few nights, it's funny now to remember. It might cheer you up to know what happened to that side of your family, the Gleeson who got away. Maybe it will make you feel worse. So many things are complicated like that. Getting twisted in our heads.

My head was twisted, Michael, when Carmel died. Of all my sisters she was the one who saved me when our father passed away. She saved my head, when I would have torn it off me in anger. Even when she was dying, she was worrying about me still, thinking about how I'd be. And I wasn't well. I didn't take it well, Michael. I never thought about you, and that's what I'm sorry for. I wanted to wreck the world, and I only thought of myself, and how the hate swelled in me when she died.

Your father was a funny man, he had the heart of Ireland in him until he went to London. He got the order to bring down Henry Blackwell's pub, as part of the campaign in the city, but he had been over too long and he said he couldn't do it. It was like he joined the other side, but it wasn't really. He just met a man he liked. A man he liked enough to go after a lord for. And then you all had to come home and – my god – I battled for him, Michael. He had disobeyed an order and things didn't look good. I battled for him, up until your mother died and the battle in me turned on him.

I'm sorry I took away your father, though I'll never be sorry for twisting the neck of the man who killed my sister. But I'm sorry you were left on your own because of me, and I hope at least you felt loved when you were with us. You have the best of him in you, the best of Carmel, and even the best of me, though you won't want to know that now.

I want to do a bit of good, Michael, to make some kind of amends. Belfast's going to hell, the army's back and the streets are starting to look like the seventies again. We don't have the minis and the flares and the collars that would take the eye out of you, but the faces are how they were then, scared and angry and murderous. The little spark hasn't come yet, that will come tonight.

I've chosen a hateful man, less hateful than what he's lined up for but not far off. I started on him a few days ago, and by now he's almost fit to shoot me when he sees me coming up the road to him each morning. He's some kind of lieutenant, I got his name, and our lads already have a background on him. They even know his shoe size, though I don't know how or why they got that.

He can't shush me away, and I've done nothing I can get arrested for. So I bring my lunch from the house that I'm staying in and I stand for hours, near enough that he can hear me telling him the stories of the Troubles and what the Brits did to us and what we did to them. How it doesn't matter how old they get or where they get to, we find them in the end. How he should watch the windows around him for the pointing gun, watch the ground for the little boxes that will blow him to bits if he stands on them. I've thought about bringing a chair out to sit with him, and I might do that today. He can't do anything but listen – it might look like the seventies again around here, but the one thing that's changed is that everyone has their phones on them. God, we would have loved them back then. It might have sped things up. He can't move but he's being shot by someone with their camera, even the few tourists who are still hanging around.

Push them enough and the beasts come out. It's the same with us all. They try and train these army lads to be mad enough to kill, but sane enough to keep control, and the two just don't work together. Two signals that have to live in the same place in their head, fighting with each other. And when you've a gun in your hand and all you see is people who want you dead, who'll do anything to get you out of their home, it's the mad signal that always wins.

So tonight is the night, Michael. If I had been a psychiatrist like yourself I might have done things differently, but I know men enough to know that this Brit is about to burst. It'll be a long whisper tonight, it'll be the names of his family and where they live and what they're doing. Probably more than he knows himself. And it won't be a bargain I'll make with him, I'll only tell him how they're going to die. And if that doesn't get him going, then he must have some disease in his head, some disease other than a willingness to go into someone else's country and hate us for trying to wrench it back.

I thought your big plan was something foolish, Michael, one man trying to remake two countries. But that was before I remembered the dream I thought was long dead. I won't say what I'm doing is for you, because it's for Belfast and the North, but if it helps toward the end you have in mind then I'll die with a smile on my face.

I'm sending you my love, Michael. You're a true Gleeson, a true McConnell, and the kings of the clanns would have been proud of you. I'm sorry I won't see you again, that I can't see into the future, but I was happy to know you and to be a part of the past.

Uncle Cathal

I felt my heart skip or jump or do something that wasn't right. A few deep breaths and I'd be okay. But when my throat tightened and my belly let me know it was about to throw up, I made a run for the sink. And that was worse, because the lightheadedness took me and spun the room around, and I didn't make it halfway before I fell to the ground.

There were sounds around me, gentle sounds, and my arms were lifted and I felt something at my side, pulling me up. Sit here, sit down, the sounds said. For the shortest moment, I thought it was my father, then I thought it was the chest of my uncle, and then I was very happy that it was not. Merriman and the police officer, helping a tall man over to a small chair. I sat and looked up at them, and Cathal's words hit me like a baton to the face and my stomach took its chance to shine. All over my knees, all over the floor.

"Is it your head, Michael?" Merriman said in fright.

"My head?"

"Is the tumor back?"

"It's just some news, Alan."

He said I was paler than the wall behind me. Sitting in my own sick in my cell, wearing a coat of lies stretching back for years. I couldn't even begin to know what Cathal had said to me that I should be wondering about now. I could barely remember one word from him. What parts of my life had been real? Cathal had murdered my father, and I'd never picked up on the lies.

"Take as long as you need," Merriman said with a cough. He couldn't have had a more worried expression.

"I think I'll need new clothes."

I found it hard to dress because my fingertips were numb. It could have been the vomiting, the electrolyte balance gone awry. I imagined it was the start of my body fading out, disappearing from the extremities inwards. When the new suit was on, I righted myself, hoping the walk to the courtroom would give me enough time to compose myself into something resembling a man. I could slow down my breathing if it got too much, take control of my physical self to force the adrenaline to wash out of my blood. I knew all that, and I still felt like vomiting where I stood.

Middle-aged, no previous convictions, an upstanding member of society, I sounded like a fine individual in the opening arguments. Merriman said everything he was meant to, laying the foundation to prize open the jury's minds. The four people who were killed were killed by a tumor, he would tell them. He would say I didn't know what I was doing and that I didn't know what I was doing was wrong. I listened to every word, and I heard nothing.

The primary prosecution barrister was a woman in her fifties whose work, I'm sure, had only got better with age. She was acute – no waffle, no lies, no smile. She would have made a good psychiatrist, but her name made her a better lawyer. Connie Nettlefield replaced elaborate opening remarks with in-depth descriptions of the killings, advising the jury of the gruesome photographs they were about to see. The Lecky scene was the least pleasant of all, with the man pictured on the floor of the pub surrounded by a halo of blood. The feet of the bar chairs were visible, along with the red and brown carpet beneath, suggesting that he had just been enjoying a pint when he was killed.

Kardonovski was given time with us after the first session, and Merriman reiterated everything he could expect to be asked. As soon as Merriman left to check when the court would resume, Kardonovski moved closer to me and said, "You know what the big difference is? It's that the demon is out, and it's left a different person. *I* believe it's a different person, but *they* have to know. And they'll only do that if you believe it yourself." And then he looked at me for far too long, until Merriman returned to the cell. I had a strong impression that either Kardonovski was trying to tell me something or else he was a lunatic. I was still wondering which it was while I was being taken to the courtroom. Kardonovski's words going through my head, and by the time I reached the dock, the only look on my face was one that said I'd no hope in hell of acquittal.

67. A Different Man

"Your father was an active Republican?" Nettlefield began.

"I believe he was."

"And he told you about the history of Ireland, what happened to it over the centuries?"

"He told me what he knew."

"And on the night on which he's alleged to have attacked John Bingham's former wife and nanny in London, you were with him?"

"I was."

"How did that make you feel?"

Merriman tried to object, but the judge let me speak.

"He shouldn't have taken me."

"Because it traumatized you?"

"Because I tripped him up when he ran after Bingham. I got a box for that."

"A box?"

"A clip around the ear."

"Your father was violent towards you?"

"Parents were quicker with the slaps back then, that was all."

"And how did you feel, seeing your father murder someone?"

Objection from Merriman. There was never a trial for that murder.

"As a psychiatrist," she changed tactic, "would you believe that if an eleven-year-old child witnesses their father attacking someone, it might affect their mental health?"

Objection again; my medical opinion couldn't be sought. The judge upheld it, on the basis that a man who admitted to murdering four people could not be assumed to have a reputable professional opinion.

"Do you personally believe your father's action had an impact on you?" she tried once more.

"I don't know what he did that night. I only know I loved him very much, and he loved me. He told me that, at a time when most fathers never said it."

"But your father starved your mother to death?"

The courtroom buzzed with shock.

"Oh no!" I was barely heard over the noise. "That was a mercy killing. She was dying, she was very far gone ..."

"He sounds like a brutal man."

Nettlefield was twisting me into a product of my environment, far away from an unwilling vessel for a malicious tumor. Merriman had told me she would, he told me that my father would be brought up, that even my mother's death would be uncovered and addressed. But hearing it in a quiet cell was a world away from hearing it in a packed courtroom.

"Mr. Gleeson? Are you okay?" the judge asked me.

"Michael?" Merriman called over.

"I deserve what I get. Wherever I spend the rest of my life is nothing to how I feel inside. I cracked my soul with this, and sitting here for one more second is a second I don't deserve."

"Mr. Gleeson, this has to be a full trial," the judge said. "This is a murder trial, so we have to hear both sides of the argument."

"I don't have a side. I wrecked that when I stood on the head of John Bingham. This was meant to be for my country, for my father. The men who starved themselves with a hopeless cause. But it wasn't any of that. I don't know why I did it, but I do know it was me."

The room was hot and tired and the session ended with a hundred faces looking at me. Somebody shouted "Murderer!" and police officers were over to them in an instant. Somebody else shouted "Well done, Michael," with just the same result.

I was hurried back to the cell. There was no panic in me anymore, it had streamed out like air from the tiny hole you don't see at the base of a balloon. Everything was out of my control. Turlough was safe and Suzanne was safe, and everything was out of my control. I sat and ate something, I think. There was a stain on the arm of my jacket. And Suzanne was shown into the cell.

I stood up but wasn't allowed to touch her. Sitting two meters away, and I couldn't even take her hand. For some reason, that would have been all that I needed.

"What's gone wrong, Michael? I don't understand." She was on the verge of angry tears.

"Don't sit in court anymore, you don't need to hear those things."

"Why aren't you talking about history, about what all those men did to Ireland?"

"I can't."

"But if you tell the court about it, the jury will know. Everyone will know. They'll understand why you did it, or at least it'll help."

"I wasn't right to do anything."

"You weren't right? You weren't right about the country and doing whatever it took to have it whole again? Right about my grandfather and the old heroes and how they'd be turning in their graves if they knew what had happened to the North? And that the men back then are the same as you are now, with so much courage it could shake a country. That's what you have to say."

"You've changed, Suzanne." I thought at that moment that she was a ghost of the women of the Rising, the *Cumann na mBan,* the female gun runners and insurgents who threw off their long skirts in 1916 to step into a soldier's uniform.

"Don't look at me like that, Michael. Think about what you have to say. You can't end up in an English prison."

"I'm sorry. I can't talk about the past, and I can't explain why."

The officer told us our time was up. Suzanne looked at me with hopeless eyes as she was forced to stand and be shown out of the cell. I moved as close to her as I could before the officer stood between us. For the first time in my adult life, someone knew what I had been and cared for me because of it, not in spite of it. And I couldn't even take her hand in mine.

*****

When the court came back into session, Nettlefield called Paul Priestley as a witness for the prosecution. I couldn't look at him as he talked about my father. I wanted everything to wash away.

"Did you know the Gleesons when they lived in London?"

"I worked with Joseph Gleeson for three years, and I saw Michael often enough."

"What was Michael like?"

"He was a lovely lad. I used to take him driving. I did a terrible thing."

"What did you do?" Nettlefield said in surprise, wondering where her witness was going.

"I taught him how to drive, or I let him drive is more like it. Across the sand in West Wittering. I'm lucky we never crashed."

Nettlefield brought him back immediately.

"Michael Gleeson's father mentioned to you that he was going to attack Lord Lucan in his former home in 1974?"

"He didn't mention it to me. I heard him say it."

"To who?"

"Our boss, Henry Blackwell."

Objection from Merriman, on the grounds of hearsay, but the objection was overruled in the best interests of justice.

"Do you know if Joseph Gleeson went to the house that night?"

"I do."

"How do you know?"

Priestley didn't answer.

"How do you know, Mr. Priestley? You're under oath."

"I met him in a pub a few days afterwards, and he cried his eyes out. He was very upset that it had turned out that way."

"That he hadn't got Lord Lucan?"

"That he'd mixed up the wife and nanny."

"And where was Michael on the night of the attack?"

"He was with him."

"How do you know that?"

"I'm sorry, Michael."

"Don't speak to the accused, Mr. Priestley. How do you know?"

"He told me."

"When did he tell you?"

"Six weeks ago, when he called in to see me."

"So the eleven-year-old Michael Gleeson was there when his father is alleged to have killed Sandra Rivett and seriously injured Veronica Bingham?" Nettlefield turned to the jury. "And now Michael Gleeson claims that this extreme trauma is not the reason why he murdered four people, but that he murdered them because of a small brain growth that has appeared recently. I think the jury will know which is more likely. Thank you, Mr. Priestley, you can sit down."

68. An Educated Man

Mikkel Kardonovski sat in the witness box with his legs crossed. He listed his education and credentials, and Merriman asked him about his specialty.

"Neurolaw."

"Is that a new discipline?"

"It's relatively new. It's growing."

"Can you explain what neurolaw is?"

"It's the application of neurology to legal matters. The way in which discoveries in neuroscience impact the law, how they should impact the law."

"So it concerns how the brain effects behavior?"

"The brain always affects behavior. Neurolaw is concerned with how damage to the brain causes changes in behavior, specifically changes leading to criminal behavior."

"Damage meaning a trauma to the head, like in a car crash?"

"It can be a physical head trauma, as might happen in a car crash, or pathological head trauma, where the brain becomes diseased."

"You're both a lawyer and a neurologist?"

"I am."

"And when did neurolaw first appear in legal cases?"

"The first appearance was in an inquest in 1966. A man called Charles Whitman shot and killed thirteen people and injured thirty-two others in one day before he was shot by police. That morning, he had murdered his wife and mother. Whitman left a suicide note in which he described having irrational thoughts. He didn't know why he'd murdered his wife, for example, because he loved her dearly. And there was no history of violence in his life."

"He had been a normal person?"

"As normal as anyone. He had a high IQ, he had been a marine, and he'd studied architectural engineering at university."

"And he had no idea why he turned violent?"

"He did suspect something. In the suicide note, he asked if an autopsy could be carried out on his brain to see if anything was present."

"And was an autopsy performed?"

"It was. They found a glioblastoma tumor, the size of a coin, pressing on the amygdala."

"Can you explain that?"

"A glioblastoma is a type of cancer, and the amygdala is a group of cells in the temporal lobe of the brain. The amygdala plays a major role in memory, but it also processes emotional reactions, such as anger and fear. We've known for at least 200 years that when the amygdala is damaged, it can cause psychological disturbances."

"Are there other legal cases that have involved the presence of a glioblastoma tumor?"

"Several, and they're appearing with increased frequency. The legal system is adjusting to new information emerging from the neurosciences."

"And what tends to be the result of these cases?"

"In the ones I've been involved with, in the States, the defendant has typically been acquitted."

"And Michael Gleeson had a glioblastoma tumor during the period of his activity?"

"He did. It has been surgically removed."

"Entirely removed?"

"There are no cells remaining at this point."

Merriman gave the floor to Nettlefield and her cross-examination.

"Mr. Kardonovski, wasn't there a pedophile who got off charges because of a glioblastoma tumor?"

"There was, in 2000."

"And he reoffended again?"

"He did. The tumor returned."

"How can we be sure that the pedophilia was a result of the tumor?"

"Because when the glioblastoma was removed the first time, the sexual deviance disappeared. The same thing happened the second time."

"Could he have deliberately masked his impulses to get an acquittal?"

Merriman objected, on the grounds that that case wasn't the case before them, but the judge allowed it.

"It's possible, but the pedophilic disease is notoriously difficult to control. The impulse is significant."

"I wouldn't like convicted pedophiles walking around just because they've had brain surgery."

An objection, rightly upheld.

"How likely is it that Mr. Gleeson's tumor will reappear and he'll kill again?"

"It's hard to say. He'll know if it reappears; he'll recognize the signs now. He was afflicted with migraines when the tumor was active."

"But you can't say for certain whether the old Mr. Gleeson will emerge?"

"I can't of course, but I'll be following him for the rest of his life. He's agreed to be part of a research project."

"And that's exciting?" she smiled.

"It's as exciting as any research project. It's about getting the facts."

And Nettlefield handed him back to Merriman, possibly thinking that it was best to leave the thought of wandering pedophiles fresh in the minds of the jury.

"Dr. Kardonovski, Michael Gleeson's brain tumor is entirely gone?"

"It is."

"I've a very simple question, and please take your time before answering. Is the man sitting there," he said, pointing at me, "is that the same man who picked up a gun and shot Evan Scott Trevelyan?"

Kardonovski considered his reply.

"In my opinion," he said, "and from what I've seen of patients who've had glioblastomas removed, Michael Gleeson is not the same man who carried out those acts."

"Would it be right to imprison him for those things?"

Objection, but Kardonovski got his words in.

"It would be like imprisoning someone for having Parkinson's disease."

"Thank you, Dr. Kardonovski. You can sit down."

*****

When I was returned to the cell, I opened Cathal's letter again, and it was the first time that I had to let it sink in that he was dead. I read it again, knowing what he was about to do when he wrote it.

The other letter he had mentioned was there too, and I opened it up. From the first sentence, it was comforting to be back with the words of Honoria Gleeson, regardless of what she would say. The letters of her childhood were written from the perspective of a pure and single thought – not the crush of constant violence, the weight of fighting for land, intrigues and information and the lies of your family – but the one and only goal of survival. It was only as an adult, safe in America, that she could reflect on what had happened, with a nature that was far nobler than mine.

69. Forgotten (1919)

(From papers discovered in July 2019 in the records department of the American Irish Historical Society on 991 Fifth Avenue in Manhattan, New York)

I'm 85 now or 86, though I'll always profess the former. Never say that an old woman can't hold joy in her heart, that her soul is too hard and aged to sing with the news that came shouting in this morning. One of the Farrells, the youngest perhaps, shocked me out of my skin when he yelled across the room that Ireland has declared itself a Republic. With his blackened dirty face, dirty faces on them all, all three of Florrie's boys. The lad ran when I waved the cloth at him, wet with my spit, and sure when could a woman not rub the face of her own grandchild? He left me laughing in the chair, laughing at his run and the thought that the old country now has only itself to think on.

I never went back, I never could. The first years here were the worst, the days we had to plea for the jobs and be happy with things we never wished for, but we helped each other out. There was always someone who'd never leave you on the road. And each year we climbed further away from what we had been and seen. Knowing that no matter what life or the heavens cast at us, it would never be as bad as what had come before. Never as bad as my family dying beside me over the days and the house torn down when me and Katie tried the

Doolough walk. Never as bad as her fair dead hair on my lap and myself so lonely I could have thrown my arms over her and waited for the wind to take my breath.

A day that happened when I was well married and with the second on the way was when I watched the men at work on the Broadway street. They were rising a new building to the sky, the Equitable Life it was called, and it was the highest thing I had ever seen. I stood looking at the wonder of it from the cemetery nearby and, standing among the dead and their graves, I should have been forlorn. I thought how few of them had graves in Doolough and Muraisc and all the places that had been laid bare on a ground of bones. But it was hard to keep low, because the sun hit down and made the white gravestones whiter, and it was like a place to celebrate what the dead had been. There had been life there, good long life, and now other lives were walking over the grass and saying the names on the stones, not knowing who they were.

And when I stood there and was happy, I found I'd forgotten the rage that had kept me through years and years and spun around those men at Delphi. I could scarcely remember their names, though I was still young. The hate had washed from me and I hadn't noticed and it was a good thing, it having been of no use to think ill of those men. Some of us survived. Many of us survived. And the lives we've had here have grown out and been more than we could ever have had at home. And that home, at last, a Republic. It would not have happened if the hearts of men were not stirred by the sight of the dead on the roads. It would not have happened if the boats of us hadn't arrived on these shores and lived and earned and sent the money back. And now that Ireland has herself to look after, the men and women who've made it so will never let the Great Hunger happen again. It will never happen again.

(Nora Farrell (née Gleeson), 1919)

70. Victims

The Victim Personal Statements were read throughout the trial, placed at intervals to avoid overstressing the jury. There was no need to be worried on its behalf. The family of Lord Lucan didn't appear, perhaps having had too much of the gossip that had been thrown at him during his missing life. A colleague from Evan Scott Trevelyan's production company spoke eloquently about his professional work ethic and aspirations for the future, as eloquently as someone who was well used to words could, but who had not enough source material to go on.

Barney Hutchinson's ex-wife read her own words from a sheet in front of her. She talked about the historical Cromwell, how proud the family was to be related to him, how great a man he was despite the ideas of some people who didn't understand history. But she also delivered beautiful words about her former husband, a generous hard-working man, and how she and her sons would never get over the savagery that was done to the one true love of her life. The court was moved to tears, and apparently I alone picked up on her body language and the lie in every sentence. But that was okay.

The tears continued when it came to the family and followers of Gareth Lecky. For a dedicated racist, he seemed to be much loved and admired. He had taken the punishment for an ancestor who may have made one small mistake, they said. And it wasn't right that Michael Gleeson had killed him, they said; Michael Gleeson should now be strung up. The judge immediately silenced them on that point, saying that such opinions weren't allowed from them in court.

For the defense, Ken Skelfington arrived as a character witness, but his skill for holding a crowd didn't come with him. He looked wide-eyed and out of place, both when Merriman encouraged him to speak well about me and when Nettlefield got it out of him that we had discussed my involvement in the IRA. He said that I told him I had paramilitary clients, that some of them were deeply broken, and that I seemed to be under remarkable stress. When Nettlefield asked him why he wasn't alarmed by my IRA connections, he told her he believed it was part of a government process. In the witness box looking shell-shocked, it seemed as if he still did.

Ken told the court that he knew I had a tumor. He'd X-Rayed it for me about a year before. Nettlefield harassed him about why he didn't report it to anyone and whether it seemed strange that I wasn't seeking treatment, but he said he was ethically obliged not to twist my arm about it, and my arm would not be twisted.

Suzanne wasn't called as a witness. Nobody knew how close we were, and to Ken and Jean, she was just an acquaintance who had come to dinner at my house a few times. In interviews with the police, the staff at St. James Hospital had said I was a very polite single man and it was surely a wonder why I'd never got married. They also couldn't believe I'd killed four people, but that was only to be expected.

*****

The jury considered their verdict for two days. I wasn't allowed to see anyone but I rang Suzanne twice in that time, asking her how her flight back to Dublin was, how Kieran and her mam were getting on, what the weather was like. Anything to hear her voice. She cried at the end of the second call, just before the jury returned, but I said I'd see her soon and went back to the warm and carpeted courtroom with a fractured heart. I didn't know what to expect for my future, I never thought I'd have room in my life for love. I thought about my big grand plan and how it caused so much hurt and had me now sitting in the dock waiting to hear my fate. A devil of cells in the wrong place in my brain. The jury saw a man who knew he didn't deserve a future and didn't know if he had one.

When the verdict was read out, I couldn't understand it. It was like something on the radio that you hear but don't take in. Merriman's arms were around my shoulders, trying to shield me from the shouts that erupted in court. It was only when I was to see the coast of Ireland from a plane window two days later that I finally knew I was free.

71. Outside the Court

Maggie stood on the steps of the court as the crowds flooded out. Half of them were singing in pleasure and half were yelling in disgust. She knew she had to get back to the station, but it wasn't happening.

"You're about to cry," Liam told her, and with both of them in full police uniform, he put his arms around her and hugged her to him.

"He got off, Liam."

"He was a sick man."

"He knew what he was doing."

"Did he do it at all?"

Maggie felt for a second that Liam didn't want to let her go, but she had to step back to look into his face.

"You don't think he's innocent?"

"Not innocent. But a posh, middle-aged man like that suddenly learned how to shoot like a marksman? Everyone thought for years that another posh man had committed a murder, but they were all wrong."

"Who's that?"

"Lord Lucan."

"You think Gleeson wasn't working alone?"

"In the interviews taken after Gareth Lecky's death, one of the witnesses said something I can't get out of my head. He said he recognized the man who had come to Gleeson's aid in the pub."

"Recognized him from where?"

"From a pub he was in beforehand, where he and Lecky got talking to an Irishman, but they left because he was a nuisance. And this guy, Stephen Madigan, thinks that was the same man."

"Is it likely?"

"The lead was followed up on, but it came to nothing because Madigan had a good few pints on him that night. But he still swears he knew the face."

"Do you have his address?"

"I do."

"Shit, Liam. This is meant to be my last week here. Do you think Booth will still want me, now that Gleeson got off?"

"Are you crazy? You had a trail that went right up to him — you were the only one. Anything that happened after that was outside our control. A brain tumor got him off, there's nothing we could have done about it."

"You think so?"

"You'll get Counter Terrorism Command if you want it."

"The only thing I want now is to see Michael Gleeson in prison for life. Instead, that bloody free man is going back to bloody Ireland. But I have to speak to him before he goes. There's a question I want to ask him. He may not have the answer, or he may not want to give it to me, but I'd regret it forever if I didn't at least ask."

72. A Release for Her

I was transferred back to Scotland Yard to wait a few hours before anyone who was offended by my acquittal moved off the streets. I sat in an interview room, with officers outside for my own protection. Officer O'Malley arrived with food. She came in again soon after, checking if I was still there maybe. By the third time, she had coffee in her hand and the aggrieved look still on her face.

"Are you finished with it all now?" she asked me.

I took the coffee and burned my mouth. She sat in a chair.

"The English over here are nice," she said. "They're all Irish anyway."

"We couldn't breathe at home, so we had to breed elsewhere."

"Ah come on. You'll have to stop it sometime. You'll have to have more in your life than that."

"I'm a different man now."

"Because your tumor's out?"

"Because I'm cured. My entire life was a panic attack and I never noticed. What do you do, apart from police work?"

"Lots of things."

"Was your father an officer?"

"Why do you say that?"

"You're young, so you must have known from the start what you wanted to do. Homicide takes a few years to get into.

You're comfortable around the station, confident around criminals."

"You're not a criminal, you're a free man," she said with acidity.

"I haven't been too pleasant recently."

She sat back in the chair and folded her arms, choosing her words carefully.

"My father was an officer, a sergeant in Wexford."

"Was he happy when you joined the ranks?"

"He was dead by then."

"When I was being interviewed, you said we destroyed him."

"I did, but you can forget about that."

"Was he on duty when he died?"

"No."

"So why did you say it?"

"Because it was his job to look for trawlers in trouble, drunks out too late, the odd bike getting stolen."

"I don't understand."

"It wasn't his job to watch for a terrorist organization using tiny Ballyhack to get their Armalites into the country."

"Oh."

We sat looking at each other, until it seemed like she was compelled to speak.

"They got eight lots in before someone informed on them."

"But how did he die?"

"He couldn't have done anything, he had no chance against them. But he was a great officer and a good man, and the shock of it all killed him. He got a stroke soon after. That's how much he hated Republicans and what they were doing, sneaking their bloody guns into the country."

"I'm sorry, Maggie, and forgive me if I'm getting it wrong, but are you blaming the IRA for him not spotting them?"

Her face turned angry. "They used people, Dr. Gleeson, they used anyone, men and women who never had anything to do with their fight, never expected it in their lives. But it affected him and it affected us. He couldn't survive it, so he wasn't around to hear what people said about him afterwards, to hear us being called 'The daughters of that fool.'"

She wasn't expecting my reaction.

"You'll never get past it if you think like that."

"Are you psyching me?"

"I'm saying you're holding a grudge against the wrong people. You may have to admit that your father wasn't the god you thought he was. He was human, like they all are. I had to do the same with my own, to see him as a henchman more than an idealist."

She turned her two hands into fists and pulled the front of her jacket down to straighten it. "The street is clear outside now. An accompanying officer can take you to the airport if you want."

"I'm fine, thank you."

She stood up.

"But your father was a great officer, in everything else?"

She shrugged.

"You're intelligent," I said, "you must have got it somewhere. Was it from him?"

"He was very good. People felt safe with him."

"I think you might be giving the IRA too much credit."

"That's the end of our chat."

"How old are you? In your late twenties?"

"Goodbye, Dr. Gleeson." She walked to the door.

I dropped my head down to think, but she must have thought I was finished because she opened the door.

"It doesn't make sense," I said.

"What doesn't?"

"He was a fine officer, yet he couldn't see the gun-running under his nose? Those boats weren't small, Maggie. They always needed help to land."

"Don't say another word."

"You probably heard everything from your mother, and if I'm guessing your age correctly, I imagine she would have told you about him in the late nineties. Around the time of the Northern peace agreement. Do you know what time that was?"

"No."

"It was the time when it was the worst thing in the world to be a Republican. Far worse than being a flawed police officer with a good track record otherwise."

She closed the door and came back to me.

"What are you saying? Because I'd choose my words carefully if I were you."

"I'm saying he may have seen the boats. He may have known about them. But your mother could never tell you that She had a choice to make, and maybe she made the right one."

"You don't know..."

"You almost caught me, Maggie. If your father was half as good an officer as you are, he knew exactly what he was doing. If you have to fault him for anything, you might have to fault him for being a Republican, not for being a bad policeman. But maybe you already knew what he was. Maybe you spotted that after all."

"I guess we'll never know," she said with feigned disinterest.

"I have contacts who could find out for you. I've been counseling a particular brand of men for years."

"I don't want anything from you."

She walked straight to the door again, but when she got there, she stopped and said something so quietly that I only caught a few words:

"...sea around it but the green..."

She placed her hand on the wall and stayed like that for many moments, and I didn't disturb her thoughts. But then she straightened her jacket and turned back around to face me.

"I do want something from you, Dr. Gleeson. I have to ask you a question, because this will be my only chance. It might help you too, which is why I'm hoping you'll answer. It's about the attack on the Lucan household in 1974."

"Ask away."

"How did your father know that Lucan was going to be in his ex-wife's house? Lucan didn't live there anymore."

"Oh." I tried to remember, but nothing came. "I don't know. He might have followed him, known his movements."

"He might have been the mystery man."

"The what?"

"There were rumors of an unknown individual who sometimes called to the house. It put another man on the scene, apart from Lord Lucan. I suppose it could have been your father."

"I suppose it could."

"So Lucan's children were right when they described someone who'd drive up in a huge silver car and call in." She took a breath and stood straight. "I have to ask you this – do you know if your father was playing around with Sandra Rivett?"

I think she was expecting me to be mortally offended, because she jumped when I laughed.

"I don't know about an affair, Officer, but I do know the man you're describing couldn't have been my father."

"Why not?"

"Because he never drove."

"Never?"

"He couldn't. He had part of his knee blown off when he was a trainee, so one leg was shorter than the other. He couldn't synchronize the pedals of a car."

"A trainee what?"

"A trainee bomb maker. It was a hazard of the job."

"So how could he work in a garage?"

"He knew everything about cars, he just couldn't drive them. His assistant collected them and left them back with the owners."

"Then the mystery man might be nonsense."

"I'm sorry I can't help you, but if you find the answer, I'd love to know."

She turned the handle of the door. "Incidentally, who was his assistant?"

"At the garage? Paul Priestley."

"So it was." She had a blank expression on her face, but it seemed her brain was firing behind it. "Before I forget, there's someone waiting outside for you."

She looked at me for a few seconds, her brain still working away.

"You know, I might drop over to you the next time I'm in Ireland, to see how you're getting on."

"Keeping tabs? I understand."

"Goodbye, Dr. Gleeson."

"Take care, Officer Ó Máille."

And she left me alone in the cell.

*****

Merriman was waiting for me outside the station. With a handshake, an embrace, and a look that told me he thought we'd both narrowly escaped death, he was off. I was a free man, and I could go anywhere I liked. And that, of course, was home. I raised my hand to hail a taxi, and someone stepped up to me, almost into my armpit. For some reason I thought it was Turlough, but it was another man, and he had a worried look on him.

"Mr. Priestley," I said in gladness, but he spoke quickly to interrupt me.

"Can we go around the side? I just want a quick word."

He brought me around the corner of the Scotland Yard building, where he immediately started shaking his head.

"I'm sorry, Michael, I honestly am."

"For what?"

"I had to say those things in court."

"You had to tell the truth, Paul. And I'm a free man now in any case."

"That you are. It's nice that you got off, whatever you were up to. I suppose you had a lot of history to deal with, maybe too much for one person."

He offered me a cigarette and lit one up himself, and the smoke that came out of his mouth was double in the heavy February air.

"What I'm here to say, son, is that it wasn't right what those papers said about your father."

"They can be brutal."

"No, I mean, it wasn't right. They said he went after Lucan for a gambling debt, but that wasn't it. I don't know what those cops would have told you, but Blackwell was Joey's pal, his good pal. So when Blackwell's girl died, Joey went after him to get back for his friend, get justice for him and his girl."

"It wasn't a gambling debt?"

"No, though Lucan certainly paid up after."

"I can't tell you how much it means to hear this." My eyes welled up. I had turned my father into someone else in my head, and now I'd have to turn him into someone else again. *A Republican, a good father, a friend. But still, a man of violence.*

Paul was ahead of me in the tears. "It didn't go well, of course, and that other poor girl was caught up in it, the nanny. You said he didn't live long after getting back to Ireland? I suppose he didn't have too long to live with the guilt."

"He didn't. My uncle killed him a few years later."

"Oh."

"I guess if that wasn't justice, it was something like it catching up with him. It happens to us all whether we want it to or not. It'll happen to me, if my early life wasn't payment enough."

"You must have seen some bad things that night."

"I didn't see anything, Paul, the place was dark."

"I'm glad to hear that, son, very glad. It's best to forget all about it."

"You were a good friend to my dad," I said. "You kept his secret for many years. But I'm happy it's out now. Sandra Rivett's family can have some kind of closure."

"She was a beautiful girl, and the whole thing was an awful shame."

"Did you ever meet her?"

"No, I never did. Her picture was in the paper for a while after."

"Did my father know her? Did they ever..."

In the middle of my sentence, Paul Priestley gave a tiny smile, a smile you'd hardly notice. A smile that stopped my heart and cut my sentence short.

"Delight," I said.

"What's that?"

"She was a delight. And you never met her?"

"Nah, like I said, I never met her." Three blinks. Four.

"Are you sure?"

He looked at my cheek. "Nah, son, not me."

"I think you did."

"I didn't."

I stared at him, working it out. I had about ten seconds to work it out.

"You know why I became a psychiatrist, Paul? Because there's another world on top of this one where I feel more comfortable. I don't really have to hear what people tell me, I just have to see how they say it. And because I can do that, there are no lies in this world for me. People tell me the truth all the time, even when they don't want to."

"So what?" His tone turned cranky.

"It's the funniest thing, but there's one person I can't read very well. She's not a sociopath or a psychopath by any means; she has a clear head and the warmest of hearts. She's also very beautiful, which at my age, is a bonus. And yet I've never seen anything like her. Her body doesn't react to her lies."

"What has that to do with me?"

"You're not her."

"What?"

"You're lying. You met Sandra Rivett."

His finger came up to my face. "I don't know what shit is going around your mental head, but I never knew her."

I didn't move my face from his finger. "You may not have known her well, but you met her. And for some reason you don't want anyone to know. What other lies have you told?"

He turned to go and I put my arm up to the wall to stop him.

"Get your fucking hand out of the way."

"Did you lie about my father? He saved your life, he deserves more than lies being told about him."

He swung around and came so close that I had to step back.

"Saved my life! Saved my life! Do you hear what you're saying! You nearly had me killed, you fucking cunt. It was the least he could do."

He started to walk. And there was no way I was letting him go. I grabbed his arm as if I'd crush the life out of it, but it wasn't enough. He brought the other one up and punched me in the face. The pain shot into my skull and I tottered back, the blood streaming into my mouth.

But he wasn't getting away. I went for his throat. I squeezed my hand around his neck and pressed him into the wall. He choked for the air and I gave him none.

"Cream leather and a silver bonnet shining in the light. You had a car, the biggest car I'd ever seen, anyone had ever seen. I remember it. There was no way I could crash it, you told me, as it'd run over anything. And it wasn't yours, so you didn't care. You'd borrowed it from the garage. You were the man who called to their house. You met Sandra Rivett. Why are you lying?"

I pressed into him with my shoulder and loosened my grip so he could talk.

"You're in the shit now," he said.

"I killed four people, Paul, people I didn't know, people who meant nothing to me. I was a different person then, but can you be sure of that? If I'm still the same man, what do you think I'd do to someone I hate?"

"I don't fucking care. Your tumor's gone, so if you do anything to me, you'll be in jail for life."

"Let me offer you something else, then." I moved right up to his ear. "I may have been a different man over the past year, but I've been working for the IRA for 24 years. How many people do you think I've counselled? How many men owe me their lives?"

Paul's eyes opened wide and he started to struggle.

"The police won't be able to help you," I said.

I took my hand from his throat but stayed up close. The blood from my nose was already drying on my face. And Paul Priestley started shaking.

"Your head will end up on a railing," I whispered, "and it won't be me who does it."

"I never saw her, I only saw the wife."

I punched him in the stomach and he started puking spit.

"Blackwell made me deliver their liquor, that's all! I'd see her with the kids but I never met her."

I punched him again and he doubled over, coughing as he slid to the ground.

I knelt down and placed my finger on his forehead. "I know a man who can shoot you here from a mile away. Shoot you right here in the head."

His mouth fell open and he stared at me for so long that it looked like he was stuck that way forever. But when he spoke, it was as if something rotten had ruptured, as if words that had been cemented inside suddenly had to flow out.

"I loved her, I would have done anything for her. It didn't matter to me that she was nine years older, but it bleedin' well mattered to her. I'd come up in the fancy car, show her what I could be, and it softened her, I know it did."

He paused, as the angry memories took hold of him.

"But then there was Charlotte Blackwell's funeral, and that was the end of my life. Your fucking little squawks outside the church brought Blackwell out, and I was battered senseless. I was lucky to get any woman after that, lucky my bloody girlfriend would still have me.

"Sandra wouldn't even look at me after the hospital, she got a fright when she saw me. Said she was getting married and moving to Australia and how did I get it all wrong? That she barely even knew me."

"And you beat her to death?"

"I was ready to kill you, more like. My head was ruined, my face smashed up, and a woman who should have been mine was leaving. All because of you. But I got a better idea than smothering you in your sleep. Your father told me he was going to rough Lucan up to get back for Charlotte, give him a few digs, and I told him Lucan was back in the house every Thursday. Lucan did show up that night, so that was a lucky coincidence for us all. Except for your father, there was no coincidence for him. I wanted him there. I wanted you there. I saved your life and ruined my own by doing it, so you owed me big time. And your father owed me for keeping you alive.

"She got a shock when she saw me, and I got another when I saw her, but after the first blow I never felt a thing. I hit the shitting life out of her, so no one would have her again. And when the Lady saw us from upstairs, I had to get her to be quiet too.

"I knew your Dad would get in through the basement door, and that had a fine lock, so I was sure I could finish it all and ring the police before he came in. But he was an expert with those locks, an expert with bloody everything except fucking walking, and in he comes and he sees me and he pulls me off the Lady. I pushed him into the wall, and that's when Lucan dropped by. A big bloody farce. I ran up to the front door and I was laughing so much I nearly couldn't get out. Lucan saw your father, your father would take the blame. But Lucan ran off, thinking he'd be blamed himself. That mucked it up for me, because then everyone thought it was him. But I didn't care. Justice is what I got. Some kind of justice."

My throat was so dry I could hardly get the words out. "Sandra was innocent."

"Yeah, like all the people you killed. Like me, when I saved you from Blackwell. Like Lucan, when they found the other lead pipe that I stuck in his car after leaving the house, not wanting to be stopped with it on me. If we're all so fucking innocent then why are we all fucking looking for revenge? So that's it. That's all of it. And I'd do it again. Do you think I'm lying now?"

"No, I don't."

"And neither do I." Another voice at the corner of the Scotland Yard building, three feet away from us. Officer

O'Malley was there, and she must have heard it all. She'd waited until she'd heard everything.

Priestley dropped his head and laughed.

As the metal handcuff went around one of his wrists, he looked up at me and said, "There's a silver lining to this."

"What's that?"

"My head won't end up on a stick."

"It wouldn't have anyway."

And Officer O'Malley cuffed his other hand.

73. Whiskey Drinking

Weeks after my release, when I was back home on the couch and Suzanne was over and asleep upstairs, I felt like a changed man, though I had a scabby sore on my head that was taking too long to heal. The fire in the grate was high against the late-spring cold, and I dozed on and off like an old man, with an old man's soapy mouth. I took every opportunity to let my brain recover, feeding it quiz shows whenever it needed them, letting it rest when it wanted. And on this dark evening, I pulled the blanket up to my chest, and the only thing I had to remember was to put the fireguard up before falling asleep for the night. But I must have dozed off, because when I woke up, the fireguard was still down, and a few chips of singeing wood had landed on the carpet.

It was a tapping that woke me, a *tip tip tip* that at first I took to be sparks popping out of the fire. But another tap came, loud and tinny enough to shake the kitchen window. It was probably the British reporters, several of whom had been over for a scoop, standing outside my house late into the evening. The police and my neighbors were kind enough to scare most of them away with cautions of arrest and a roar of thick curses, respectively.

I prepared to send them off with a few polite words as I shuffled over to the window. A face looked in through the glass, lit by the security light to the side. I smiled before opening the door. He went for a handshake, but I could give no less than a hug. It embarrassed the hell out of him, and it did me no end of good.

"You'll have a whiskey?" I said.

"It's not my kind of thing."

"You'll be fine with a small one, Turlough. You were never an alcoholic."

I poured him a small one and me a larger, something to hold in my hand for as long as I could. We sat in front of the fire, me on my makeshift bed and him in the huge armchair. He was comfortable there, and I was comfortable where I could see him entirely.

"How have you been?" I asked.

"I've been fine, everything's fine. How have you been, with your head?"

"It's good now, it's better. It was only a small lump, but you'd be amazed at what they can do."

"The lumps or the doctors?"

"Both. I'm glad to be over both of them."

"And the case worked out alright?"

"It did, indeed."

"Unanimous verdict."

"I was surprised by that."

"It was the right thing."

We both tightened our lips, thinking and staring at the fire. I didn't know what he was mulling over, whether it was a job, something sweet and personal, or nothing at all. Happy to be warm.

"I met my son," he said, his face brightening up, more than I'd ever seen. "We see each other all the time now."

"That's great news, Turlough, great news. I'll have to meet him."

"Ah yeah." He sipped at his whiskey. "He knows you already."

"He knows me?"

"He's moving up now, almost the head of it all. Terry's his name, same as me, though I go by the Irish."

"Terry's your son? And he's the head?" I didn't know what to do with the information.

"He's getting there. Brought in a few changes, got the bad lot out. Calming things down before the referendum on the North."

"Terry's your son?" I said again.

"I've a few of them. I've met them all. The accountant, my daughter, she's an oddball but nice enough. Lovely children, don't look a bit like me. And the other boys are grand. One's a bit of a drinker, but we'll have to knock that on the head. It was nice to see them. Tough at first, but all's well now."

"I only met Terry, but he seemed a decent young man."

"He is. I'll be there to help him now."

"He wouldn't have helped in any court cases?"

"He told me he did you a wrong, alright. And he was glad it worked out the way it did. But that was the jury who got you off."

"It was a bit too unanimous for my liking."

"There was no tampering, you can't do that these days."

"If there *was* any funny business, never let me know."

"I'll never let you know, Dr. Gleeson. But you had that tumor thing, and people see sense these days. That brain fella did great for your cause. I read all about it on social media. Social media is what it's called."

"Kardonovski was clever. He knew exactly what to say."

"To the jury?"

"To me. You know, it's funny, I can spot a lie in most people, but I'm no good at telling them myself. So I was the only person I had to convince. And I had to do it completely."

"Convince yourself of what?"

"That I was so different from the person I was before, that I didn't deserve an acquittal."

He looked as if he wasn't quite sure what I meant, but he just said, "I think it worked."

"It did indeed. Though if I'd been on the jury, I would have convicted myself."

"That reminds me," he leaned in, "I just wanted to say that you were very good, taking that pressure off me. I could have been in the soup."

I smiled at the thought of Turlough standing in a barrel of soup.

"There was no need to get you in the soup. And you saved my life on more than one occasion."

We sipped again and I wondered if we'd be sitting here in the future, many years away, passing pleasant time. But I took the chance to break the peace. I stretched my legs before me and moved to the end of the couch, nearer to his chair. A hand rub to my chin, a tricky subject coming up.

"Turlough, I've been thinking about something. About this whole thing." My eyes returned to the fire, there was no rush. "I've been thinking about it since the hospital, and it's just such a funny little thing that I don't know why I didn't think of it sooner. I don't know why I missed it."

He looked at me with those wrinkled eyes that had seen so many places and things I never would. I had known him as a patient for over two years and as a person for only a short while, but we totally and entirely trusted each other. We had too much to lose.

"And this silly little thing, it keeps jumping into my head, and it would be the perfect way to end this chapter of our lives. Do you know what would be the perfect end to this whole thing? The perfect fire and whiskey at the end of the night?"

He raised his eyebrows to hear whatever I was going to say. I made sure my throat was clear and the room was silent apart from the odd sparking wood. And like that first time, when I asked him to find Lucan and it never occurred to him to refuse, I brought up a subject that I could never have broached with anyone else. I looked at him, at his old, veteran face, and I said,

"The royals. We never got the queen."

And he smiled.

THE END

Acknowledgements

Thanks to you, the reader, for taking a chance on a little black book from a debut author with a funny name.

Thanks to my family for not minding that sometimes I'm thinking about heads on spikes when I'm talking to you.

Thanks to Margaret Sutherland Brown – I couldn't thank you the way I wanted to, but your help is never forgotten.

Thanks to my late grandfather and grandmother, who fought to make sure their six daughters lived in a free Ireland.

Thanks to Turlough for appearing out of nowhere, though I suspect you've always been there.

And thanks to you, Michael.

Siobhan